Trigger Warning

Dear Readers,

While this book is a work of fiction, it contains storylines that may be triggering for some of you.

My goal is to handle these topics with care, but I want to make sure you have all of the information before diving into this book.

This book touches on sensitive topics, including alcohol use, a notable age difference in a romantic relationship, and some emotional abuse within a family. These issues are thoughtfully resolved.

Please consider your own triggers when deciding whether to read this book.

Love, Kaylene

tender TEMPTATION

KAYLENE WINTER

CILLIAN

Prologue - Present Day

Jesus. Will the rain ever fucking stop?

Hustling down Second Avenue, with little reprieve from the endless downpour, I try to pull my heavy canvas jacket closed, my flannel shirt and black jeans are practically plastered to my body. Water sloshes into my work boots as I try to navigate glistening puddles pooling on the sidewalk.

I'm soaked to the bone.

Like most native Seattleites, I don't own a fucking umbrella.

Stubbornly stupid.

Ah, fuck it. I deserve to be wet and uncomfortable. After the day I've had, I might as well get the flu on top of it.

Finally, I spy the green awning up ahead despite the darkened skies. A few more steps and I push through door of the Metropolitan Grill, a Seattle steakhouse institution. Veering left to avoid the hostess, I take a seat at the bar in all my damp glory.

Settling onto my usual stool with embarrassingly practiced ease, I'm self-aware enough to realize it's an act of defiance against my wicked cravings. My eyes, inadvertently—or advertently, who the fuck knows—drift to the rows of amber bottles gleaming against the under light of the glass shelving.

Particularly to the whiskey. Lord, what I'd give for a fucking taste. How I'd savor it. Vanilla and smoky oak. Sweet notes of caramel and honey. A hint of fruit, either orange zest or a slice of crisp apple. I shut my eyes and practically feel the warmth enveloping me in a comforting glow, radiating through every vein and easing the burdens of my mind. Soothing the aches of my soul. Wrapping around me like a soft, fluffy blanket on a shitty Seattle night.

It's been over a year since I've had a sip. Even though every day is a battle, I haven't been tempted in months. Today, though, the fight feels harder. The liquor more alluring.

Freddy, the bartender whom I've known for years, sets down a tonic water with lime in front of me. I grip the cool, clear glass tightly, hoping the lime's sharp scent will override the memory of peat and warmth. The guy in a suit two seats down orders a Red Breast neat. My jaw clenches with envy. The liquid gold catches the light as Freddy pours it with an easy flick of the wrist.

Mesmerizing.

Tamping down the old, familiar ache, I turn away. Focus on the clink of glasses and the murmur of conversations around me—anything to drown out the noise in my head. It's a silent struggle, unseen by the laughing customers in the busy restaurant.

I take a sip of my tonic, the fizz biting at my tongue. It's a pale imitation of what I truly crave, but at least it's safe. *Necessary.* I'm fully aware of the consequences if I were to give in to my demons. I've lived and breathed them and won't live one more day with regret coiling in my gut. Still, I need something...more.

"Hey, man. Can I get a hot coffee?" I tap the polished wood with my finger to get Freddy's attention. "I'm soaking wet and fucking freezing."

"Sure." Seconds later he hands me a steaming mug. "Cream or sugar?"

"Both." I slide a twenty toward him. Coffee is no substitute for the nectar of the gods, but at least it will warm me up and keep me sober.

Hell, it's no small feat considering what happened today. Suddenly, I'm on the brink of losing my shit and I have no one to blame but myself.

Well, maybe my stupid, inherited addiction genes. Memories of my da's spiral into alcoholism invade my thoughts. Barely a teenager when he crashed and burned. I was instrumental in helping him rebuild the business he founded once he got sober. A decade ago, I took over as CEO and now McGloughlin Construction, is the biggest game in town. For what?

A terrible mistake I made three years ago coming back to haunt me and destroy all my hard work?

"Kill." An undeniable presence, Brennan, my entrepreneurial younger brother uses the nickname my family calls me and takes the stool next to me.

Stocky with piercing brown eyes and a determined gait, he effortlessly commands respect in every situation. Today, his head is shaved close and he sports a meticulously groomed beard. Despite his imposing appearance, Brennan's demeanor is easygoing. He's perfected a balance of serious professionalism with well-timed jokes, which endear him to everyone he meets.

He and I are the closest of all my brothers. My Irish twin. Through it all, we're always there for each other, no matter what.

I curve my lips into something resembling a smile. "'Bout time,"

"You look stressed, Kill. Everything okay?" Brennan is far too perceptive for his own good.

I hesitate then point to a secluded booth at the back of the bar we sometimes use for confidential conversations. We take our seats on opposite sides of the table and are promptly interrupted by a server. There's no way I can eat right now, but Brennan's always hungry.

He orders his usual Porterhouse while I dig my thumbs into my temples to try to quell the throbbing in my head. "I'm fucked."

"Dramatic much?" Brennan drapes his arm along the back of the booth and purses his lips. "Who'd you piss off today?"

I shake my head. "My past has come back to bite me in the ass. I'm struggling, man."

A familiar tug of anxiety and regret fills my chest cavity as I remember the best—and worst—summer of my life. "Do you remember the day I landed the first Vander contract, and we spent the entire spring celebrating? Partying every night. Fucking gorgeous women. Waking up and doing it all again? Never missing a beat."

"Oh, I remember." Brennan arches an eyebrow and takes a sip of his Diet Coke. "We were on quite the tear. I had a hard time keeping up with my fuck-boi older brother, pardon the pun."

Wincing, I nod and look down at my clasped hands. I'm stalling. He doesn't need a recap of our past debauchery. He was there. "Yeah, well I ignored the warning signs. Despite our family's history of alcoholism, I thought I could control it."

"You're a year sober now. If you're beating yourself up about the past...don't." He taps the back of my fist with his finger.

I stare him dead in the eye. "No. You don't understand. I fucked up. *Really* fucked up."

"How so?" Brennan's eyes nearly pop out of their sockets.

I nod sadly. "She broke my fucking heart..."

"The girl you were seeing? Yeah, I remember the petite blonde, but I'm still not following you. You never told me it was serious." He furrows his brow.

Ah, well, we were private. Too private. And it blew up in my face.

Still, the first time I saw her will forever be tattooed on my brain.

The second she stepped through the doorway of Kell's Irish Pub, time slowed to a halt, like in the movies. The spotlight from the stage illuminated her from behind and cast a glow-

ing halo around her delicately sweet face. Thick, golden hair cascaded down her back in soft waves. Her flawless, milky skin made her look ethereal. Angelic.

Her body was sculpted for temptation. Short, cut-off shorts showed off her long, muscled legs to perfection. The black bodysuit she wore clung to her curves, leaving nothing to my imagination. Her tits. God, her tits. Creamy mounds of deliciousness spilling out of her top. Her nipples practically poked through the fabric.

She was, without question, the most exquisite woman I'd ever laid eyes on. The ultimate paradox of innocence and allure. A saint cloaked in the clothes of a siren.

I couldn't look away. Not for a second. I knew I had to have her.

The way she moved through the crowd—poised and self-assured with a hint of awkward—reminded me of a newborn fawn taking in the world for the first time.

I watched her, transfixed, like a schoolboy.

Then, as if compelled by a gravitational pull, she turned to me and her turquoise eyes caught mine.

And it was all over.

Brennan listens with rapt attention. He doesn't interrupt or give any indication he's judging me. I drop the bomb.

"I should have known better." My voice is a whisper of shame. "I wasn't thinking about the consequences. Hell, I didn't even register there *could* be consequences until it was too late."

"Shit, man. You never told me the whole story. *Heavy.*" He leans back in the booth and scrubs his stubble with his big paw. "Things make more sense now."

I'm not a man who cries easily, but my eyes sting with unshed tears. I'm nauseous with desperation. "At the time, I thought I was justified. But, what I did...how it ended. I'm ashamed." My admission is raw and frightening. Brennan well knows about my descent into hell after it all went down—he's the one who helped pull me out.

My brother reaches across the table and grabs my wrist. "People make mistakes. It wasn't your fault. Work your steps. Forgive yourself; it's in the past."

"Easier said than done." I shake my head sadly.

He arches an eyebrow. "Why?"

"Because she's back." I wince and recap what happened earlier today.

Brennan's skin pales. "Oh, *fuck*..."

"Yeah." I slump back into the booth, defeated.

The agony of seeing her has unleashed a storm of emotions whirling through me all at once—panic, despair, bitter anger, and heartache.

Bottomless, all-encompassing sorrow for what could have been.

I'm spiraling. Tormented. Caught in a vortex of longing and impossibility. My defenses are crumbling into oblivion.

My resolve to stay away forever is dissolving completely.

Because seeing her again confirms what I've always known.

There's no moving on, not in this lifetime.

One

Three Years Prior

I JACKKNIFE UP WITH a gasp, heart racing, as blinding light floods my bedroom.

I never get used to this.

Each morning, ever since I returned home from Hedge Academy, Hilde, our house manager, slips in and sweeps open the curtains to make sure I'm awake. A strict instruction from my father. He expects me to be up early.

Even on Saturday morning. It's barely 5:30 a.m. on my 18th birthday.

Hilde scoots out and shuts the door behind her. She doesn't need to say anything more. I'm expected to be an obedient little girl who follows her daddy's rules.

Which makes me cringe, though I tamp it down and play along.

On the way to my en suite bathroom, I take a moment to gaze out the floor-to-ceiling windows at the expansive view of Lake Washington. Below the meticulously manicured gardens, a stone path leads to the place where laughter once echoed from a bustling dock and fire pit. All of it has been removed, replaced with thorny shrubs blocking access to the waterfront.

The altered landscape is a constant reminder of what was lost there. Every joyful memory has been overshadowed by our family tragedy. My brother, Forrest, drowned in the lake five years ago today. My birthday is now the anniversary of his death.

Forrest was the golden child, destined to take over my father's business. Our family and friends were celebrating my thirteenth birthday with a barbecue. Suddenly, laughter turned to eerie silence when he dove into the lake and didn't come up. Not only did my brother's future end, but all happiness in our family drowned with him.

Every birthday since, the air in this house thickens with unspoken grief, making me feel invisible. Neither my mom nor dad will acknowledge it's my birthday today. It's as if my existence has been muted by the past.

Life as I knew it ended the day I entered my teens. Now, I'm expected to take over Bright Shipping before my dad retires. I'm not allowed to have typical teenage friendships. I've been under the strict and watchful eyes of nannies and tutors, even while away at boarding school. My father also strictly forbids me from dating. He says the distraction will derail my focus and compromise the rigorous path he's laid out for my future.

I know the truth. He doesn't want anyone to defile his precious daughter. God forbid I have fun.

I'm fucking lonely.

In therapy, I'm learning to navigate my grief and resentment by reclaiming parts of my life to learn what feels authentic to me. Including my birthday. This year, though I feel like I'm a million years old, I'm technically an adult. She tasked me to take some small, but significant steps toward asserting my independence.

I have a plan.

After a quick shower, I pull on a pair of joggers, a simple tank top, and tie my hair into a high, messy bun. On my way downstairs, I catch a glimpse of myself in the mirror. This isn't the sculpted and polished Ivy Bright my dad prefers. My version of Ivy is ready to grasp some semblance of weekend normalcy.

My version of Ivy is going to enjoy *one day* free from a legacy of tragedy and expectation.

Descending the back staircase to the breakfast room, I spot my dad, Stanley Bright, already seated at the head of our sleek, glass-top formal dining table with his back to the panoramic view. The spread before him is mouth-watering—organic fruits, artisan bread, imported cheeses. I'm used to the many silent displays of our family wealth.

"Good morning, Dad." I try to keep my voice neutral as I approach the table. To pull this off, I need to be clever. And not mention my birthday.

My dad barely looks up from his tablet, where he's no doubt been reviewing market analytics or shipping news. "Morning." He surveys my outfit, his eyes narrowing slightly. "Interesting choice for breakfast attire."

Typical. I choose to ignore the slight, pulling up a chair. "It's comfortable."

"Yes, well, remember the importance of maintaining a polished appearance." He returns his attention to his breakfast, but not before adding, "Your position will demand a certain standard of professionalism, best get in the habit now."

His words sting. A reminder my life is a series of stepping stones with no deviation from his plan. "Actually, I was hoping we could talk about the summer."

"What's to discuss? You're leaving for Stanford Business School in a couple of months." He sets down his fork. "Until then, I'd like you to start your training..."

"...Dad, stop." I push around a slice of kiwi on my plate with my fork. "I need a break and I'd like to take the summer off. I've worked hard to get both my high school diploma and my undergrad degree in four years. Stanford will be intense. I'm not planning on lying around watching reruns on Bravo. I have an idea for a productive, but more creative way for me to spend the next few weeks. Art class. Dance. Things I used to love and won't have time for once I start school again."

My dad sighs. "Ivy, you have the intellect and the education. Why squander your time on frivolous dreams? Reality has much more to offer you."

"I don't see it as squandering," I counter softly. "I want to live a bit. It's not a lot to ask. You play golf every Friday and Sunday. Do crosswords. I've even see you watch *Shark Tank* a time or two."

My father pauses, considering this. "Well...."

"Please." Leaning on the table, I rest my chin on my palms and give him my best puppy-dog eyes. It used to work all the time. Now we're about 50/50. No, 70/30 in his favor.

"I don't want you to waste time you can't get back." He pauses and I almost think he's going to wish me a happy 18th. He doesn't, but he does surprise me in a different way. "You know what? You're a good girl. This summer you can do your little hobbies. Your mom will probably be thrilled."

"Thank you." I ignore the backhanded dig. "Where *is* Mom?" I glance up the staircase and back at him. No sign of my mother, Allison Bright.

Dad clasps his hands. "Packing. She's coming with me to Asia. We're leaving in an hour." He gets up from the table. "She needs a change of scenery to....refresh."

Wait, what? They're leaving? *Today?*

His carefully chosen words remind me, painfully, my birthday is irrelevant to them.

Will I ever get used to how badly it hurts?

"I do have some conditions. While we're gone, other than your classes, keep to your usual routine here. We don't want to worry about you. I'll leave you several books I'd like you to read, which are vital for your future." He places his hand on my shoulder, the only sign of affection he's shown me in years.

I look up at him. "Would it be okay if I stayed with Emma Rogers? From the academy? You like her and her parents are clients. Maybe not all the time, but it would be nice to have company from time to time."

"Well…" He scrutinizes me so I'm careful to keep my puppy-eyes fixed with sincerity. "Only if you're not imposing. Make sure to let Hilde know—and Ivy?" He narrows his eyes on his way up the stairs. "I'm trusting you. Don't make me regret it."

I'm shocked, I never thought he'd go for it. Trudging back up to my room, I'm actually confused at this turn of events. Did my parents think it was acceptable to abandon me for the summer to live with the house staff? With restrictions to boot?

Ridiculous.

Thank God for my quick thinking. At least now I'll have someone to hang out with and activities to look forward to this summer. I pull out my laptop and search for dance workshops. A three-hour session late this afternoon catches my eye—perfect. I register, but, truthfully, it hardly feels like a victory.

As I'm scrolling through some art classes, I hear a *thump thump thump* of a suitcase on the stairs. A car engine starts. My parents chatter past my bedroom door and down the hall until I can't hear them anymore. Peering out the window, I watch them get in the car. Then it disappears down the long driveway.

Neither of them bothered to say goodbye. *Wow.* I'm lost in a bit of woe-is-me for a few minutes. Tears prick my eyes and it takes a while to tamp them down. I'm *not* crying today, though. *No way.*

Then it dawns on me.

I've been handed the greatest gift I could ever ask for. A summer of freedom.

At least for eight weeks.

Which is a lifetime. Fifty-six days. The possibilities are endless.

I might get a tattoo. Try sky-diving. Oooh, maybe a concert...or a festival. Yes! I can take a road trip to the Olympic Mountains and go hiking.

Wait.

Am I going to do all of these activities with *Emma*? How *depressing*.

She's nice and all but we're not close. Actually, she's immature. It's understandable, I guess. Most of my boarding schoolmates hung out like normal students while I earned my diploma, got a business degree, and learned the fundamentals of our shipping business.

Without playing a tiny violin, in a couple of months, I'll be fast-tracking an MBA while my so-called peers have the time of their life, joining sororities and living the college life. Activities I'll never get to experience.

Yeah, Emma and I are a million miles apart. It's a pretty sad state of affairs.

Wait. A. Minute.

I don't need to hang out with Emma. Hilde doesn't have Emma's phone number, and I'm not about to give it to her. Plus, with my parents being in a completely opposite time zone, they won't call to check up on me—my dad will be too busy working and my mom barely acknowledges I exist. If I tell Hilde I'm staying nights at her house, no one will be the wiser.

With Emma as my unwitting alibi, I'll be able to do whatever I want.

Ooooh. The possibilities are endless.

I don't have to be Ivy Bright, heiress and perpetual goodie two-shoes. I can be whomever I want and do whatever I want, whenever I want to do it. No one is going to stop me.

Oh, the adventures I'll have this summer! I'm going to try everything I'd never be allowed to do under the oppressive rules of my dad.

Maybe after dance class tonight I can hang out in a coffee shop...or, a *bar*. Somewhere casual, where I could strike up a conversation—I'm surprisingly adept at small talk. I don't want a nightclub vibe or anything too precious or too divey. Definitely not somewhere where my parents' friends might see me.

Hmmm.

The studio is close to Pike Place Market. There's bound to be somewhere nearby to stop by after class is over. I Google that shit and, bingo, there's an Irish pub called Kells a couple of blocks away. I launch their website and it's perfect. Casual. Low-key. Nondescript. Tonight there's even a live band. There's no chance anyone will know me there.

Except...I have to be twenty-one to get in.

Well, I didn't get perfect grades for being stupid. It takes me all of thirty seconds to find a video on YouTube on how to make a fake ID.

It's surprisingly easy. I upload my driver's license into Photoshop. Change my birthday so I'm twenty-four, not eighteen. Then, it occurs to me...I should also use a fake name. On the off-chance I get caught, I can't risk dragging the Bright name through the mud. I decide to use my mother's maiden name.

I type in "Ivy Davies," save my handiwork in the cloud and locate a place where I can print and laminate the card. It's amateur, sure, but hopefully it will pass.

Holy shit.

I've never dared to defy my father completely. I've never kept secrets—other than the fact I own a vibrator which—*eww*—is frankly none of his business. What's a girl who isn't allowed to date supposed to do?

Anyway, the excitement of doing something scandalous is intoxicating. I find myself giddy at the possibilities the next eight weeks will bring in my journey of self-discovery and adventure.

Self-discovery and adventure...

I look at myself in the mirror. As my counselor says, tune into what you want and don't let anyone make you feel bad about it.

Tell me, Ivy. What do you really want? If you could have anything?

I'm not going to lie. I know, but never dreamed it would be possible.

I want to be touched. Loved. *Adored.* I don't want friends, I want a summer fling. Someone to hold my hand and kiss. Someone to explore my sexuality with, before I hit Stanford.

Let's be honest, I'm a horny, eighteen-year-old virgin and I will never, ever, ever get this opportunity again. The rest of my life will be dedicated to running the family business and marrying someone my dad approves of.

Starting today, I'm finding a slice of happiness.

On my terms.

And, I'm not going to feel bad about it.

Two

The Same Night

I BOTH LOVE AND dread these dinners.

My family is everything, I love seeing them. On the other hand, I sometimes feel invisible. Overshadowed by my brothers' towering achievements.

Bounding up the concrete stairs to my parents' Craftsman mansion on Capitol Hill, I'm exhausted from a last-minute scramble to resolve a sudden crisis at one of my construction sites. From the time I can remember, I dreamed of running my family's business, McGloughlin Construction.

Truth be told, I had no idea how the constant demands and pressures would weigh me down some days.

It's a pleasant, early summer Seattle evening, the warm glow of the sun radiates off the large windows. Inside, I can see it's already buzzing in the spacious dining room where my ma has prepared a lavish dinner to celebrate my oldest brother Connor and his wife Ronni. They're having another wee baby in a few months.

Connor is the bass player in Seattle's most famous band, Less Than Zero. Ronni is an actress and producer and is, arguably, more famous. Aside from their security detail, who largely remain in the shadows, neither of them are precious about their celebrity status, thank God.

I open the door and survey the scene. Twins Liam and Padraig are also rockstars. Their band Fireball is not as famous as LTZ, but are critically acclaimed in their own right. They're chatting with Seamus, our youngest sibling. He's a surgical resident, fresh from a hospital shift. He's still in scrubs and looks like he's about to fall asleep standing up.

"Where've you been?" Brennan, a year younger than me, is the founder of an Artificial Intelligence tech company. He slams an arm around my shoulder like he hasn't seen me in weeks.

I hug him back. "Ah, work stuff."

"You okay?" He tilts his head and scrutinizes me. "Need to talk?"

I love Brennan, he and I have always been like two peas in a pod. We're Irish twins, after all. Sometimes he needs to back off, though. "I'm fine, you've got to quit worrying. I've got everything under control."

My da spots us and sidles over. Brennan tenses but pastes a smile on his face. All of my brothers but me have a love/hate relationship with him.

Somehow, I seem to understand my father. Empathize, maybe.

Rory McGloughlin founded McGloughlin Construction shortly after he immigrated from Northern Ireland. With his hard work ethic and quick wit, he turned it into a power-house—until a car accident nearly killed him and threw our family into turmoil.

At eighteen, Connor was forced to run the company he hated to keep the family afloat. He sacrificed college and pursuing his own music dreams for years so all of his brothers could finish high school and attend college.

Meanwhile, my father was in constant pain. He turned mean. *Really* fucking mean. Depression led him to struggle with alcohol and he developed a gambling addiction that nearly bankrupted the company and our family.

Right around that time, Connor hired Jennifer Deveraux, his then-girlfriend, to help out with the business. At first I was pissed, I'd been working part-time for years and wanted to run McLoughlin Construction myself. Connor wouldn't hear of it but promised I'd have a bigger role once I obtained my BA in Construction Management from the University of Washington. Seemed like a decent compromise to me.

By the time I was in my senior year of college, Da sobered up enough for Connor to feel comfortable following his dream of touring with LTZ and managing things from afar—with the idea Jen and I would serve as backup to keep an eye on Da. Of course, none of us could have predicted his band exploding into the stratosphere. Connor did his best, but was gone for two years solid with only a couple of visits in between.

Needless to say, Da relapsed and Jen and I were faced with the same issues Connor dealt with. Jen wanted out and my ma threatened to move back to Ireland.

It was a wake-up call for my father. He became serious about his sobriety and McGloughlin Construction. Although his health conditions continued to dog him, Da turned things around for himself. The company thrived and, to make amends for his years of neglect, he gifted all of us a town-house in one of his developments. At that point, Connor turned the company back over to him and Da brought me in as CEO on my twenty-fifth birthday.

Unfortunately, because Da's behavior had been abhorrent for years, it took a while for my brothers to forgive him—but they haven't forgotten. There's still a rumbling of resentment every so often.

Not from me, though.

In my eyes, Da is a hero. His entire world was ripped out from under him at thirty-eight, which is hard for me to comprehend. He fought through injuries, addiction, and PTSD, only to nearly be felled by a stroke and a substantial stint in a rehab clinic not too long ago. Now he's tackled his demons and is stronger than ever, both emotionally and physically. Our family means everything to him and he's been an incredible mentor to me personally.

For the past decade, I've worked side by side with my da and have seen firsthand how a strong work ethic and high standards are the backbone of every successful company. He taught me the construction business was more about relationships than bricks and mortar.

"Making every client feel like the most important person in the room is the real secret to a profitable business," he'll say.

Over the years, despite my own social anxiety, I've taken his advice to heart. Even with the pressures of running a multi-million-dollar business, McGloughlin Construction is my life.

I love it—I've dedicated all my time into making it more and more successful and I take great pride in my work ethic. My ability to forge instant connections to turn lucrative deals into lifelong partnerships has been instrumental in getting us to where we are now.

Da is semi-retired now, though he stays in the know on all our projects and helps out on occasion.

"Cillian, you made it, so you did. Tell me about the new shipping project. Have you heard if we got it?" Da's eyes shine with excitement.

I shake my head. "Nah, I still have a ton of pre-interview paperwork to complete. There's all sorts of environmental and tribal considerations since it's on the Duwamish river. I'm not meeting with the guy until later this summer anyway."

"You're always prepared." Da slaps me on the back. "There's no doubt in my mind you'll get the job."

Connor, Ronni, and my ma emerge from the kitchen, each carrying serving dishes heaping with utterly delicious-smelling grub. My stomach growls. "Need any help?"

"Aye, lad. Will you grab the colcannon? It's on the counter." Ma's brogue is still as thick as though she lives in Northern Ireland. I find myself speaking like her from time to time.

All of us do, I reckon.

Sitting around the dining table, we pass thick slices of fresh brown soda bread to go with the lamb stew and buttery mashed potatoes with kale. Amidst vivid tales of my brothers' success, which eclipses mine by a mile—three famous rockstars, Seamus's surgical miracles, and Brennan's tech innovations, I find myself longing to chill with two fingers of Midleton.

There's no alcohol in this house anymore, for obvious reasons. Most of my brothers don't partake, but it's never been a problem for me. Besides, I'd never put my father's sobriety at risk by bringing my own bottle, though.

Hmmm. After dinner, I think I'll head over to Kells, a local Irish pub at Pike Place Market. It's only a few blocks away from my loft and has a great selection of Irish whiskey. I love that it's in a tourist area—makes it easy to hook up with an out-of-towner who's down for a quick fuck without any commitment. My ideal situation, always.

I'm too busy for anything more.

Yeah. I'm definitely in the mood to get laid. Shit, it's been a couple of months. Catching a nice little buzz and sinking my cock into a beautiful woman's sweet heat will definitely take the edge off.

As the evening begins to wind down, I'm ready to execute my plan, but Brennan catches me by the elbow, guiding me away from the others into the quiet of the living room. His voice is low and serious. "Cillian, hang back a sec. Da interrupted us before— Is everything alright?"

"Yeah, of course." I hesitate, the concern in his eyes seems to come from nowhere. "Why do you keep asking me?"

"You didn't speak much at dinner. It looked and felt like you'd rather have been anywhere but here." He crosses his arms.

I'm taken aback. "Where's this coming from? With everyone here tonight, it's hard to get a word in edgewise."

"I guess, um... Look, you're expanding the business fast." He grips my shoulder. "You and I hardly hang out anymore and I want to make sure you're holding up okay. We saw how things got with Dad. Be mindful, alright?"

His words piss me off because, unlike Da, I've never done anything to jeopardize McGloughlin Construction. Who is he to judge? I'm not about to pick a fight with my brother, though. "Thanks, Bren. I'll keep your concerns in mind."

Now, I *really* need a drink. I hate rehashing our family history.

Brennan claps my shoulder then squeezes it reassuringly. "All I'm saying is we're all here for you, not just for the good times. Don't shoulder it all alone."

Jesus. *Whatever*.

Rejoining the family in the living room, we land in the middle of Seamus recounting a run-in with his new boss. The laughter and stories continue but Brennan's words linger, reminding me of the delicate balance I must maintain keeping my family and personal life separate.

It's time for me to go.

"Everyone, I'm gonna head out." I scoot to the foyer.

"What's the rush, Kill? Got a hot date or something?" Connor raises an eyebrow with a knowing grin.

Seamus, snickers. "He's always sneaking off—probably leading a double life we know nothing about!"

"Oh, let the boy have his secrets; everyone needs a bit of mystery." Ma joins in with a playful twinkle in her eye.

Liam nudges Padraig. "Yeah, Kill's the mysterious one."

Their laughter and lighthearted slags fill the room, and while I know everyone's being playful by trying to pry a bit of information out of me, I'm annoyed.

Though he's amused by the family's banter, Da gets me. He catches my eye and nods toward the door, releasing me.

I step outside into the cool air and feel an immediate sense of relief.

A hour later, I'm sitting alone at the bar in Kells as three shots warm my system. I nurse a glass of Red Breast, relishing how the smooth liquid coaxes the tension from my shoulders. I find such peace in a buzz from the alcohol. For the first time today, my mind settles and I can simply exist.

Only one thing could improve my evening. It's time to find my fuck-buddy—a woman who won't expect more than a few orgasms, which I'm more than happy to provide.

Looking around, no one catches my eye. I'm patient, though.

I've got all night.

Three

IVY

Later that Evening

"*SLANTE!*"

A group of older men slam their pints of Guinness to toast the end of a workweek. They aren't the only ones. Kell's Irish Pub is packed with people of all ages and ethnicities on Friday evening. It's unlike anything I've ever experienced in my entire sheltered life.

Thrilling.

It's been an epic day filled with indulgence. The best I've had in such a long time.

I'd forgotten what it's like to be, well, happy.

Three hours of dance class was an emotional, cathartic release. It felt like layers of my structured life were shed away forever, allowing my mind to heal a bit. Making me feel open to possibilities.

No, making me eager to pursue them. I'm brave. Confident. Comfortable in my own skin.

After class, I enjoyed a leisurely dinner at Matt's in the Market, sitting at the big picture window overlooking the fish mongers. A beautiful girl with an incredible voice was busking. The halibut melted in my mouth. I was so content, I nearly didn't follow through using my new fake ID.

Then I thought, why play it safe? A night out is my way of throwing caution to the wind. Today's a milestone birthday and I deserve to have one drink to celebrate, even if it's technically illegal.

The music is lively. The atmosphere is fun. It's perfect here.

Tonight, my new identity, brave Ivy Davies, is going to dance with a cute guy, maybe two. Boring, scared Ivy Bright, heiress to Bright Shipping and Daddy's puppet belongs in my mausoleum of a home. The tragic girl whose brother died on her birthday can stay there, as far as I'm concerned.

I make my way to the bar with a nervous flutter in my stomach. I already know what I want—an Espresso Martini. I hope the bartender doesn't look too closely at my ID. Then again, why would he? The doorman scrutinized it and let me in without a second glance. Pushing my way through the crowd, I feel another jolt of independence.

It's addictive.

Rounding the corner, I zero in on the most handsome guy I've ever seen. He's tall, roguish and radiates a powerful magnetism. Everything about him captivates me and I find myself heading toward him.

The pull is primal.

Undeniable.

As inevitable as the tide is drawn to the moon.

He wears worn jeans and a black, fitted T-shirt emblazoned with a construction company's logo. Every muscle in his body is chiseled to perfection. A dark, unruly mop of hair nearly touches his shoulders and the stubble shadowing his square jaw gives him a wild, almost untamed look. He carries the confidence of someone who's used to getting what he wants. Power radiates through every pore of his body.

His eyes, though. They're kind and complicated. When they lock on mine, I'm enthralled by swirls of rich, earthy browns meshing with vibrant greens like a fairytale forest promising both danger and sanctuary.

The entire room fades away because our connection is instantaneous.

A jolt of electricity races through my body, rooting me in place a few inches in front of him. He takes me in with a slow, appreciative scan as though I've finally arrived. By the time his eyes return to mine, his lips curl into a naughty smirk and he nods. Like I passed his inspection. Immediately, my nipples harden into points and my pussy throbs with a need I've never known.

For a fleeting second, I forget why I'm here and who I'm supposed to be. And then, my entire world shifts on its axis forever. "*Mo shíorghrá*, I've been waiting for you." His deep slightly slurred voice has a faint hint of Irish lilt.

I'm momentarily taken aback because I don't know what *muh HEER-grawh* means, but decide to play along. "Here I am." I hardly recognize my breathy, flirtatious voice. "I'm sorry I'm late."

His raucous laugh fills the space between us. He leans in and his hand brushes against my arm, sending a surge of warmth through me. I'm acutely aware of every detail of this *man*—the breadth of his shoulders, the firmness of his arms, the dimple on his chin. He smells wonderful, like a hike through the woods on a clear day. "I'm Cillian. Are you ready to dance with me?"

"I thought you'd never ask." I playfully push his arm.

Cillian intercepts my hand and leads me to the middle of the dance floor, where he pulls me against his granite chest and spans my waist with a firm, possessive grip. We begin to move in perfect sync to the rhythm of a slow, haunting melody. His breath is warm against my ear. "You're absolutely captivating. Are you gonna tell me your name?"

I can't help but stifle a giggle. It's absurd to be intoxicated by an older guy who I've just met, but there's no denying my attraction to him. I'm not usually a believer in woo-woo stuff, but meeting him weirdly feels like my destiny. Like I manifested this shit.

"Ivy Davies." I run my fingers along the strong lines of his back, feeling his muscles flex with each pass.

"Eye-veeee." He draws my name out. "Darlin', you move incredibly well."

His lips trail down to the sensitive skin below my earlobe, sending shivers down my spine straight to my core. His hand rests against the small of my back and he urges me against him as we sway. Oh God, is that the hard bulge his cock? It's nestled between my legs like it belongs there.

He wants me.

I want him too. I'm literally soaked with arousal.

"I could say the same about you." Looking into his hazel eyes, which twinkle with mischief, I roll my hips against his. "It's almost like you know what I want before I do."

I don't even recognize myself. I'm operating on pure, carnal instinct. Judging by his surprised—yet amused—expression, my deliberate gesture is charged with an unspoken promise.

Groaning, Cillian cradles the back of my knee and lifts my leg to rest against his hip, aligning our bodies as we swirl into a graceful, flowing dip. "Maybe I do." His other hand grabs my ass and squeezes with a thrilling boldness. "Or maybe we're exceptionally in tune with each other."

The next song is a vibrant, traditional jig. Something in the music calls to me and I get lost, throwing my arms above my head and swaying my hips. Dancing over to Cillian, without breaking eye contact, I drag my fingers across his shoulders. He captures my hand and twirls me into his side and guides my arms around his neck.

"Jay-sus, you're a very sexy girl." Cillian's hands span my hips and he wedges his leg between mine, holding me there.

Once again, our movements are fluid, like it's natural for our bodies to align like this. Ignoring the tempo of the song, we rock slowly in perfect harmony. He takes my hands in his and draws them over my head. Our eyes bore into each other's as he runs his hands from my wrists to my shoulders and fists my hair.

Angling my face beneath his, Cillian hovers his lips against my neck, causing my breath to catch. The backs of his fingers trail back down my ribs and he clutches my hips and lowers his cheek to mine. Shamelessly, I grind my aching pussy against his thigh as we sway sensually.

I lose track of how many songs we dance to or at what point the crowd begins to thin, but for the next couple hours, our movements merge into one fluid motion and we're in our own world, vibing to our own rhythm. Teasing. Flirting. Touching.

I'm only vaguely aware of the band packing up because we're so lost in each other. I don't care if we're surrounded by dozens of people, he captures my mouth and spirals of ecstasy pirouette throughout my body.

Cillian's intense, decisive gaze locks on to mine. "From the moment you walked in here tonight, there's been no one else but you."

My heart races at his admission because I feel the same way. The air between us crackles with anticipation. His strong, gentle hand cradles my cheek. His ever-present erection throbs between us.

Not once tonight has he tried to hide what I've done to him, and I know what I want.

Him.

Impulsively, I close the distance between us and brush my lips against his. Cillian's guttural moan sends a shiver through my soul, igniting a profound yearning. His lips part slightly to invite me into the warmth of his mouth, allowing our tongues to slide in a slow, sweet exploration.

Our kisses intensify. Grow more urgent. Cillian's hand moves from my cheek to the back of my neck. His fingers lace their way through my hair, anchoring me to him as he devours me. My breath is quick and ragged and I press against him, not wanting a millimeter of space between us.

With a swift, assured motion, he lifts me off the ground. Instinctively, I wrap my legs around his waist and sling my arms over his neck. He supports me effortlessly with a firm grip on my ass, rocking me against his hard cock as our frenzied lips and tongues continue to explore.

"Do you want to get out of here?" he eventually murmurs against my lips, his voice low and husky.

There's no reason to play coy. I nod. "More than anything."

I wanted a summer fling. Why wait another minute? With only eight weeks of freedom, I'm diving headfirst into whatever experience he's offering. This guy is sex personified, the perfect person to show me the ropes. Maybe, even literally.

Tonight, the shadows of my past and the weight of my future can wait.

I want *this*. I want *him*.

As we leave the pub, hand in hand, I know I'm making the right decision. With every fiber of my being.

Something tells me, he's my destiny.

Four

CILLIAN

A Few Minutes Later

IVY'S GOING TO BE such a hot little fuck.

I can hardly believe my luck at meeting someone so...perfect.

When we leave the bar, the cool summer breeze does nothing to temper the heat coursing through me. Half hour from now and I'll be balls deep inside her, which is fucking awesome.

At the same time, I kind of like how Ivy's hand feels tiny in mine as we navigate the bustling downtown streets toward my loft. It's weird, we've only just met, but the mere act of walking back to my place with her feels like a gift—one I shouldn't take for granted.

We stop at the crosswalk, giving me a chance to steal a glance.

Her face, illuminated by the soft glow of street lamps, is a vision of serenity. Her big, blue eyes blink up at me, wide and shimmering with adoration. *Desire*. Her golden hair is tangled and wild from my fingers. Her lips are plump from my kisses. She even has beard burn on her upper lip.

God, she really is perfection.

It knocks me back.

I certainly didn't plan on this turn of events, but I'm not going to look a gift horse in the mouth.

Seeing her like this, vibrant and alive, stirs something hidden within me. Something more than lust, though my dick is hard as a pole. *Yeah*. Somehow, we've made a profound connection. It's tugging at the core of my being.

I've always thought love at first sight is a myth—and maybe it is—but with her, I can totally understand how people catch feelings quickly. Ivy makes me feel alive in ways I can't comprehend.

Ten minutes later, we arrive at my building, which has been renovated by McGloughlin Construction into a blend of historical architecture and modern design. I close the industrial elevator door behind me then gently tug Ivy toward me. Our bodies align with a shockingly familiar ease. Our lips touch except, unlike at the bar, now there's a deliberate slowness in how I kiss her. I want to savor the moment and heighten the connection we've been weaving all night.

The elevator comes to a stop, I hold the door open so Ivy can step inside. Her gaze sweeps across the high ceilings and custom fixtures. "You live *here*?" Her voice is tinged with awe. "It's *gorgeous.*"

Ivy's enthusiasm fills me with pride. I spent nearly two years making this not a just a cool place to live, but a showcase of what my company is capable of. Every detail is to my taste, from the old brick walls intersecting with vast, floor-length windows to the contemporary kitchen to the rich, warm wood floors.

"Thanks, darlin'. I renovated it myself. Moved in earlier this year." I caress the side of her face and nuzzle her ear, whispering, "For the record, the only thing gorgeous in here is you."

Ivy's chest heaves and she grips my elbows, sighing as she melts into me. "Cillian, the way you touch me, it feels incredible."

My cock throbs against my jeans. My God, Ivy looks sweet and innocent, but the way she speaks is direct. To the point. Clear with her intention. Her physical cues are there too.

The way she was grinding against me tonight has given me a permanent hard-on.

Although, under my loft's high-end lighting, it's apparent she's younger—much younger—than I originally thought. Or maybe, the buzz from the many Guinnesses I consumed earlier has faded and I'm able to see her more clearly now.

Shit.

I can't deny how much I want her, but it's time to do some due diligence before things go further. I'm not going to fuck her until I'm sure we're both on the same page. The last thing I need is a scandal.

"Hey." I take her hands in mine and step back. "I think we both know where this is headed and it's important you feel safe. Do you want to text someone where you are?"

A flicker of uncertainty flashes across her eyes but is quickly masked by a quick, nervous smile. Ivy's cheeks flush an intense shade of pink and her lips part as if she's about to say something. She stops and instead bites her lower lip. I hope she's not having second thoughts, but I won't pressure her if she is.

"Um. Yeah. Great idea. Give me a sec." She efficiently types into her phone and looks back at me. "For the record, I'm nervous at the situation, not at you. I *want* to be here." Ivy reaches for my belt like she's done this a few times before. "I want *you*."

"Whoa, hold up for a second." I capture her hands, bring them to my lips and kiss her knuckles. "Let's talk about this. I can be pretty intense during sex. If there's anything you're not on board with, I'll stop. No matter what. Okay? I'll always respect your boundaries."

Ivy blushes adorably. "How can you be so perfect? I've been wet all night thinking about what you're going to do to me."

Alrighty, then. Green. Fucking. Light.

"Oh, sweet Ivy." I take a step away and look at her. "You're killing me with your naughty talk. At least let me be a gentleman. Would you like something to drink? Wine?"

She slides onto a stool at the counter, twirls a lock of her hair around her finger and looks off into the distance. "Uh...Sure."

"Red? White? Rose?" I crouch my six-foot-six frame down to check my wine fridge, then peer up at her.

Ivy shrugs. "Whatever you like is fine with me."

"Rose, then." It's usually the wine of choice for the women I've dated—*errrr*, fucked. "Tell me. I've never seen you at Kell's before. What brought you out tonight?"

God, the way she blushes. Pinkness spreads from her cheeks to her chest. It's adorable. "Well, I actually have a confession. I was celebrating tonight."

"Oh yeah?" I set out two glasses and fill them with wine. "What's the occasion?"

"Well…" Her laugh echoes like music in the spacious loft as we clink our glasses together. "It's actually my birthday. Today's usually a sad day, but I decided to reclaim it."

I don't need to be a detective to read between the lines. There are secrets hidden beneath her carefully chosen words. It's probably not the time to delve into it now, though. "Well, then. Happiest of birthdays. How old are you, sweet Ivy?"

"Twenty-four." She looks me in the eye, then takes a large swig. "How about you?"

Good God, the relief. She's eight years my junior, but well within the fuckable range. Then it occurs to me. If she looks young to me, the opposite must be true for her. She probably realized I have a gray hair or two.

Maybe she thinks I'm too old for *her*.

"Thirty-two," I admit, watching her closely for any sign of concern. It's a big age gap. We're in different decades and different stages of life.

"How utterly and completely perfect." Her laughter fills the room again. "Guys my age are immature and selfish. I've always wanted to be with someone who knows how to treat a woman. Someone with *experience*."

Oh, this is on. If she wants experience, I'll show her every trick I know. Ivy's going to come many, many times. She'll never want to leave.

Whoa.

I circle the island, swivel her stool so she's facing me and step in between her knees. "You're young and beautiful, shouldn't you be celebrating with your friends instead of hanging out with me?"

"Um…" Her gaze flicks toward the window before returning to mine. "I used to. Not much anymore. Usually, I spend it with my family but they're out of town."

"Families can be complicated. Mine has its own set of issues." I cup her face in my palms.

She grips my wrists, as if to keep my hands in place, but looks down. "The truth is, something happened a few years ago on my birthday and we really don't celebrate anymore."

Her voice trembles, indicating some profound sadness that ignites a protective urge within me. I angle her face so she's looking into my eyes . "I'm sorry to hear. I'm glad I could bring a little cheer to your special day."

"You have. More than you know. It's been the best birthday in a long time." Ivy's contagious smile returns, drawing me in.

I step closer until my thighs hit the edge of the chair. The air between us crackles. "I'd like to make it even better, if you'll let me."

Her eyes meet mine, flickering with desire. Encouraged, I tuck a loose strand of hair behind her ear. The rough pads of my fingertips graze her skin lightly. My simple touch sends a shiver through us both, reigniting the electric current that seemed to pulse only for us on the dance floor.

"How?" The word catches on her breath.

"Maybe like this." My lips latch on to the sensitive spot on her neck and I suck gently before I kiss my way to her mouth.

Things between us rapidly escalate and she responds with an urgency matching my own. She yanks me to her by my beltloops. I rest my palms on her parted thighs, my thumbs work their way under the hem of her cutoffs, deliberately moving closer and closer to her sweet little pussy. I can smell her arousal from here and I need to taste her. *Now.*

I feel her fingers thread through my hair as she moans against my mouth, "More."

Encouraged, I intensify our kiss. Her tongue tangles with mine. My fingers trace the hollow of her upper thigh and slip inside her leotard, finding her absolutely drenched. My cock fills to a capacity I didn't know was possible. "Are you sure you're okay with this? I'm getting past the point of no return with you..."

"Yes!" Her hand clamps around my wrist to hold me in place. "I want this. *Please*..."

"Everything?" I pause and press my forehead to hers to stare deep into her soul. For some reason, I want to really check in with her. I'd die if I hurt her.

She hooks her legs around my hips. "This wouldn't feel so incredible if it was wrong, Cillian."

Ivy releases her grip on my wrists, unbuckles my jeans and slips her hand inside my waistband. Her palm presses against my engorged cock over my boxers—I nearly come on the spot.

Okay. *Fine*. I'm convinced. She wants this as much as I do.

"Oh, no. I'm taking care of you first." I remove her hand from my pants and place it on the counter. "I've been dying to taste your pussy all night."

Ivy moans, "Yes, *pleeeeeasssse*."

I graze her lower lip with my teeth and slide through her wetness to locate her slick little clit. "What have I found here?"

"*Ahhhhh*," Ivy cries out, squeezing her eyes shut, squirming at my touch.

God, she's incredible. This will the best sex I've ever had. Hands down. The initial flirtation in the noisy ambiance of Kells has turned into something neither of us expected, but maybe we both desperately need.

I work two fingers deep inside her tight channel and stroke. "Remember, tonight's about you. You'll have so many birthday orgasms, your head is going to spin."

"*Yes*. I want all the birthday orgasms," she whimpers. I withdraw my fingers and plunge them back in. "Ohhhh, God. *Ohhhhkay*."

Fuck. She's responsive. One night won't be enough. The thought lingers as my fingers catalog every millimeter of her velvety pussy. The thought is tantalizing and terrifying all at once.

I want to be in this moment now, though. I push thoughts of the future to the side.

For now.

Tonight, my focus is on Ivy.

I'll make her twenty-fourth birthday one she'll never forget.

Five

A Few Minutes Later

I MUST BE CERTIFIABLY insane.

I've turned my body over to a man I just met.

And, it's better than I ever could imagine.

Cillian's fingers are doing magical things to my pussy—how can something feel so incredible? I've had fantasies about what my first time would be like, but it was never this. I'm pretty skilled at getting myself off, but—until now—I had no idea how much pleasure my body was capable of.

Cillian's thumb circles my clit in time to his fingers plunging in and out of me. I'm squirming. Writhing. Moaning like a porn star. I can't control my reaction to expert manipulation of my pleasure spots. Everything is raw, natural and intense. His face hovers over mine, studying me intently, almost like he's cataloging my every reaction.

Almost like he wants to memorize me.

For someone like me, who's grown used to feeling invisible most of the time, Cillian's focus on my pleasure is addictive. Every detail of his face is sharp and clear. The concern. The intensity. When the wet sounds he's eliciting from down below make me tense with embarrassment, he whispers encouragement. Tells me how beautiful I am. How fantastic I smell.

I'm sure he senses my inexperience, because he describes everything he's doing to me. It makes me feel safe. Cared for.

Seen.

I'm not an idiot, he's a stranger. An incredibly handsome stranger whom I'm willingly going to have sex with, no matter what the consequences. I should be scared, but I'm not. Every instinct tells me I was supposed to meet Cillian tonight. He's my destiny. He's my person.

Except, for one thing. I've backed myself into a corner with the lie about my age. I had to do it, though. It's what's on my fake ID.

Besides, if I tell him the truth now, he'll stop finger-fucking me, which can't happen. If I don't tell him, then I risk...God. This can't be a one-time thing.

"Where'd you go?" Cillian smooths the hair from my face with his free hand. "Are you not enjoying this?"

I nod vigorously. "It's *soooo* good, I'm, *uh*..."

"It's okay. I'll get you there, sweet Ivy." Cillian's thumb presses my button and circles furiously. "You're going to cream all over my fingers and I'll lick up every drop."

"Ohmygod." My pussy convulses at the thought of his mouth on me and I find myself bucking against his hand like a wild woman, seeking something to push me over the edge. I don't know what I need. Yet, I feel frantic to figure it out.

Light crow's feet etch the corners of Cillian's eyes when he smiles down at me patiently. His jawline is dusted with stubble, a mix of dark hair with the occasional reddish thread. His thumb grazes the apple of my cheek. "Don't chase it, baby. All you have to do is relax. I've got you. I promised birthday orgasms and I always keep my promises."

Cillian lowers his head to the curve of my neck. His lips hover over the sensitive spot behind my ear, then he flicks his tongue on my earlobe while his thumb moves faster and his fingers hit a spot inside me I didn't know existed. In seconds, there's no choice but to give in. Warmth pools in my core and spreads like a radiating brushfire. My thighs shake. My nipples feel like they're piercing through my leotard.

Then I explode. Grip his hand and hold it in place so I can ride this out. My head thrashes from side to side and I hear myself screaming unabashedly. I've never in my life been this free. Felt this *much*.

Throughout, Cillian holds me. Slows his fingers to long, soothing strokes as I come down. The softest sighs escape his lips every time I shudder. His raw, natural, woodsy scent permeates my senses. Everything about this moment will be burned into my memory forever.

"My God, you're sweet as pie." Cillian removes his hand and sucks on his fingers. "Delicious."

I watch him, transfixed. I'm not sure how I expected to feel, but I'm not embarrassed. I want more. I want it all. I reach up and thumb his scruff. "Can we do more?"

"Jay-sus, greedy woman." Cillian smirks, but his hazel eyes never leave mine. He slips one arm firmly around my lower back and the other beneath my knees and, in one fluid motion, lifts me from the stool.

His hold is protective. Possessive. His chest muscles flex under my touch. Instinctively, my arms wrap around his neck and I rest my head against his shoulder. He leans his head against mine and carries me with a confident grace down a softly lit hallway. Cillian pauses at the double door, his eyes searching mine for a moment. I nod and grip his nape.

I've never been surer of something in my life.

Cillian nudges the door open with his foot, revealing his masculine bedroom washed in the gentle glow of ambient lighting. He lowers me onto the bed and kisses my lips before slowly releasing his hold. He doesn't break contact, though. His hands trail lightly up my waist, across my chest to my face.

Leaning down, he holds himself inches from me. There's a slight catch in his breath. "Are you okay?"

"Yes." I tilt my head up until our lips are barely touching. I grip the hair curling at his neck. "You've already made this the best birthday ever."

Cillian's mouth crashes down on mine roughly. Our tongues slide over each other as he cups my breasts and thrums my nipples through the fabric. He tastes like wine and...*me.*

The realization is overwhelming.

We break apart and I rest my hands on his hips. His jeans are still unbuckled, I undo the button, unzip them and slip my hand inside his boxers. Tentatively, I grip his cock and slide my fist up and down like I've seen on porn videos. He's thick. Weighty. I want to taste the liquid leaking from the tip, so I engulf his crown.

"Oh, fuck." Cillian's hips jut forward. "What a hot little mouth you have, baby."

Encouraged, I lock my gaze with his and lick him from root to tip. Kiss up his shaft and repeat. Jack him. Suck and swirl. Cup his balls. I don't know what I'm doing, but he seems to like it. Cillian grips my cheeks and watches himself disappear in and out of my mouth, uttering anguished groans every so often.

Abruptly, he pulls out. "Ivy, I'm on the brink. If you don't want me to come in your mouth, now's the time to tell me."

"I want you to." I don't hesitate to guide his length back into my mouth as far as I can manage.

Cillian thrusts himself to the back of my throat and I feel hot liquid pulse out in spurts. I swallow every salty-sweet drop and lave his cock with my tongue until he's clean. Another first, and I love it. Making him lose control makes me feel powerful

"There's no going back from this, Ivy." Cillian steps out of his jeans and boxers and sits next to me on the bed. Pulls off his T-shirt and tosses it on the floor. He's gloriously naked and looks exactly like a marble statue in Rome. "I have a feeling if I fuck you tonight, you're gonna be mine forever."

Tingles flutter up and down my spine at his words, which make me even more confident in my decision to be here. On paper, the idea of forever with Cillian after knowing him a few hours is absurd. In reality, his words ring true. "I think I might already be yours."

"Well, since you're mine, I've got to mention you're wearing too many clothes." Cillian unbuttons and unzips my cutoffs and I lift my hips so he can slide them down my legs.

I bite down on my lip and watch him peel down my leotard. My breasts spring free and he kisses and sucks on each nipple while he rolls the clingy fabric down and off my body. A horrific thought permeates my body. I never thought to shave because I had no idea I'd be naked in a man's bedroom tonight, but even someone as inexperienced as me knows I should groom my pubic hair before sex.

I can't help but panic and place my hand over my mound. "I'm sorry, I didn't plan..."

Cillian grabs my hand and presses me back on the bed. "You're my every fantasy. I dig your hairy little pussy. Never hide yourself from me."

"Are you sure?" I press my thighs together and try to twist away.

He grasps under my leg and presses up toward my ear exposing...everything. He runs a finger through my soaking folds and I quiver. Despite how nervous I am, he makes me feel desirable. Mature.. "You're very wet, *mo shíorghrá*. Do you want me to lick your pussy?"

My voice trembles. *"Yesssss."*

His licks his lips. "And then, do you want me to fuck you, Ivy?"

"*Yessssss.*" I'm exposed, but the way my body responds to his touch, I can't wait to feel him inside me.

Cillian's eyes skim my body then meet mine, quirking with amusement. "I don't know..."

"Do you believe in fate?" I cup my breasts and pinch my nipples, somehow knowing I'm safe in expressing my sexuality with Cillian. "I've loved everything about tonight. I didn't expect to meet the sexiest, kindest, most handsome man in the world, but I'm glad it happened. There's something between us. I'm not going to question it. Don't worry, I'll never regret anything we do."

Cillian spreads my lower lips with his fingers and inserts his finger deep inside me. "Giving yourself to me is a precious gift. I'm honored. Remember, you can stop at any time."

"I don't want to stop," I plead. "*Please.*"

He brings his finger to his lips and sucks. "I want this too. And, I was serious earlier, this is not a one-night thing. I have a feeling we're going to be magic together."

"*Mmmmmm.* I can't think of anything better than spending the summer fucking you." I'm startled when I utter such brazen, but truthful, words.

Cillian slides down my body until he's eye-level with my pussy. He breathes me in and sighs. "Well, I can't think of anything better than spending my *life* fucking you."

He hooks my thighs over his shoulders, settles into this new position and gazes up at me as he sucks my clit between his lips.

My entire body shudders and it's official.

I belong to him.

Six

CILLIAN

Minutes Later

I'VE NEVER TASTED ANYTHING better in my life.

Ivy blushes as she watches me feast on her. I fucking love the way she bites down on her lip when I lick her cream. No one's ever responded to me this way. It's like I hold the key to her every pleasure. God, I can't wait to feel her perfect pussy fluttering around my cock every time I make her come.

I'm quite certain I don't deserve her, but opportunities like this don't come around often. I don't intend on doing anything to fuck this up. I've never wanted a girlfriend. Never believed in love at first sight.

Until now.

There's no doubt in my mind. I want Ivy to be mine. Full stop.

"How can this feel so incredible?" Ivy cries out. My tongue tunnels into her and I drag it through her glistening pink folds to her clit. I suck on her little bud until she starts moaning. She covers her mouth with one hand and buries the other in my hair.

I grin up at her. "Maybe because you're my favorite flavor, hands down."

She's gorgeous, writhing and panting as I devour her. Between long licks, I flick her clit with the tip of my tongue until she grips my hair hard. Her thighs shake and she shatters again, drenching my face.

I lap up every drop. "You're going to have to pry me off your perfect pussy. You'll have to beg me to stop."

"It's too intense." Her head thrashes from side to side, but I dive back in and edge her to another peak.

"You can take it. You're tight, I want you wet. My cock will slide in easily." I resume my feast, this time inserting two fingers and locating her spongy bundle of pleasure.

I'm not gentle. I'm relentless, rubbing her spot and lapping at her delectable pussy. Every muscle in Ivy's body trembles.

Her heels dig into the bed on either side of my shoulders. She bucks wildly against my lips and moans, low and keening, "*Cillian*, oh God."

I place my other palm on her lower stomach and press down. Suck on her clit. Thrust my fingers in and out. Ivy finally gives in and loses all semblance of control. It's beautiful to see. She's a wild, feral woman owning her own pleasure, which I draw out and out and out. I'm exhilarated. I want to spend every waking hour making her come.

She bites down on her lip hard and her eyes practically roll back in her head when she goes over again. Tears stream down her cheeks as wave after wave rolls through her. My face is soaked with her essence, but I love it.

Shifting my position so I can wrap her in my arms, I cup her perky breast with one hand. The other pets her mound in light caresses to ease her off the ledge. "I wish you could see yourself come. You look beautiful."

"I do?" Ivy blinks up at me.

I close the small gap between us and press my lips against hers. It's a gentle kiss, soft yet intentional, allowing me to savor her. To slowly explore with deliberateness. Her soft hand threads into mine. I'm not sure how long we make out but Ivy snuggles closer, tucking herself against the curve of my body. Her leg slips between mine. Her head finds the perfect spot on my chest. We're a tangle of warmth and comfort, our bodies fit together perfectly.

I melt.

"If you're tired, we don't have to go further, love. I'm happy to hold you all night." I kiss the side of her head. I'm dying to be inside her, but she's allowed to change her mind.

She tenses for a second. "Are *you* tired?"

"No, but I want to make sure you're still on board with...everything." I squeeze her tightly, trying to play it cool. The truth is, I want her more than I've ever wanted anything in my life.

Ivy doesn't look at me, just trails her fingers along my arm. "Yes. Completely."

"Okay." I lean up on my elbow and tip her chin up so I can look at her.

"I'm not someone who ordinarily takes risks. Me being here with you is...uncharacteristic, to say the least." She moves my hand to her breast. "You make me feel wild and uninhibited and also safe and protected."

I thumb her pink nipple into a hard peak. "So...would you like me to make love to you now?"

"Oh, we're making love now, not fucking?" She reaches for my cock, which is hard as steel.

I clasp my hand over hers and, together, we stroke. "We'll do both before the night is over. Maybe twice."

I roll over and kneel between Ivy's legs. She reaches down and uses two fingers to spread her lips apart. "I want to feel like I'm full of you. Like our bodies are one."

I nearly ejaculate on her stomach.

"Ivy, Jesus," I groan, working my shaft. "If you keep saying stuff like that it'll be over before it begins."

The look she gives me burns with such intensity, it makes me tremble. "I want you." Ivy spreads her legs wider and rubs her clit. "I can't wait to feel you in me."

I glance over at my nightstand. "Let me get a condom."

"I'm on the pill." She grabs my wrist. "I'm, uh...clean. Please tell me you are too."

The thought of being inside her raw causes my dick to twitch. "I've never *not* used a condom."

Ivy leans up on her elbows. "Good. I want to feel all of you."

Her words are all I can take. No man could resist this woman in this moment, including me. I give in, reach under Ivy's legs and yank her up so her perfect ass rests against my thighs. My cock presses against her wet pussy.

"Holy fuck." I tap my dick against her clit. "You're dripping for me."

Slowly, I feed my cock into her narrow channel. Inch by inch. I can't look away. "God, you're so fucking tight and wet." I rock my hips to push in deeper, though I'm only a fraction of the way in. "Look at how you're taking me, Ivy. Watch us."

"*Ohmygod.*" Ivy's transfixed. "I'm not sure you're going to fit."

"You're stretched around me like you can't possibly fit another inch, but you will. You can handle all of me. Keep playing with yourself." I circle my hips to work myself farther in.

Ivy clenches around my cock. Her stomach ripples. She rubs furiously until she gasps as another orgasm rips through her body. As she comes, I snap my hips and use her release to easily fill her up.

"*Wow.*" Ivy's eyes flutter closed.

"You own me, Ivy." I stop moving and reach up and pinch her nipples. "Tell me what you want. Help me make this good for you."

Ivy gasps and wriggles around me as she adjusts to my size. "It doesn't hurt, it feels...like I need you to move. Give me everything. Don't hold back. I trust you."

She fits me like a custom glove. I drive into her, using my grip on her ass to control our movements. She clings to my arms and watches me impale her over and over. Every now and then I shift my angle until my crown nudges her pleasure spot and she screams out in utter ecstasy. My cock is per-fectly positioned, I pick up the pace and fuck her hard until her tits bounce between us. Every now and then I capture a nipple with my lips and suck.

I'm a madman. Nothing's ever felt this phenomenal. "You're going to come on my cock again, aren't you?"

"Yes!" she rasps, already trembling.

"I'm coming in your tight pussy and I'm not pulling out. I'll fill you up." Ivy's walls clench around me tightly as I hammer into her.

"*Ahhhhhhh*. Oh, God. *Ahhhhh*." Ivy unabashedly screams at the top of her lungs.

Shit. The onslaught of sensation is too much and I follow without any warning, heaving and grunting until I'm empty.

I gently lower Ivy to the bed and cage her in with my arms, but I don't pull out. We're both slick with sweat and panting for breath, but I cradle her and press adoring kisses to her face. "Holy shit. This is the best it's ever been for me, sweet Ivy. How do you feel?"

"Perfect." She grips my face, guides me to her and kisses me passionately. "It's the best it's ever been for me too."

I snap my hips to burrow my still-hard cock into her wet heat. "I'm honored."

"I loved every second. Orgasms with your big cock inside me are...intense." She giggles. "It finally makes sense why people become addicted to sex."

Something about her words niggles at me. She's talking as if she's never made love before, but that's not possible, is it? Nah. She's a sexy little thing. There's no way. As I look down into her gorgeous, flushed face, my heart swells with a mix of emotions. Happiness. Lust. Longing.

Fear.

I can't regret what happened, but I've got to be careful with her.

"Let's get you cleaned up." I ease out of her, a pool of our release floods the sheets. "I'll be back."

Ivy watches as I get out of bed and return with a warm washcloth. I carefully wipe us up and climb back next to her. As we lay entwined, I savor every moment. Holding her close. Breathing in her flowery scent. Enjoying her heartbeat against mine.

She falls asleep against my chest and I can't help but think—I want this to last...*forever*.

Jesus. I've got to slow my roll. I'm operating on emotion. We don't know each other. With our age difference, we're likely in very different places in our lives.

Chances are, she'll move on from me. Probably sooner rather than later.

I'd better not get too attached.

Or, is it already too late?

Seven

IVY

The Next Morning

I WAKE UP TO the warm glow of sunlight on my face and a man's arm slung around my body.

Something stiff is poking me in the ass.

At first, I panic because I'm in an unfamiliar place and my body is sore...everywhere.

Then, I remember where I am and whom I'm with. Every wonderful thing about last night comes back to me in an instant.

Yesterday, even though I knew the day would suck, I didn't anticipate I'd be abandoned by my parents. In planning my grand adventure, it never occurred to me I'd stay out all night, courtesy of my oblivious friend, Emma. Let alone lose my virginity to a guy who's fourteen years older than me.

Funny how life can change in an instant.

Heat sears through my core at the thought of Cillian worshiping every inch of my body. I've given myself a lot of orgasms over the years, but nothing remotely compared to the pleasure he was able to coax out of me. He talked a convincing game last night about spending more time together, but I wonder if he'll feel the same way this morning. Maybe I'm a one-night stand.

It could go either way. I'm self-aware enough to realize how crazy it is to think I found my soulmate at eighteen. On paper, he and I don't make sense. Especially because he doesn't know I'm six years younger than what I told him. Or that I was a virgin. I have mixed feelings about keeping secrets from him, but I need to see how things play out before I come clean.

I wonder if he'd have made the same choice, if he'd known.

For now, I'm exactly where I want to be.

Cillian's cock twitches and I can't help but smile at the thought of waking up like this every day. God, am I insane?

Am I this infatuated with a man I met hours ago? I turn to face him. His eyes are still closed, his handsome face relaxed.

Wow. An overwhelming sense of rightness overtakes my thoughts. He's been inside my body. I can't imagine my life moving forward without him.

I lean in and kiss him gently. His eyelashes flutter before his hazel eyes slowly open. He brushes his thumb over my cheek and tucks a lock of hair behind my ear. "Morning, beautiful."

God, his deep, sexy baritone. My stomach flutters. "Good morning."

"Did you have sweet dreams?" He trails his hand to my waist and pulls me closer.

I snuggle in, caught up in the cozy intimacy of waking up in someone's arms for the first time. "Yeah, and they all seemed to involve you."

The corners of his eyes crinkle as he tightens his embrace and kisses my forehead. "Then, I hope I played my part well."

Before he can stop me, I smash my lips against his. As our tongues tangle, Cillian's hands trail down my sides and around my ass. He drags me closer until his erection is flush between our bellies. I moan at the thought of having sex with him again and wrap my fingers around his cock.

"Is this okay?" I sling my leg over his hip.

Groaning, Cillian kisses a path along my neck as I glide him through my folds. "Fuck, baby. You don't need to ask."

"Good." I hold his tip to my opening and try to guide him in, but quickly realize this position isn't going to work.

Without saying a word, Cillian rolls onto his back, taking me with him, and suddenly I'm straddling his hips. As my legs stretch across his body, I feel small muscle aches from yesterday's dance class and our own sexy gymnastics, but I don't care. He grips his cock and helps me position myself so his crown presses against my entrance.

"Now, ride me, sweet Ivy." He holds me by my waist as I lower myself on his thick length.

Once he's a few inches in, I brace myself on his stomach and watch as his cock stretches and fills me. "Oh...this is *awesome*," I sigh the moment my pussy rests on his pubic bone.

The pleasure blooms immediately, especially because Cillian expertly cups my tits and squeezes them, then pulls and pinches my nipples. I feel myself creaming around him, allowing me to move up and down on his cock more easily. Then, I roll my hips. Undulate. Swivel. Grind. I experiment until my clit hits just right, then I rock back and forth, keeping the friction. My orgasm builds immediately as I start to ride him harder.

Cillian growls and grips my ass in his big hands. "Yes, baby...use my cock however you want. It's yours!"

"*Ohhhhhh.*" My movements are almost frantic. I can't get enough of him.

My mouth lolls open as we stare into each other's eyes. My tits bounce as I grind my pelvis into him. His cock hits a magic place inside and I'm going to explode. Cillian seems to sense I'm about to go over, and he pulls me down until my tits are smashed against his chest. Then he kisses me hard as his hands wrap around my back to press my pelvis against his.

Before I know it, he flips us over, presses my legs together and pistons his cock into me from behind. He's embedded so far into my body at this angle, every inch of his cock seems to have been designed to fit me perfectly.

"You're clamping around my cock like a vise. It feels so fucking awesome." Cillian continues to fuck me with everything he's got.

My orgasm hits like a bomb, and I collapse like a noodle, completely spent. Cillian rolls us over and clasps my hands in his, bringing them over my head. His hips piston for a few more thrusts until he fills me with his hot release. We remain locked in place, kissing and stroking each other for a while. Eventually, he finally softens and slips out, leaving me empty.

"Sex with you is amazing. I hope I'm not a disappointment. You've probably been with a lot of women." I snuggle closer to him, enjoying the feel of our combined release dripping between my thighs.

Cillian cups my cheek. "What's happening between us is something special. I could spend every day of my life filling you up over and over." He kisses my forehead. "But, will you do me a favor? Let's not talk about other people when we make love."

I'm mortified. "I'm sorry…"

"No." Cillian presses a finger to my lips. "Don't apologize. I understand we may be at different stages in our lives. I'll say this once out of respect for you. I've been with a lot of women over the years. If you'd have asked my brothers a few years ago, they'd say I was a serial fuckboy. Those days are long gone, but I promise, I've never, not once, felt such a strong connection with anyone. It's confusing. You entrance me, Ivy. I want to see where this goes. I don't care about our pasts. Let's focus on what we have in the here and now."

His words are music to my ears. I run my fingers through his hair. "I want to. I asked because I never expected to feel like this and I wanted to be sure we were thinking the same things this morning."

"We are." Cillian tweaks my nipple and his dick lurches against my thigh. "Now look what you've done. You've got to be sore. I should give you a break. Can I make you breakfast?"

"Sure, but maybe we can shower after we eat." I slap his butt as he eases out of bed.

He pulls on a fresh pair of boxers and tosses me a large T-shirt. "You're insatiable. And I like it. Why don't you wear this for now. Should I throw your clothes in the wash?"

"Sure." I pull on his T-shirt while he gathers up our clothes. It's natural being here with him, I'm more comfortable in Cillian's loft than I am in my own home.

How funny.

Cillian shakes his head, laughing, and backs out the door. "Oh, and to answer your question, we'll shower after breakfast. I'm not done with your birthday orgasms. Not quite yet."

I'm stretched and achy, but want everything he has to give me. As I follow him into the kitchen, my mind races. Last night, I wasn't truthful with Cillian because I wasn't sure what this would be. This morning, I've caught feelings and I feel guilty about the lies between us.

We can't build a relationship on a foundation of deceit. I need to tell him the truth if this has a chance of being more than a one-night stand. Starting our future off on the right foot means coming clean, no matter how daunting the conversation might be.

But, seriously, now that he's fucked me, how can I possibly tell him I was an eighteen-year-old virgin who's pretending to spend the night at a classmate's house so my dad's house manager doesn't rat me out?

Carefully. Very carefully.

Soon, the aroma of coffee and bacon fills the room. I lean against the counter, watching him. "Are you sure you're in construction? You have mad cooking skills."

"Well, with six boys in the family, my ma taught us all how to cook a few things." He carefully plates our breakfast. "I actually started working at my father's construction company when I was eighteen. My brother ran it for a few years, but he's in a band and had to go on the road. My dream was to take over one day and when I was twenty-five, I gladly stepped in permanently."

Huh. Sounds really familiar. We have another thing in common. "Is your dad alive?"

"Aye. He's semi-retired now. For years he struggled with alcoholism. Had some health problems. Blah. Blah. Blah. Now he's doing well and I run it and he helps out from time to time." Cillian sets a plate down.

His openness tugs at me, encouraging me to share a few of my own truths. "My dad expects me to take over the family business in a few years. I'm off to start my MBA at Stanford Business School in a few weeks." I keep my voice steady to try to ease into who I really am.

"You have quite the responsibility." Cillian looks at me with respect. "Sounds like we've both been pushed into deep waters early."

"Yeah, I'm overwhelmed sometimes," I agree, trying to smile. My whole truth is on the tip of my tongue, but something holds me back.

"We're great in bed, we both love to dance and we're trying to keep family legacies afloat." Cillian takes a bite of bacon. "With so much in common, it makes me wonder if you like spontaneous getaways. I have to check on something at one of my jobsites, but maybe we can take a drive and spend tonight somewhere fun?"

Is he for real? I'm thrilled, except...I've got to let Hilde know I'm spending another night at Emma's. Probably better to do it in person rather than by text. "I should go home and pack a change of clothes. My car is parked in the lot at the Market."

"Amazing. I'll drive you over and you can go grab some things while I work. I'll pick you up in a few hours." He takes my empty plate and puts it in the sink. "We can postpone our shower until later."

Uh...*shit*. I have to at least come semi-clean. "This is embarrassing, but I still live at my folks' house. I don't really want to explain to them—" I gesture between us. "At least, not yet."

I can't risk him showing up on the security cameras.

"Uh, yeah. Wouldn't want a strange man to show up at your house, would you?" Cillian grins. "Will they be worried you didn't come home last night?"

Aha. Perfect opportunity to be honest-*ish.* "Well, my I told my dad I'd be staying some nights with a friend."

"Makes sense. For now, he's none the wiser." Cillian embraces me from behind and nuzzles my neck. "I won't give you away...yet. How about you meet me back here at three."

Fifteen minutes later, wearing Cillian's T-shirt and a pair of his running shorts, I'm on my way home, giddy as fuck. I've met a man who adores me. Wants to spend time with me. I'm smitten, and who wouldn't be? The way he worshipped my body is a fantasy come true.

Plus, even if he doesn't know it yet, he made me a woman.

My summer will be filled with Cillian McGloughlin.

Scratch that.

Cillian is going to fill *me* up all summer.

I can't wait.

Eight

CILLIAN

A Few Hours Later

GOD, I NEED A drink.

I'm having second thoughts. Third thoughts. What the fuck am I doing?

Pulling into the familiar confines of my building's garage, I'm like a live wire. The apprehension's been intensifying throughout the drive home.

All morning there was one problem after the other on the jobsite, yet the image of Ivy's smile, how we danced—how we fucked—replayed incessantly in my mind. My dick was at half-mast for most of the day, which was annoying AF. I've never caught feelings for someone I picked up at the pub before. It freaked me out and, at some point today, doubt crept in.

I'm so goddamn stupid. I can't go out of town with some woman I met last night.

Woman. *Hah*!

Ivy Davies is twenty-fucking-four. Far too young for me. It's not like we have a future, she's moving to California in a few weeks. Our timing sucks. She's only beginning to explore adult life, while I'm buried in responsibilities and feel stretched thin. I don't have any space for…whatever might be blooming between us.

I need to nip this in the bud.

I kill the engine to my truck and sit for a moment, trying to sort out my thoughts. I'm a no-strings, no-complicated-entanglement kind of guy. *Fuck it*, I'm canceling. I'll tell her I didn't book anything yet and let her down by claiming I couldn't get a reservation.

There's no need to hurt her. She can go home and this madness between us can fade into the ether.

My phone buzzes as I make my way from the parking garage to the coffee shop next door, where Ivy is waiting.

> ***Ivy:*** *Still feeling you from last night…I'm ready for a repeat. ;)*

Jesus fuck. My dick springs to life from her flirty text. I promised this sweet Ivy a getaway and she's probably been excited all day. Meanwhile, I've spent the past couple hours scheming how to get out of it.

The rational part of me knows, without a shadow of doubt, all the reasons why letting this continue is a mistake. The bottom line is, I'm not the guy for her. Last night I had too much to drink. I didn't even bother with protection. I'm clean, but gave no thought to the potential consequences in my rush to get my dick wet.

She said she's on birth control, but maybe she lied.

Fuck. Ivy could be pregnant.

I'm not ready to be a father.

Why would she lie about it, though? I can't imagine someone as genuine as Ivy would be less than truthful. Pretending to spend the night at a friend's aside… But, I'm a friend, right?

We'll go with that.

Yeah. I'm spinning. Like I always do if someone outside my family threatens to get close.

Let's be honest. Despite the swirling doubts and panic, an inherent, truer part of me yearns for this to be real. Everything in my being wants to hang out with her some more.

Get to know her. Hold her hand. Run my fingers through her hair. Wrap her in my arms by a roaring fire. Watch her come apart every time I fuck her.

Jesus. *Shut. The. Fuck. Up.*

Each step toward the coffee shop is a battle between my desires and my fears. Then I catch a glimpse of Ivy standing on the patio.

She's bathed in the soft afternoon light, her white dress catches the breeze—it's a vision. Ivy is so starkly beautiful it's like a punch to my gut. With a small, pink overnight bag at her side, Ivy waits. Blonde hair glimmering with golden highlights. She turns her clear, turquoise eyes toward me and smiles, and it's as though my world reorients itself around her.

Only her.

All the arguments, all the reasons why this shouldn't happen, fade into insignificance. The sight of her wipes clean any doubt. She's what matters to me now.

Mine.

Mo shíorghrá

"Hey," I manage to choke out as I approach.

"Hey!" Her voice bubbles with infectious joy. "I was thinking about how much fun we'll have in a hotel room."

The way her eyes light up talking about our unmade plans unravel me. How could I have thought to deny her this? "Well, let's head upstairs. I need to pack."

In the elevator up to my loft, Ivy presses against me. Her boldness sends a thrill through my veins. I wrap my arm tightly around her, pulling her flush against my chest, as if trying to meld her into my body. If there were any lingering thoughts to get out of this, they dissolve in this instant.

Instead, a new determination takes root. I'm making tonight unforgettable. But, I've gotta come clean.

"About this trip," I say as we step into my living room. "I haven't actually booked anything yet. I got caught up at the site and then, well, it was time to meet you."

Her laugh in response is light and forgiving. "What do we do, Mr. Spontaneous?"

"Give me twenty minutes to shower and pack. I promise I'll line something up." Her trust in me, despite my own stupid doubts, bolsters my resolve to honor our burgeoning connection with the sincerity and effort it deserves.

An hour later, we're in my work truck on the nearly deserted road to Willow's Lodge in Woodinville. One hand rests on her thigh and my fingertips tease beneath the hem of her dress.

I lean in close. "Since we're in the middle of half a dozen vineyards, I thought tomorrow we could spend the day wine tasting."

"Sounds perfect." She kisses my upper arm, which drives me out of my ever-loving mind. "Though, I wonder if we'll make it out of bed."

Holy. Mother. Of. God.

My hand clamps on Ivy's leg and instinctively she lifts her hips to release the fabric, giving me better access. My fingers push beneath her panties and find her drenched. I nearly veer into a ditch when she places her hand on mine and presses my fingers into her slickness. Moaning, she grazes her teeth on my arm.

We're only about a mile away from the lodge, but this can't wait. I manage to safely pull to the shoulder of the road and Ivy crawls into my lap before I even cut the engine. She straddles me and we feast on each other's mouths as I grip her ass and grind her against my aching cock.

Sweeping her beneath me, I lower her across the bench. Her blonde hair fans across the seat and I yank up her dress to her waist and nestle between her legs. Her delicate hands roam all over my chest and arms. Sunlight filters through the windows.

"Ivy, you're magnificent." I lower my mouth to hers, kissing and sucking my way down her neck, earning one enticing moan after another.

I pull down the bodice of her white dress, revealing the swell of her tits straining against a plunging pink-lace bra. I press a kiss to her ribs and unhook the front clasp of her bra, pushing the fabric to the sides. She watches me, her expression both awestruck and innocent, as I cup one perfect breast and lick her raspberry-pink nipples into points.

"You're so good. Don't stop," she begs.

I roll my hips against her. "It's broad daylight, I'm only gonna take the edge off. I want us to go all night."

Ivy's hips rock up and she moans and writhes, bowing up beneath me as I swirl my tongue around her nipple and squeeze her other breast. I kiss and taste and worship her plump tits, teasing and taunting her by grinding my cock into her core. Her skin is flushed. Her breathing is shallow. She's exquisite.

"Cillian, please..." The ache in her voice sends me into overdrive.

I push my hand into her damp panties, her juices coat my fingers like molten lava. Pressing against the magic spot inside her, my thumb circles her clit and she gasps. I crash my mouth to hers, wanting to capture her passion and drink it like fine whiskey.

Ivy shudders and grabs my wrist, rocking her hips against me. The cab is filled with her long, keening moans as I work her pleasure points. She bucks against me, whimpering. Her body trembles with my every movement. Lowering my mouth back to her nipple, I suck hard and her inner muscles clamp around my fingers.

"*Sooooo* good. *Ahhhh.*" Ivy's head thrashes from side to side and she explodes, coating me up to my wrist.

My cock is swollen painfully behind the zipper of my jeans, desperate to get in on the action, but now's not the time. I want Ivy to come apart for me again. I kiss her harder. Rougher. She matches my rhythm, fucking my fingers until she screams, "*Cillian, I'm coming.*"

I feel her tugging at the button of my jeans and my cock lurches with joy. The thought of Ivy's fingers wrapped around my dick nearly makes me come on the spot. We have all night, though. She gently squeezes my swollen crown, I groan and grab her hand and pull it from my pants. "Not here. I can wait."

"Why, though?" Ivy pouts and pulls her panties to the side, giving me a glimpse of her glistening pussy. "See? I want you now. Fucking you is all I've thought about today."

Fuck. This woman's sex drive is like a dream come true. "Me too, but let's get to the hotel. We're two minutes away."

Leaning down, I press kisses all over her face. Then I try to re-clasp her bra over her pretty tits, to no avail.

"Here, let me." She takes over and quickly pulls herself together, then leans back in her seat. "I'm sorry. I didn't mean to be pushy, you make me feel all the things."

My heart nearly bursts and I bring my fingers to her lips. "I dig you're not afraid to ask for what you want. It turns me on and, believe me, we're on the same page."

A minute later, navigating the winding road to the lodge with Ivy's scent all over my hand, a powerful realization settles in.

Every reservation—the age gap, my workload, the practicalities of dating someone generally—seem trivial now. In the span of twenty-four hours, Ivy has ignited something fierce and protective in my soul. I can try to deny it, but she's the real deal.

This isn't some fleeting romance. What we have is something profound.

Tonight, we'll lose ourselves in each other.

Tomorrow, we can talk about what lies ahead.

Nine

IVY

The Next Day

THE SUN IS BEGINNING to set over the Olympic Mountains.

Cillian's hand rests on my thigh as if to remind me whom I belong to now. Every part of my body tingles.

Our ride back from my first overnight getaway is tinged with a soft, comfortable silence. The kind that settles over you when you're content to be in someone's presence. A feeling I haven't had in years.

Which is weird, considering I didn't even know who he was three days ago. Since then, Cillian's hands, lips, and mouth have touched me everywhere, inside and out. He's claimed me, though I doubt he has any idea of how profound this weekend has been. I've given him all of my firsts.

Even now, though I'm sore—really sore—I want more of him.

I want to give him more of me.

"Are you okay?" Cillian squeezes my knee. "You seem restless."

I'm not sure how to answer. I decide to flirt. "Let's just say I'm not used to having a huge cock impale me for three solid days..."

A slow grin spreads across his face. "Oh, yeah?"

"Don't get a big ego." I swat his arm.

His expression changes abruptly. "Seriously, are you uncomfortable? Did I hurt you? Tell me the truth."

"I'm a bit uncomfortable, but no, it doesn't hurt." I thread my fingers with his. "I kind of like it. The soreness reminds me of all the fun we had."

"Do you need a night off?" He squeezes my fingers.

My heart thuds to my stomach. Tears sting the backs of my eyes at the thought of not waking up with him. Dramatic much? Maybe. We've only had two nights and I can't imagine not sleeping in his arms. What do I say, though? I don't want to come across as too needy. "Um...if you do."

"Baby girl." Cillian brings our hands to his lips and kisses my knuckles. His signature move, I've discovered. "Don't deflect. I was asking what *you* need."

I gaze into his eyes. "You. I need you."

"Aye, sweet Ivy. *Mo shíorghrá.*" Cillian's depth of sincerity and warmth makes my heart flutter. "Then spend the night with me, if you want. Spend *every* night with me, if you can swing it. Life is short, we should grasp happiness when we can."

His offer tugs at every corner of my soul, stirring intense emotions I've never known. "Really? You don't think this is going really fast?"

"I mean...yeah." He glances over. "Your life is more complicated. If you need to slow down, we'll take this at your pace."

"What if I like the pace and want to stay tonight? Stay with you every night? What if there's nowhere else I'd rather be?" The prospect of more time with Cillian is too tantalizing not to inform Hilde I'm staying with Emma until my parents get home. Thank sweet baby Jesus I cleared it with dad before they left. A moment of accidental genius. "Will I freak you out if I say being with you feels like finding a piece of myself I didn't know was missing?"

"Oh yeah? Well, I feel the same way." Cillian's hazel eyes sparkle. "And since you're moving to California in a few weeks, why waste any time? Let's soak up every minute we can."

A thread of dread weaves through my excitement. Does he see me leaving for grad school as an end date for us? *Ugh*.

"Yeah. Let's make the most of every moment." I smile at him, hoping to savor the present, even if my heart yearns for a future I'm uncertain how to secure.

"I have a question." Cillian pauses as we merge onto the freeway. "Why Stanford, anyway?"

His tone is genuinely curious, but do I detect an undercurrent of something else?

"My dad's choice because of the caliber of the business school," I admit. "As I mentioned, he likes to control most of my life. Well, at least since my brother..."

Cillian squeezes my knee. "Tell me. I'm an excellent listener."

"Well, Forrest—he was supposed to take over the family business," I sigh, the anguish of his death ever-present and heavy on my chest. "When he passed away, it changed everything. My parents became more protective. *Overprotective*, really. It's only recently started to wear on me, but I don't want them to worry. I'm all they have left."

"We have lots in common. The challenge of living up to family expectations because of a tragedy." Cillian nods.

"Really? You too?" My heart swells at the thought of him truly understanding what I'm going through. "I guess the reason I'm excited to go to Stanford is to get away from the constant scrutiny. My dad is powerful. He's used to everyone around him bending to his will, and I'm no exception. He doesn't see me as an adult, able to take care of myself and make decisions. He likes to control who I spend time with. With them being away all summer, it seemed like the perfect opportunity to seize my moment. Expand my horizons. And, there you were."

"Seize your moment, huh? Are you telling me I'm a convenient excuse to rebel against your dad?" he teases gently, giving my hand a reassuring squeeze.

I shake my head. "You have no idea."

"It sounds like you're carrying a lot on your shoulders. At your age, you shouldn't let anyone control you, Ivy. Even your father." Cillian's eyes narrow with concern.

I tense up. How do I navigate this? "Yeah...I get what you're saying. In his defense, my dad's been through a lot and he wants to protect his little girl."

"Still..." He catches my eye. "You're twenty-four. A grown woman with your own needs and desires."

This is getting sticky. I should confess. It would clear things up.

It would also end things.

I'm not willing to risk it. "I know, but trust me. I have my reasons. All I was saying is, with them out of town, I have more flexibility outside of his watchful—and judgmental—eye."

"Look. I'm sorry." He moves his hand closer to the cleft between my legs and grins. "Whatever your reasons, I'm glad it led you to me. If you hadn't figured it out, I'm fishing a little bit. Is this a summer fling for you? I'm already missing you and you haven't left yet. I was secretly wondering if you'd be open to attend a business school closer to home."

My heart bursts with joy. I read this conversation all wrong.

"I guess it depends." I massage the top of his hand with my thumb. "He probably won't be a fan of me dating anyone during grad school, since he's covering the cost."

Cillian returns both hands to the steering wheel. After a moment, he looks over at me. "Well, he definitely won't be a fan of you dating someone eight years older than you. Right?"

I don't need to answer him. We fall into another silence, this one not quite as comfortable, considering the air is filled with unasked questions and the echo of my half truths.

A few minutes later, Cillian shifts the topic to his own family. "Connor, my oldest brother is the bassist for Less Than Zero, the rock band. When I was in my early teens, my da wanted him to quit high school and to help him run McGloughlin Construction. Then, Da had a terrible accident, got addicted to pain meds and Connor didn't have a choice.

He saved our family, really. Sacrificed his own dreams for nearly a decade to keep the company afloat and become the breadwinner to get me and my brothers through high school."

"Wow. He was under lot of pressure." I'm astounded. Not only at the parallels in our lives, but holy shit. His brother is really, really famous.

"He was," he agrees. "Connor hated construction and everything about the business, but felt bound by duty. On the other hand, from an early age, I knew it's what I wanted to do so I relentlessly weaseled my way in. At first, he'd only let me help out on the weekends, but once I turned seventeen, he realized I was serious. By this point, LTZ was starting to get well-known and he started to teach me how to run the business."

"Wait, you were that involved in your family business before you were eighteen?" I'm blown away. More things we have in common.

"Yes and no. I think I mentioned, I took over completely at twenty-five—because Connor insisted I go to college first. I lived at home while I was at UW and worked in the business until I graduated with a degree in Construction Management. His ex-girlfriend, who's now married to a woman named Becca, took over when Connor left on tour. I worked with her until she moved to the Kitsap Peninsula."

Connor's so open. Engaging. Honest. I'm fascinated by his life. "It sounds like your brother is pretty special."

"You're spot on. He sacrificed his own happiness for years to put all of us through school. I'm not sure any of us appreciated it at the time because Da was such a distraction, but we all respect the shit out of him. He inspired us and the rest of my brothers found their own paths early on too. Liam and Padraig are also musicians, they're in a band called Fireball. Brennan founded an AI company during his freshman year of college. The baby, Seamus, completed early start in high school and is finishing up his surgical residency."

His description of his brothers makes me miss Forrest and how our family used to be normal. "How cool. You all sound very driven."

"Yeah, we're quite the bunch." He chuckles, then turns serious again. "May I pry a bit more without upsetting you?"

"Oh-kay..." I tilt my head and brace myself.

"Why is your birthday tough? You've alluded to it a few times." Cillian's thumb continues to trace patterns on my inner thigh, making me tingly.

He's been open with me, I want to do the same as much as possible. "My brother died on my thirteenth birthday." I suck in a quick breath because I nearly blurt out "five years ago" accidentally. "We were swimming and jet-skiing and celebrating with a load of our friends at my house. He hit his head on a rock and drowned. My birthday turned into the day we lost him instead of the day I came into the world."

"I can't even imagine." Cillian pulls off into downtown Seattle.

"It's been awful." I squeeze my eyes shut to stop myself from crying. "I loved him and he was such a light in our family. It's a struggle sometimes not to feel sorry for myself. Or, angry at the world. My birthday is now forever associated with his death but I can't make it about me or my loss because then I'm an asshole. There's not a day that goes by where I don't mourn him. He'll never be able to fulfil any of his potential. Get married. Have a family. There are no words for how much it hurts."

Cillian squeezes my thigh. "Ivy, this might sound crass, but it needs to be said. Your brother's death doesn't need to define you. You're still alive and you have your own hopes and dreams, right?"

"Yeah." I nod, touched by his empathy. "I do. It's the reason I was out at Kells the other night. I decided to reclaim my day."

"I'm glad you did." He kisses my temple. "Maybe meeting was our fate."

As we drive toward his loft, I know I have to tell him everything. He deserves to know the truth.

How, though?

Tonight, I want him to make love to me, lie in his arms and bask in the afterglow of our weekend. Enjoy the feeling of falling in love for the first time. "I'm really glad we did this. I know we just met, but being with you means a lot to me."

"Me too, sweet Ivy. Me too." He pulls into his parking garage.

On the way up to his loft, Cillian's arms wrap around my waist and I lean back into his broad chest. His cheek rests on top of my head.

Everything about being with him feels perfect, yet the secret of my age hangs like a shadow. What happens if he finds out I'm eighteen?

My biggest fear is the truth will shatter our beautiful illusion.

Leaving us both to pick up the pieces.

Ten

CILLIAN

One Week Later

IN ONE WEEK, Ivy has burrowed her way into my heart.

We've been virtually inseparable since the day we met and I'm not entirely sure what to do with all the feelings swirling inside me.

The credits of the murder-mystery news show we've been watching roll across the screen. I haven't really been paying attention because she's all I think about. When I'm not with her, I miss her. When I'm with her, like now, I'm already planning the next time we'll be together.

How can this be? None of it makes sense, yet my feelings for Ivy are the truest I've ever felt.

"Seriously, how did she stay with him. I mean, come on! The guy was creepy." Ivy sits up from where she was resting comfortably in my lap. It's dark outside now, and the soft glow from the big-screen TV casts shadows across her cheek, highlighting her serene beauty.

Chuckling, I playfully tickle her ribs. "We've only been seeing each other for a week. Should I be glad you're not getting creepy vibes from me?"

"Oh, give it time." Ivy giggles, her eyes sparkling with amusement. "I'm sure you have at least one or two mysterious quirks I've yet to discover."

As Ivy's laughter fades, I lean in, captivated by the sparkle in her eyes. "Mine aren't so mysterious. How do you feel about nipple clamps? Or a remote clit vibrator?" I whisper before our lips meet.

The contact sends a shiver through me. Her lips are soft yet insistent, and as I intensify our kiss, my world seems to narrow to the warm, sweet taste of her mouth. It's a revelation each time—this feeling of rightness. Of wanting to linger in the moment forever.

My hands find the small of her back, pulling her closer so her legs are on either side of mine. As we make out, I'm overwhelmed by a rush of emotions—affection, desire, and a burgeoning love that feels both exhilarating and terrifying in its intensity.

We break apart. I hold her gaze while I pull her tank top over her head, cup her breast and suck hard at her nipple.

Ivy moans, low and husky, and wraps her arms around my neck. "We can't. I'm on my period, remember?"

"So what?" I kiss up her chest to her throat.

She slides from my lap. "Let me take care of you."

I'm about to protest but her hands dip beneath the waistband of my joggers and she yanks them down, freeing my cock. Licking her lips, Ivy's turquoise eyes pierce mine. She wraps her fist around me and strokes up and down my length. The next thing I know, her lips are wrapped around me and she engulfs my shaft, bobbing up and down and swirling her tongue along my slit.

"Jesus, *fuck*." I grip her hair into a tight ponytail as she worships me with her hot little mouth. I can't even comprehend how incredible this feels.

She kisses down my shaft and sucks on my balls as she jacks me. My hips jerk and twitch of their own volition. I bite my lip hard when the zaps and zings build at the root of my spine. Moments later, Ivy guides my cock back into her mouth, humming along my shaft. I'm on the edge of utter and complete insanity.

"I'm gonna come. Ivy. Baby, if you don't stop…" I tap her shoulder furiously.

Undaunted, she clings to my thighs and doubles down on the suction. I'm lost. I thrust up into her like a madman. Her tongue swirls along the veiny ridge on my crown and she cups my balls and gently squeezes, causing every ounce of control to go by the wayside. I hold her in place as I cant my hips one last time, coming in long spurts.

She looks into my eyes as she swallows it all, then licks me clean and releases me. "Delicious."

This woman. She has me endlessly turned on. Infatuated. Probably, madly in love.

Rolling Ivy backward onto the couch, I push her panties to the side. "Your turn."

"Ewww. No, Cillian." She wriggles to get free.

I grab her ankle and drape it over the back of the couch and press her other leg to the side. She's glistening with arousal. "*Yes*, Ivy. Chalk it up to one of my mysterious quirks because I don't give two shits if you're on your period. You'll never go a day without me going down on you as long as we're together."

Leaning over, I dip my tongue into her slick folds. Ivy's hands thread into my hair and her hips rock against my lips. I circle my tongue around her swollen little nub. She tastes salty. Sweet. Slightly tangier than normal, but still my favorite flavor. Her back arches and she tries to wriggle free, which isn't going to happen. I slide my hands under her ass and hold her against my mouth and suck on her clit.

"Oh, oh, *ohhhhh.*" Ivy grips my scalp as I lap and lick her into a frenzy, fascinated at how her pussy darkens, then blooms and swells as she becomes more aroused with each passing moment. Until Ivy, I haven't been consistently intimate enough with a woman to bear witness to the subtle signs of her stimulation. It's addictive. Makes me want to discover everything that turns her on.

Spreading her lower lips apart with my fingers, her engorged clit pokes out from under its tiny hood. Her sweet musk permeates my senses. I swirl my tongue around it then lick like a madman. Ivy's thighs start shaking and she tightens, then lets go with a loud, keening, throaty moan.

Throughout the numerous contractions, I soothe her clit with the flat of my tongue. When her pussy stops convulsing, I kiss my way up her stomach, pausing to lick her nipples into hard peaks. Once our centers are aligned, I pull out her tampon, toss it on top of her T-shirt and slam inside her. Gripping her hands with mine, I look down at her, all flushed and plump-lipped from sucking on my cock and having a world-class orgasm. Ivy wriggles her hands free and caresses my face, never looking away as our bodies mesh in perfect harmony.

"You're my everything," I choke out, and I mean it.

Afterward, we lay on the couch still wound together. Ivy plays with my hand, rubbing the calluses on the tips of my fingers before pressing her palm against mine. "You've become my everything, too."

Half hour later, we're showered and snuggled in bed. She rests her face against my chest and I comb my fingers through her wet hair.

I've never felt close to someone outside my family, yet despite the revelation about her brother, there's a big part of her life shrouded in mystery. We're hurtling toward something official, it's probably an appropriate time to gently, cautiously, get her to open up a bit.

"You know," I keep my tone light, "I know why I can't come over to your house, but when you mentioned the swimming and jet skis I realized I don't know *where* you live. I've been inside your body about a hundred times at this point, if you're comfortable sharing—I'd love to learn more about you.""

Ivy shifts slightly to look up at me. She hesitates, as if choosing her words carefully. "It's complicated. My dad...*um*... I'll say it. My family is very, *um*...wealthy. We live in Medina and my house has its own private entrance within a gated community and an intense level of security."

I raise an eyebrow, intrigued. "Security? Like, bodyguards and surveillance?"

"Yeah. State of the art," she admits, with a small, almost apologetic smile. "We have a house manager, housekeepers, groundskeepers... It's like a small fortress sometimes. They all report to my dad, not an optimal place to break the rules."

The mention of her breaking rules niggles at me. I'm still finding it hard to comprehend why a twenty-four-year-old woman, who's going to Stanford Business School, can't tell her parents she has a boyfriend and is staying at his house. Then again, I don't have sisters. What do I know?

"What would he do if he knew you were with me here and not at your friend's house?" I probe gently, wanting to understand but not push her too far.

Ivy shifts away from me and rests her head on her palm. "If he knew about us, I honestly don't know what he'd do. He has this idea of who I should be with, and it definitely doesn't include anyone outside his circle of approval."

"Ahh, so I'll be your dirty secret." Kind of hurt, I roll on my back, but don't look away.

My words hang in the air. She looks down. Her fingers nervously toy with a strand of her hair. "Cillian. If I'm being honest, I'm not sure what will happen after they get back. All I know is I can't lose you."

Her response raises more red flags for me but I try to put myself in her shoes. It can't be easy for her to be a surviving child with overprotective parents. I'm patient, though. Hopefully, she'll open up and we can figure out a solution.

God knows, I don't want this to end either.

"Ivy." I turn back on my side to face her fully. "Whatever happens, I'll be here to help. Okay? If your dad is anything like my brother, who will do anything to protect his wife and kids, he wants to make sure you're safe and happy."

Her eyes widen. "Yeah. You've hit the nail on the head. He didn't used to be this way. All of this craziness started after my brother died. He's petrified of something happening to me, and I don't want him to worry. As annoying as all of this is, I love my parents."

"Let's take things one day at a time. I'm enjoying getting to know you and I love having you here. You told the staff you're staying with your friend Emma for the summer so we have time. Stay with me until they get back and we'll deal with your parents later." I clasp her tightly.

Ivy circles my nipple with her finger. "There's nowhere I'd rather be. We have a plan."

"Tell me the truth, though. Are you worried about this plan?" Raising an eyebrow, I can't mask a flicker of concern.

"You're lying to them. I'd hate for any kind of deceit to put you—or us—in a tough spot. If they find out you've been staying here, I'm not an idiot, they'll blame me for corrupting you. It's important we're on solid, truthful ground as soon as possible. It's something my da drilled into me after his troubles."

Ivy bites her lip and squeezes her eyes shut. "Yes. I'm a tiny bit worried and I definitely don't want there to be any lies between us. I wanted to tell you about my relationship with my parents, even though I know it probably seems bizarre. I'll figure out a way to tell them about us too."

"Truth is important, baby." I kiss her forehead.

"Yeah." Tears well in her eyes as she traces my lips with her finger. "It is."

"Don't cry," I reassure her, "It'll be okay. *We're* okay."

I hold her close and pat her trembling back as she cries. Her breath eventually steadies and, despite my earlier concerns, a protective warmth floods through me. Ivy's vulnerability and courage in revealing her tangled realities makes me feel even closer to her. We're building trust as we navigate our budding relationship.

My God, how I cherish this woman. My mind returns to the bird analogy.

She's trying to spread her wings and escape from the gilded cage her parents have kept her in. What a fucking gift. I do not take it for granted I'm the man she's entrusted her newfound freedom with.

Above all else, her honesty tonight reassures me.

It's early days, but we're building something special.

Two Weeks Later

HOW DID MY LIFE get so complicated?

Perched on a cushy stool in the airy kitchen of my empty house, I'm sipping a mango smoothie after my dance class, waiting to start my session with Dr. Martin, my therapist. Hilde knows I take my therapy calls at the house, so she's out running errands.

Today, I need some perspective. It's been three weeks since my parents left, and they haven't checked in on me once.

I'm not stupid. Hilde is probably keeping track of my comings and goings and, if she's asked, will tell them I've been at Emma's this entire time except to come home to pick up new clothes. Thank God, I've been such an obedient and dutiful daughter, maybe that's why they haven't checked up on me.

It doesn't really matter though, I'm in big trouble either way. I've tried to be truthful, but I'm still lying to Cillian. I'm lying by default to my parents.

It's not who I am, and for the past three weeks, I've selfishly justified the reasons why it's necessary.

I've never been happier. I'm head over heels in love with Cillian. We haven't officially defined our relationship yet, but we're a couple. The only time we're apart is when he's working and I'm in dance or art class. Even then, we text and talk to each other all day long.

Gah, this double life is taking its toll. I want to come clean with everyone but I'm scared to death I'll lose it all. I thought it would get easier, but I was wrong. Now, it seems impossible.

My phone buzzes. It's a text from Cillian.

Cillian: *Can't wait to ditch my family dinner and devour something far sweeter…See you later, trouble ;)*

Aaaand…I'm wet.

I swear, this man has me in a perpetual state of arousal. I've gotten used to my pussy pulsing with need, my panties being damp and my nipples puckering into tight little bullets. All in anticipation of what we're going to do the second we see each other.

My virginity is a distant memory. I've embraced my sexuality in ways I could never have imagined before Cillian. My contraband vibrator is a pale imitation to Cillian's beautiful cock. My man's the perfect partner—caring, loving, and makes me feel safe to try anything I want to explore.

Oh, do we *explore*.

He and I have fucked, made love, had sex—all of the above—at least twice a day since we met. Some days we don't even get dressed. There's not a place in his loft we haven't christened. Or, his truck. We've fucked at a secluded cove on the beach. During an impromptu picnic in the woods. In the stairwell at one of his buildings. Against a wall in the alley after a concert. He got me off in a movie theater—oh, and at a fancy restaurant. I gave him a blowjob on a ferry ride. Anywhere and everywhere is fair game. We're insatiable.

When Cillian's inside me, I'm complete.

My phone pings again with a calendar reminder, snapping me out of this startling realization. It's time for my therapy session. I launch the Zoom meeting and prop my phone up so I can be hands free.

Dr. Martin's kind face fills the screen. When I'm feeling shaky, her calm presence has guided me through the depths of despair ever since my brother died. She's helped me find a sense of self amidst my family dynamics. Now, I need her guidance to unravel the threads of deceit I've woven with respect to my relationship with Cillian.

"I've never meant to lie." My words tumble out. "Asking my dad for a small amount of freedom started as a way to feel normal. To reclaim my birthday. It unlocked a rebellious streak, I think."

Dr. Martin nods, her pen paused over her notebook. "Tell me about what you define as rebellious."

"I met a guy three weeks ago, slept with him on the first night and he's become my whole world." I bury my face in my hands then look into the screen. "I won't give him up. I think I'm in love with him."

She smiles. "How wonderful. Why is falling in love with someone rebellious?"

"Cillian is thirty-two, fourteen years older than me. I met him in a bar—don't judge—on my birthday. I got a fake ID to get in. I went home with him, lied about my age and my last name. Now he thinks I'm twenty-four and my last name is Davies, not Bright. I'm fully invested in this relationship and while it's long past time to come clean, I'm terrified of how Cillian will react. If my dad finds out I haven't been at Emma's, I'm toast. I could lose everything." My words whoosh out in a flurry.

"Hmmm." Dr. Martin taps her finger to her chin. "It's good you recognize your lack of truth impacts both of you. Let's break it down. Why are you scared of Cillian's reaction?"

I take a moment to gather my thoughts, appreciating her ability to guide me through this process. "Honesty is very important to him. If I tell him I'm only eighteen and was a virgin, he's going to feel deceived. Betrayed. Misled." My voice falters slightly. "I've kept a huge part of myself hidden and now we're getting closer to an official commitment. He won't understand. And, if he finds out I'm six years younger, there's no doubt he'll break it off."

Dr. Martin nods thoughtfully. "It sounds like you don't believe the foundation you're building is strong enough to bear your truth."

"How could it be? I'm not naive. It's only been three weeks. Putting myself in his shoes, I'd be sketched out if I found out he was, say, forty. I'd wonder why he lied." My words taste bitter, but I continue. "I'd also be worried there were other things he was lying about. While my reasoning for, uh, keeping my age and identity secret started out innocently, we're getting serious. There's no question he'll view our relationship—*me*—differently when I tell him. He'll probably question my maturity and motives."

"A valid concern," Dr. Martin agrees. "However, do you think it's possible he'll understand why you felt compelled to alter the truth? Have you discussed your family dynamic with him?"

I pause. "A bit. He knows about my brother. And about parents' protectiveness. He knows I'm getting my MBA to help run the family business. I'm always careful not to go into too many specifics to avoid more lies. If he presses, I change topics. I've also found blowjobs are a great distractor."

"Ah. Using your newfound sexuality to avoid tough conversations." She tilts her head. "Interesting. I hear everything you're saying, but have you considered trusting Cillian? Owning up to your lie and explaining the extreme pressures you face with your family? You're not a typical eighteen-year-old. Your situation is unique, as you're aware."

Hmmm. Could my background help him see why I've done what I've done? "Maybe. In my ideal scenario, once the initial shock passes, he'll see our connection goes beyond age. We share similar values and ambitions and we challenge each other intellectually. Oh, and our chemistry is...*unbelievable*." I sigh. "It's hard. I *know* what drew me to him was *not* the age on our driver's licenses. The question is, will he feel the same way?"

"Given what you know about him, what do you think is the best way to broach the topic with Cillian?" Dr. Martin shifts forward in her seat, never taking her eyes off me.

"He needs to know how much I value what we have—how important and real our relationship is for me," I begin, trying to articulate a plan on the fly. "Then I'll tell him I've been feeling guilty, especially as we've gotten closer. How I care about him immensely and respect him as my partner. Keeping this secret doesn't feel right anymore."

Dr. Martin smiles slightly. "Sounds like a great approach. Sincerely acknowledge your mistake."

"I hope he understands it was never about deceiving him, it was about asserting my own independence." My nerves flutter. "I didn't expect to find someone like Cillian on my birthday, but it happened. I don't regret it. I've never felt like this about anyone. I won't—can't—lose him."

She adjusts her glasses then asks softly, "Ivy, could this be a situation where you're more invested in the relationship than he is? You've never had a boyfriend before."

"No, I think he feels the same way, at least he tells me he does. Cillian claims he hasn't had a serious girlfriend because he's been busy with his business. He's also been honest about his sexual history—there've been lots of women." I hear myself say the words and panic. He's so much more worldly than me. God, I'm in over my head. "I don't have any experience with an adult romantic relationship other than this one." I'm caught between anxiety and hope. "Maybe I desperately want to believe that somehow I'm different—that I'm the 'one.' Am I being delusional?"

"Do you think physical attraction is driving your relationship?" Dr. Martin focuses on my biggest fear. "Sex seems to play an important role in your day-to-day relationship, which is understandable for two young, attractive people who have explosive chemistry. If he's been with a lot of women, do you worry it's overshadowing emotional and intellectual connections you could be building?"

"No, actually, I don't think so," I say, with confidence. "We talk about everything—from pop culture, to politics to philosophy. He tells me hilarious stories about his huge family—which is filled with genuine rockstars, by the way. We know each other's hobbies and discuss places we want to travel together. That kind of stuff. We're already making plans for him to visit me at Stanford." I take a breath. "We also encourage each other. He seems to value my thoughts on his plans to expand his construction company. He's even implemented some of my ideas. Our sex is amazing, but I've fallen hard for the whole package. For the first time in my life someone sees me for me. It feels like we're equals."

Dr. Martin glances at her wrist. "Well, it seems like if you don't want to risk losing a man who means the world to you, it might be time for a discussion. Now, I hate to do this, but we have about five minutes."

"Okay, one final question. How should I start the conversation?" I already feel stressed.

"I'd choose a quiet, private time. You should both be relaxed, but I'd avoid having the talk after you've been intimate. Don't confuse the two. Start by reaffirming your feelings for him and describe what the genuine parts of your relationship mean to you." She scribbles something on her notepad. "Then, once you feel the moment is right, share your truth. Be clear, direct, and prepared for any response. Remember, Cillian isn't your father—he probably won't react with anger. Revealing your age and sexual experience should be about reinforcing your trust in him and a commitment to honesty in your relationship moving forward."

"Thank you." A sense of resolve builds within me. "I can't do it until I rehearse a bit. I'll be ready soon. At the very least, I have to be honest with him before I leave for school."

"Try not to wait too long." Dr. Martin's voice is kind. "You've been carrying a heavy burden, Ivy. Your relationship with Cillian—I'm glad you've found someone special. Remember, —it's best to remove obstacles before they become too big to overcome."

Nodding, I feel the corners of my mouth lift slightly at the thought of him. "Yes, he's the only person in my life who sees me for me. Not the Ivy Bright who's supposed to take over Bright Shipping or the tragedy-touched girl whose brother died on her birthday. Cillian has become my everything. I owe him the truth."

Hanging up with Dr. Martin, I head upstairs to take a shower and get ready to meet Cillian later. He gave me a key to his loft and I bought a new sexy bra and panty set to surprise him.

Facing him and confessing will be the hardest thing I've ever done, but it's necessary.

I owe it to him. I owe it to myself.

For the woman I am now. For the woman I hope to become.

Cillian deserves the truth.

Twelve

CILLIAN

The Same Night

GOD KNOWS, I LOVE a surprise.

Looks like I'm in for one later, a text came in from Ivy.

> ***Ivy:*** *Wrapped up in something sinful at your loft...no rush. You're in for a treat later. ;)**

The woman's made a home in my heart. I admire the way she barrels through life with a spark lighting up everything around her. She's sharp. *Really* sharp. Her wit keeps me on my toes, there's never a dull moment. And, holy fucking shit, there's the way we click. We have some kind of wild chemistry I've never felt before.

Being with her is both a comfort and an adrenaline rush. She's got me hooked, always wanting more. I finally get what all the sappy love songs are about. I've stopped worrying about our age difference. It doesn't matter. Ivy is special.

I'm keeping her around for as long as she'll have me.

"Kill, are you actually smiling?" Connor, who has his own gruff tendencies, nudges me.

I'm at Daniel's Broiler at Leschi with my brothers, Connor and Brennan. We're here to feast on a thick steak and start plans for our own grand surprise— a party for our father Rory's 60th birthday later this year.

I try to play it cool and shrug. "Thinking about work." I know a smirk has unwittingly spread across my face and betrays my attempt at nonchalance.

Connor and Brennan exchange a glance. Neither are fooled for a second.

A knowing grin spreads across Brennan's face. "Don't try to hide it, brother. I saw the hot blonde duck into your office last week. Carries herself like she owns the place. Doesn't take her eyes off you. Sound familiar?" He winks and takes a sip of his cocktail.

"Yeah. I'm seeing someone. Sue me." I raise my glass of whiskey in a toast. "Let's get down to business."

Connor claps me on the shoulder. "Hey, if she makes you half as happy as Ronni makes me, then I'm all for it. Who is she?"

"Her name's Ivy Davies." I pause for a second, realizing I don't have many specifics about her past to share. "We met at Kells. It's only been a few weeks, but I dig her."

Brennan rolls his eyes. "Another McGloughlin down. Next thing you know, she'll be at family dinner."

Funnily enough, I don't hate the idea. Other than our obvious age difference, she's perfect. My folks will love her.

"Maybe. Full disclosure, she's a lot younger than me." I flick my eyes to the menu.

Brennan leans back in his chair. "Don't tell me you've robbed the cradle, she's not still in high school, is she? There are laws."

I wince at Brennan's comment. Connor's wife, Ronni was exploited in Hollywood as a teenager, it's a sensitive matter in our family. Sure, Ivy *looks* young, but it's only eight years. She's an old soul.

"Fuck off. You shouldn't even say something like that out loud." I shake my head, pissed. "Twenty-four is not jailbait."

Connor's tone is soft as he covers for our younger brother. "It was supposed to be a joke."

"I was out of line, sorry Kill. Sorry Connor." Brennan hangs his head. His mind works a million miles a minute, we're all used to him speaking before he thinks.

Connor waves him off. "Yer alright. Let's focus on Dad's birthday, aye?

The three of us dive into details. We plan to invite a few people here at the restaurant and that's about as far as we get. Well, I guess we have a general idea of the guest list, but it's clear none of us are party planners. Brennan offers to reach out to Stevie Hayes, Padraig's and Liam's childhood friend who owns a thriving party-planning business.

Our chatter drifts to Da, unearthing memories filled with sawdust, sweat, and the strict discipline of our youth.

"Say what you will but, in my opinion, Da's work ethic shaped us into the men we are today." I'm on my third whiskey and don't bother to tamp down my unpopular point of view.

"Your perspective is skewed," Connor scoffs. "You were a kid."

"Nah, I think you carry resentment," I fire back. "I knew what I wanted at fifteen. You refused to believe me because you hated it so much."

Connor strokes his beard. "I never knew whether you genuinely loved it or wanted to impress Da."

My mind drifts back to long days on jobsites as a boy with the smell of fresh timber and the sound of nail guns echoing around us. "Oh, I love it. Always did. Still do. The building, the creating. My favorite childhood memories are of helping Da."

"I hated every minute of it, too." Brennan shakes his head. "Physical labor isn't my thing. It felt like endless torture. But, you're right. I guess it taught us a lot about hard work and responsibility."

Connor sighs, his expression hard to read. "I'm probably not the one to talk about this. It's no secret I resented Da for years. I'm guessing you guys never knew how bad it got before I took over. One night I came home to find Ma in tears because he'd withdraw ten grand to stake one of his illegal poker games. It got to the point where, at least once per week, I'd be up all night scouring the worst neighborhoods and the seediest places only to fight like hell to drag him home. The next day, I'd wake up and be back on the jobsite."

"Jesus, Connor." Brennan's eyes widen in horror. "We all knew things were rough, but shit. You really took the brunt of it, didn't you?"

Brennan and Connor go back and forth discussing Da's downfall, recalling nights of violent, drunken outbursts and several incidents where the family nearly lost everything due to his gambling addiction.

They don't know it, but I've had many conversations with Da about these worst years of his life. He's confided in me about how much those times haunt him and the shame he feels for the chaos he brought into our lives. He's come through it all—and is healthier than he's been in years. Even after recovering from a near-fatal stroke not that long ago.

In listening to my brothers, though, I realize my relationship with him has strengthened over the years. We're together a lot, with time for open discussions and a shared interest in McGloughlin Construction.

Clearly, Da still has a long way to go with my older brothers, particularly Connor, who hasn't fully forgiven him. Understandably.

Connor puffs out a breath. "Ma almost packed up to go back to Ireland. She was close to moving all of you."

"Seriously? I didn't know she considered leaving." Brennan looks between us. "Losing Ma would've torn Da apart. I doubt he'd have ever recovered."

"Yeah." I feel the need to bridge the gap of our varied experiences. "I remember her talking about needing a fresh start, away from all the memories and the mess. But she stayed, for us and for Da. We all owe her a lot for holding things together."

Connor nods slowly. "Aye. I never really understood why Ma put up with him. Then Ronni stood by me during my whole deep fake mess. Having a good woman at your side, someone to stick with you through the storms. Hell, it changes everything."

His acknowledgment of Ronni's support resonates, stirring a feeling I can't quite pinpoint. I find myself thinking of Ivy waiting for me at my loft. I can almost smell her fresh, citrusy scent. Feel her small hand stroking my stubble. Her soft lips against mine.

I've grown accustomed to her vibrant presence and the undeniable connection we share. Is she the one who'll stand by me through anything? Would I do the same for her?

The thought both excites and terrifies me as I consider our burgeoning relationship.

Speaking of which, I glance at my watch and am surprised to see it's nearly ten p.m. Time to go home and make love to my girl. "Let's settle up, I've got an early start."

"No worries, I've got this one." Brennan pulls out his wallet, flashing a knowing grin at Connor. "Go on and get your 'early start' with the mystery blonde We all know what that means."

Twenty minutes later, I step into my loft and stop short.

Ivy's curled up on the couch, fast asleep in a skimpy piece of lingerie consisting of nothing but hot-pink straps and silk.

She snores softly, her hand rests across her soft belly. One perfect breast has escaped. Her blonde hair is spread out on the cushion, making her look almost ethereal in the dim light.

Seeing her like this—peaceful and vulnerable—something shifts inside me. This isn't lust or a summer fling, it's so much more. I feel it in my gut.

She's the one.

Ivy Davies has my heart, full fucking stop.

I absolutely want to be the one who's there for her, always.

Quietly, I drop my keys and jacket. Moving closer, I gently lift her. She doesn't wake up, but instinctively nuzzles against my chest as I carry her to the bedroom. Laying her down, I slip off my clothes, slide in beside her and pull her close. The feel of her, so right in my arms, cements what I've been reluctant to admit.

I'm all in.

Completely, irrevocably in love with her.

I'm keeping her around for as long as she'll have me.

Two Weeks Later

I WOULDN'T SAY I'M panicking.

No. I don't need to say it. I *feel* it in every part of my body. Queasy stomach. Shaky hands. Exhaustion.

My parents are due back in three weeks and I still haven't told Cillian the full truth.

I *suck*. I'm disappointed in myself. With each passing day, the reality of my situation sinks in. The freedom I've grown used to is about to evaporate. So is my relationship with the man I'm falling in love with.

The thought is unbearable and there's nothing I can do to stop it.

Today's been particularly rough. Hilde stopped by my room and caught me packing a bag for the week and made a point to ask if I "would be sleeping at home anytime soon." Though I've been expecting some sort of blowback, her comment took me by such surprise. I wasn't sure what to say except to reiterate I was enjoying my time with Emma.

Her disapproving look sent a chill down my spine.

Made me wonder if the jig is up.

Still flustered, now I'm in rush-hour traffic on my way to a Belltown construction site where Cillian is overseeing the latest phase of one of his high-rise development projects. My stress level is through the roof, which isn't helped by the fact no cars are moving. It would be faster to walk, at this point.

Aaaaaarrrrgh. I'm fucking frustrated. I should be excited to see Cillian, he always has something fun planned for us. Instead, the butterflies, which threaten to burst out of my head, aren't from anticipation of spending time with my man, but from the crushing weight of my secrets and what will happen when they're exposed.

Something tells me I've run out of time. If I don't tell Cillian soon...

I can't even think about the alternative.

In an attempt to distract myself, I rehearse our conversation in my mind. I could be straightforward. Or, try to make a joke out of it. Maybe I could give him a "what if" scenario to see what his reaction is. The reality is, there's no way to confess and at this point, it probably doesn't matter. Either way, he'll be upset.

Upset. *Ha*!

I'm totally screwed.

Fifteen minutes later, I pull into a stall across from the construction site. It's unseasonably hot in Seattle this summer, I'm wearing a lightweight, knee-length chambray skirt paired with a soft, sleeveless white blouse and white sneakers. My hair is tied back in a high ponytail to keep it off my neck. He said to dress casual, I hope this is okay.

Once I pay for parking, I stop and take a couple of cleansing breaths. Try to center myself. Prepare for the worst, hope for the best sort of thing. Something catches my eye at the jobsite. I glance across the street and my heart stops.

Cillian is waiting for me, beckoning me over. A smile stretches across his face when our eyes lock. His hard hat tips slightly over his wavy, dark hair, which has grown a bit since we met. It nearly touches the broad contours of his muscular shoulders. He wears jeans and a McGloughlin Construction logo-tee, an outfit identical to the one he wore on the night we met.

I'm so in love with this man, I can't see straight. Dashing across the street, I leap into his arms.

"My God, you're a vision." Cillian catches me effortlessly, whirling me around before setting me on my feet. "You missed Brock, I was hoping to introduce you."

"Some other time." Cillian is willing to include me in his world and here I am—the asshole—keeping him separate and secret in mine.

My elation at seeing him comes crashing down to reality, but Cillian doesn't notice. He takes my hand and guides me to a rickety, industrial contraption of metal and cables. "We're heading up to the top floor. Don't worry, this is safe."

Inside, we're pressed against each other. Cillian's hand rests lightly on my back. His warm, reassuring touch always makes me feel more grounded, somehow. I wrap my arms around his waist and bury my face in his chest. Breathe him in. He smells like sunshine, the outdoors, and a bit of musk from working all day.

He kisses the top of my head as we ascend. "Are you okay? You seem off."

"Yeah." I nod against his pecs, though I'm far from okay. My mouth opens and closes like a fish several times, ready to spill everything, but no more words come out.

Then the doors jerk open and the expansive Seattle skyline surrounds us. The rooftop scene takes my breath away. I spot a portable card table and a couple of folding chairs positioned on a platform overlooking the waterfront. *"Cillian*! What did you do?"

"Nothing much." He winds his arm around my shoulder and walks me over to the setup. "I thought it would be nice to have a sunset picnic."

He pulls out my chair and leans down for a kiss when I'm seated. My hands tremble slightly as I pull Cillian's face closer, pressing my lips to his with a fervent, intense urgency. I'm desperate to savor this perfect moment because I'm afraid we won't have many more.

We break apart and a tear spills down my cheek. "Thank you, baby. This is perfect. I'm *touched*."

"I'd do anything to make you happy, my sweet Ivy." Oh, his eyes. Those intense, mesmerizing hazel pools flecked with green and gold find mine, warming me from the inside out.

I can't do it.

"What are we celebrating?" I watch Cillian uncork a bottle of white wine and fill two plastic cups.

He pulls out two dishes of Alaskan king crab salad from the cooler. "I remember you mentioned you loved this."

My favorite food. I mentioned it the night we met. My God, it never ceases to amaze how closely he listens to me. He cares about what I think. Goes out of his way to make me happy.

I can't lose this man. I will do whatever needs doing, but I *will not* lose him.

"Every day with you is better than the last." I mask my turmoil with a smile. "I can't believe you remembered. You make everything special, Cillian."

"Well, I agree, at least about every day being better than the last." He sits next to me and takes my hand. "You asked what we're celebrating. Life, baby. Life. My company's doing great. We're final contenders in the biggest project yet and I'm pretty sure we're going to get it. My family is doing well. But, none of this matters without you. *You're* the difference. You make everything better. My life was incomplete until we met. You're my missing piece."

Overwhelmed, I murmur, "*Me?*"

"Yes, you." He takes my hand and kisses it. "You bring this...energy into my life. Being with you makes everything feel more intense, more vivid."

Even though my lies are a lingering shadow that threaten this perfect moment, I'm not going to shatter the fragile joy we've found. "I feel the same."

"Look, I know you're heading to Stanford soon and we'll need to navigate your weird family dynamic. I've also been worried about our age difference, and whether we're in two different stages of our lives." Cillian's voice falters slightly, a hint of nerves he never usually displays. "The thing is, I've never been more sure about something. I want you and I to be a real couple. Can we make this official?"

Tears prick my eyes, not from his words, but from shame of keeping the secret I can't seem to spit out. "I want to. More than anything."

"Then let's make it happen" He gently wipes a tear from my cheek with his thumb. "Whatever obstacles come, we'll face them."

The sincerity in his voice makes my heart swell even as it aches with the weight of my unspoken truth. "I love you, Cillian. I hope it's not too soon to tell you. I really mean it."

Cillian's eyes soften, surprise and warmth flood his features. He tugs me up from my seat and onto his lap. "*Mo shíorghrá*. I didn't want to freak you out, but I love you too. I've never felt like this about anyone."

Shifting so I'm straddling him, with my skirt billowing around us, Cillian's thick, hard cock presses against my core. I slip my hands under his shirt and glide my palms up his muscled chest and back down to the waistband of his jeans. "I want you. Now. *Please...*"

"Yes." His fingers find my pussy and I roll my hips so he can pull my panties to the side. "How perfect would this night be if we come at the same time while the sun is setting?"

In seconds, his jeans are undone and I'm impaled. We move as one, though not in any sort of frenzy. Instead, we stare into each other's eyes. My arms are wound around his neck, he cups my ass to hold me tightly in place and nudges up into me until I'm as full as can be. One of his hands slides up to my lower back and he presses my pelvis against him. We find a slow, intense tantric cadence and every nerve ending in my clit blooms and pulses with every gyration.

"I love you," he says as the sun dips below the horizon and the sky turns into a vibrant canvas of orange and pink, reflecting off the glassy waters of Puget Sound. The Olympic Mountains in the distance are silhouetted against the fiery backdrop.

My core spasms and tingles. I lean in until Cillian's breath mingles with mine. "I love *you*."

Our lips connect, but our exploratory, sensual kisses are also deliberately slow, matching the rhythm of our hips. As the last streaks of the sun paint the sky, it's like we're the only two people in the world. We climax in pulsing waves, leaving me dizzy.

I love—and I'm loved by—this amazing man.

Moments later, after we straighten our clothes and pack up the remnants of our rooftop dinner, we're walking hand-in-hand toward the elevator and a sudden, bold thought strikes me.

What if there were a way to protect what we have? To ensure nothing and no one could ever come between us, despite my secrets and the looming deadline.

Gripping Cillian's hand tighter, I stop in my tracks. My heart beats wildly in my chest. Yet, what I'm about to say feels as right as every step we've taken so far.

"You ready to go home?" He presses the button to the elevator.

My entire body buzzes with excitement and nerves. I bounce on my toes and grab his other hand and face him. He tilts his head and looks at me curiously.

"I have a crazy idea." I thread his fingers with mine.

He pulls me against his body. "Oh yeah? Lay it on me."

"Let's get married."

Fourteen

CILLIAN

One Week Later

I'M DISCOMBOBULATED.

Stunned. Conflicted. Also, tempted...

Leaning back in my chair in my office at the jobsite, I stare at the ceiling. The low hum of the portable air conditioner fills the silence as I collect my thoughts.

Since Ivy blurted out the idea of getting married last week on the rooftop of this very building—moments after we first declared our love for one another—I'm more confused than ever.

I almost took her up on it. Summer's going to be over before we know it and neither of us are ready for the inevitable changes ahead. Our entire relationship has been impulsive, why not whisk off to Vegas?

Not wanting to quash her passion and impulsivity by telling her no, I spoke my truth, though I tried to handle the delivery with care. We have something special. I see us having a future. I also explained I didn't want her to make a hasty, life-altering decision she might regret later.

She was disappointed, but we agreed to revisit in a week—tonight.

I know we're not ready to take this step. We have too many obstacles and realities to contend with. She's leaving for Stanford in three weeks. Her parents have no idea I exist. My family doesn't know much about her either, for that matter. Ivy and I have been living in our own bubble since we met, but our lives are not fully melded yet.

Until then, why add the pressure of marriage?

My phone buzzes, pulling me from my thoughts. It's a text from Ivy.

> **Ivy:** *Six more hours. Can't wait to show you how much I've missed you...*

Attached is a close-up of her sucking on her index finger.

My dick digs what I see and fills to capacity. Jesus, the effect this woman has on me. It's unbelievable.

How am I going to get by without her? I can't imagine not waking up with her wrapped in my arms. For nearly two months, the first thing I do every morning and the last thing I do at night is make love to her. She's everything I didn't know I needed.

But, am I that person for her?

My chest tightens. The thought of her discovering who she is, on her own terms, fills me with a mix of pride and fear. Pride for the strong, determined woman she's becoming. Fear she might outgrow me and the love we share.

Fuck it. She's mine now. I'll make the most of every moment we have left. I type my reply

Me : *You've made my day a whole lot harder...*

The bottom line is, I don't want to break up. I'm also not going to hinder her from reaching her full potential before we make such a big commitment.

For the next few hours, my concentration is needed on the business. Specifically, my upcoming meeting with Peter Vander, a renowned green architect with whom I've worked extensively over the past few years. His firm was chosen as the architect for the project I'm up for, which means my chances of getting this job went through the roof.

Peter's connected to me in other ways. He's married to Jordan Deveraux, whose brother, Jace, is in LTZ with my brother Connor. We met a couple years ago when we were both recruited by LTZ's guitarist, Zane Rocks and his wife Fiona Reynolds, to help design and build their business, The Mission and its sister restaurant, Gus.

Since then, I've handled many of Peter's builds in Seattle. I'm extraordinarily familiar with his aesthetic and commitment to the environment, making us a perfect team.

Glancing at the clock, I realize if I don't leave now, I'll be late. It's only a ten-minute walk, but I'll definitely need a coffee pick-me-up. Fifteen minutes later, I step into the airy, modern lobby of Peter's architecture firm with a Venti sweet cream Cold Brew. The receptionist greets me with a professional smile and guides me to the spacious conference room. While I wait, I admire the minimalist, yet stunning decor, which is not only VA's signature, but indicates their commitment to sustainable design.

Peter pushes through the glass door and holds out his hand. "Cillian, always a pleasure."

"Great to see you, Peter." We shake and I settle back down into the chair across from him.

The table between us is strewn with blueprints and eco-friendly material samples. Peter wastes no time, his enthusiasm evident. "This new project, Cillian—it's more than a structure. It's a vision. Imagine a shipping facility serving not only as a benchmark in environmental design, but this one will truly revolutionize operations."

"A project like this feels like my next logical step. I'm looking forward to diving into something this complicated, I hope I'm selected." I trace my thumb over a piece of roofing material.

With a conspiratorial grin, Peter leans in slightly. "I'd love to give you more details about the client, but you know how these NDAs can be. It'll be quite the reveal, you might be surprised."

"Understood." I chuckle. "I feel proud of what I submitted. I wanted to pick your brain about next steps, without pushing your boundaries, of course."

Our discussion shifts to the technical—solar panels doubling as architectural features. Innovative water recycling systems, and green roofs teeming with native plants. We spend the next two hours going over details. The project is ambitious, a complex puzzle fitting perfectly with our mutual goals.

"Well." Peter's eyes burn through me. "If we nail this, we're looking at potentially revolutionizing how shipping hubs are built worldwide. I have an inkling our work together will open up opportunities we never dreamed possible. Are you on board?"

"Definitely." I nod.

As he walks me out the door, Peter nods, his smile broad. "Good luck in your presentation. Let's make this happen."

I start back to the jobsite but realize it's past four. Considering the conversation I need to have with Ivy tonight, maybe it would be better to go home early. She should be back from her painting class by now. Spinning on my heel, I walk seven blocks to my place.

By the time I step into my loft, I'm feeling lighter than I have all day. The meeting with Peter went better than expected and the thrill of a potential breakthrough project pulses through me. At the very least, I'll have something to concentrate on while Ivy's away at school.

"Ivy?" There's no answer. The loft is quiet, the late-afternoon light spills through the windows casting long, warm shadows across the hardwood floors. A smile tugs at my lips as I head toward the bedroom, anticipation building with each step.

The door is ajar. I push it open and I almost need a moment to compose myself. There, before the full-length mirror, stands my girl. Ivy hasn't heard me come in, she's too absorbed in adjusting the delicate straps of the black lingerie she's wearing. I'm rooted to where I'm standing, struck by her beauty and the intimate vulnerability of the scene.

"Ivy," I say, my voice a low rumble. I'm already unbuckling my jeans as I approach.

She whirls around and both surprise and delight flash across her face. One arm instinctively covers her breasts, the other her pussy. "Cillian! You're early."

"Let me see." I kick off my jeans and boots and fling my T-shirt to the ground. "Don't hide your beautiful body from me."

Ivy drops her hands and standing before me is my every fantasy come true. She's wearing some sort of lacy contraption. The top is like an open-cup bra with thin black straps framing her tits, just enough to hold floral-shaped appliqués in place over her nipples. The rest is essentially lacy fabric that crisscrosses over her body in a geometric pattern and is fastened with miniature black ribbons.

Pumping my engorged cock, I close the distance between us in a few strides, my eyes not leaving hers. "I couldn't wait to get back to you, and this is what I find?" My hands span her waist, my fingers maneuver their way under the soft fabric and caress her even softer skin. "You're stunning. Is this for me?"

"Of course. Welcome to your private show." Her arms loop around my neck, pulling me closer. Her turquoise eyes sparkle with mischief.

Sliding my palms down her hips and around her ass, I effortlessly lift her off the ground. Her legs wrap around my torso and I walk us to the mirror. Reaching between us, Ivy guides me into her slick heat and we both watch her pussy stretch around my cock.

I capture her lips with mine and the rest of the world fades into insignificance.

A potential Vegas wedding. My meeting with Peter Vander. Her leaving for school. None of this is important when we lose ourselves in each other.

An impromptu fuck, in our own sanctuary, allows the complexities of our lives outside these walls to be suspended in time.

Challenges are momentarily paused.

Discussions are on hold.

Nothing matters but this moment.

Fifteen

IVY

The Next Morning

FEAR CLAWS AT ME like a slice across my gut.

It worsens every waking day.

Mornings like this are going to end forever if Cillian doesn't see things my way.

Sunlight filters through the blinds, casting long, warm stripes across the bed where he and I lie tangled in the sheets after making love this morning. He stirs beside me, his arm tightening around my waist as he plants a soft kiss on my shoulder. The digital clock on the nightstand blinks 7:30 a.m., a blatant reminder of the real world waiting outside.

There's only two weeks left until my parents return. Two weeks until the hammer comes down. Two weeks to make our relationship permanent. Two weeks will change the trajectory of my entire life.

"Whoops," he mumbles against my skin, his voice thick with satisfaction. "I fell back asleep."

"I like cuddling after sex." My mind is a chaotic mess with thoughts racing faster than my heartbeats. "We only have a few more of these mornings left. I want to cherish them."

"Sweet Ivy, we have millions of these mornings left." Cillian shifts, propping himself up on one elbow to look at me. His hazel eyes are soft with affection but clouded with thoughts of his looming workday. He kisses my shoulder again. "It's time for me to jump in the shower. Big day ahead."

Cillian slides out of bed, his muscular frame unfolding as he strides toward the shower. He moves with a fluid grace. I blatantly ogle the defined lines of his back down to his sculpted ass.

Lately, I find myself desperately cataloging every detail about Cillian, trying to etch every moment we have into my memory. Last night we were supposed to talk about getting married, but we fucked all night instead.

I'm not complaining, but a sense of urgency feels like it's choking me. Somehow, it hasn't seemed to register with him.

"Cillian, wait." My voice is sharper than I intend.

He pauses, then turns with towel in hand. "What's up?"

"We didn't talk about Vegas." I sit up, clutching the sheet to my chest. "About...everything."

Cillian's expression tightens and the air between us charges with unsaid words. "Ivy...I, uh, thought we agreed to give it a week."

"It *has* been a week. If you don't want to marry me, say it," I blurt out, the fear of losing him twists my stomach.

He sighs and returns to the bed and sits. His eyes search mine. "Ivy, that's not fair. It's not about wanting to marry you. Of course I do. It's about making sure we're both ready for something that big. This—us—it's been fast. Amazing, but fast."

"I *know* it's been fast," I shoot back, feeling desperate and frustrated. "Don't you get it? If we wait, everything could fall apart. My parents will be back in two weeks. What if they force me back into the life I had before? I couldn't bear it."

Cillian rubs his temples, clearly struggling to keep his composure. "We *cannot* base this decision on fear. Or your parents. Marriage is a huge step. It's not a quick fix."

"Are you looking for reasons to avoid it? Are you embarrassed by me? Is this just a game to you?" The words tumble out before I can stop them, each one laced with more accusation than I intend.

He winces, hurt.

God, I sound like an immature teenager. Because I am.

Cillian's voice softens. "Ivy, I'm not embarrassed. This is not a game. Part of me would like nothing more than to throw caution to the wind. We're clearly compatible, you've been living here for nearly two months."

"Then why don't we just go for it?" I feel tears sting the backs of my eyes.

He brushes my hair back with his fingers. "Because there are other people to consider. We haven't met each other's families yet and family is, clearly, a huge part of who we both are." He presses his finger to my lips when I try to interrupt. "Let me finish. We owe our parents an introduction before springing such big news on them, but it's not the only reason. You're committed to Stanford this year—it's your chance to explore who you are outside of your family's expectations. Outside of me. You'll grow tremendously as a person." He removes his finger. "I don't want to hold you back. You might find new passions and meet new people. I love you and we'll see each other as much as possible, but I'd never want you to rush into such a big commitment. I want you to choose me with no doubts. If you still feel the same next year, maybe you can transfer to University of Washington or, who knows, we'll figure it out."

"So, you don't want us to be exclusive." I'm anguished and can't stop a tear from falling. "You're saying, 'go out there and fuck other people.'"

Cillian's jaw clenches, and he takes a breath before speaking. "What the hell? Ivy, *no*. I love you. Why would you think I'd send you off to fuck someone else?"

"I don't know. Maybe so you can? You've been with a lot of women. Maybe I'm not enough." Then the truth slips from my lips before I can catch it. "You're my *first*, Cillian—my first *everything*."

The words hang between us. I've revealed one of my secrets.

Shit. Should I go ahead and reveal it all?

Cillian pauses, his expression tightens with shock. "Jesus. *What. The. Fuck*? Other women? And, correct me if I'm wrong, but are you saying you were a virgin the night I met you at Kells? Why wouldn't you have told me, Ivy?" He runs a hand through his hair, visibly angry but conflicted. "The first time you have sex is not some small detail you omit to your partner. Without being crass, my cock isn't small. I could've really hurt you."

"Okay. Fine. *Yes*. I was a *virgin*. I kept it to myself because I didn't know I'd end up falling in love with you. As far as hurting me, I wasn't worried. I've been using toys for years, I just hadn't...*um*." My voice is shaky and intense. Too much. Taking a calming breath, I shake my head sadly. "I'm being defensive and you're right. I'll take accountability. It was wrong not to tell you. At the time, I couldn't have predicted how important you'd become to me." I grip his wrist. "I wanted it. I wanted you. And, baby, my first time was everything I could have ever dreamed of. *More*."

"I'm glad to hear. I wish I could have shared the experience with you," Cillian snarks, then softens. His gaze flickers with concern. "*Please* don't lie to me again. If we're going to be in a committed relationship—which is what I want, by the way—we need to be honest with each other, no matter what. Secrets don't fade away. They grow. And I want us—this," he gestures between us, "to be built on trust. Nothing you can tell me will make me love you less."

I feel his words press on my chest. It's time. "I promise no more secrets. There's actually something else I want to tell you, it's no big deal." My voice trembles slightly, I know the gravity of what I'm about to say.

"Can we continue talking while I get ready? I'm running behind, but we're not done talking and this is important." Cillian gets up and strides toward the bathroom. He flicks on the faucet and the sound of cascading water fills the space between us.

Following close behind, I feel the steamy heat wrap around me like a thick blanket. We step into the shower and he continues as he soaps himself up. "I'd like to address what you tossed at me before you dropped the virgin bomb and finish up the discussion about Vegas. First, I have no goddamn interest in fucking any other woman and if you have any doubt in your mind about my intentions toward you, we're not ready for marriage yet."

"Cillian..." I clutch his elbows.

He gently grips my face between his palms. "Let me finish. Second, I consider us to be exclusive, I'm sorry if I wasn't clear. Third. I love you. So goddamn much being without you scares the fuck out of me. I would like nothing more for us to spend our lives together but, the truth is, we're faced with an upcoming separation, whether we like it or not. All we can do, for now, is focus on growing as a couple and figuring out how often we can see each other while you're at school. Assuming we still feel this strongly in a few months and our families are on board, I'm all in."

"I'm worried. My dad is strict, I don't think he's going to approve. Getting married would help us bypass at least one obstacle." The edges of my vision blur with unshed tears. I'm going to tell him. It's on the tip of my tongue...

He pauses, the water streams down his shoulders onto me. "Baby, isn't part of your journey to stand up for yourself and make your own decisions? Going to Stanford, becoming independent—that's part of it, right? Didn't you tell me it's what your grief therapist suggested?"

I press against his gorgeous body, my heart both heavy and hopeful. "Yes, but I'm scared. You haven't met my dad. Ever since my brother died he's pinned all of his expectations on me and he has a funny way of making me want to gain his approval. I don't want to let him down and I don't want to lose you. This feels impossible. I want you to be part of my life so badly."

"You won't lose me, Ivy." Cillian's eyes lock on mine with a sincerity that takes my breath away. "We'll tackle this as a couple, one step at a time. We'll make it through by understanding and supporting each other Not by rushing into marriage as a means to avoid the hard conversations. When we get married, I want it to be a momentous occasion celebrated by everyone who loves us."

Emotions so complex I can't comprehend them overwhelm me. I can't ever remember having a conversation this rational about something so important. *Then why can't you just tell him the whole truth?*

"I know you're right. It's hard and I'm sorry for trying to rush you into marrying me. I trust you're committed to me and I'm committed to you. I guess it feels like everything's closing in on me and I got panicky." My entire body aches with love for this man who is so wise. So understanding.

We get out of the shower and he hands me my towel. We dry off and he kisses my forehead gently. "Apology accepted. We'll figure it out. I'm not going anywhere, and I'm not letting anyone take you away from me. But let's do it with integrity. Okay?"

"Okay." Even as I say it, a part of me dies knowing I'm still being duplicitous by keeping my real age from him.

It's time.

No, long past time.

I return to bed and watch Cillian as he finishes getting dressed. His movements are unhurried, though now he's way behind schedule. Even though I've disappointed him and put pressure on our relationship, he's taking his time to make sure I'm okay. My feelings are more important to him than anything else—*gah*. Each glance he throws over his shoulder is filled with such warmth. It bridges the gap of our earlier tension.

He needs to go to work. I'll tell him tonight.

"See you later?" He approaches the bed, buttoning his flannel.

"Absolutely," I manage a smile despite the forthcoming confession about my age. "I love you, baby. I really, *really* love you."

He leans down and plants a sweet kiss on my lips. "I love you too. We'll figure this out. I promise."

Cillian strides out of the bedroom and I hear the door to the elevator close behind him with a loud click. The loft immediately feels emptier. I linger in bed for a moment longer, clutching the sheets we messed up all night. Feeling comfort in the lingering scent of him.

The scent of us.

My phone buzzes on the nightstand. It must be Cillian. Excitedly, I reach for it and see the screen light up with twenty missed notifications from when I was in quiet mode. Fifteen missed calls. Five texts. Starting at nine last night.

My entire body freezes.

My father. He's home. One week early, without warning.

9:45 pm Dad: *Where are you, Ivy?*

11:15 pm Dad: *I know you're not at Emma's. It's critical you come home now.*

12:30 am Dad: *Ivy. Stop the bullshit. Respond immediately.*

2:45 am Dad: This is unacceptable. Get your ass home now. You're putting us through undue stress. We need to know you're safe.

8:00 am Dad: If I don't hear from you by 9 am, I'm involving the authorities.

The last one, time-stamped minutes ago, sends a cold shiver down my spine.

Panic clenches my gut as I scramble out of bed and throw on some clothes. I'm out the door in minutes, the looming threat of my father's control spurs my every step. Before I get in the car, I text Cillian.

Me: My parents returned early. I'll try to call later.

On my way home, as the city rushes by, a heavy dread settles over me.

I'm not ready for this. Today, I have to confront everything I've been running from.

The hourglass has run out.

Sixteen

CILLIAN

Three Days Later

BRAAAAAANNNNNG. BRAAAAAAANGGGG.

Jesus fucking Christ.

The sharp blare of my phone alarm slices through the haze of my whiskey-drowned slumber, dragging me back to a reality I can't face. I jam my finger on the off button with more force than necessary to shut it off.

My head is pounding. A thumping reminder of last night's poor decision. Trudging out to the kitchen to take some Tylenol, I spot the empty whisky bottle on the kitchen counter. It glares at me accusingly. Last night, I drained it in a futile attempt to quell my escalating panic about Ivy.

I'm a mess. A shell of a man. I've endured three days of unbearable silence from my girlfriend and the uncertainty is crushing. Ivy has vanished. She sent me a text telling me her parents were home early, and then nothing.

No texts. No calls. Nothing.

I've called and texted her a million times and still...nada.

Did I push her away?

Not knowing is killing me. It's like she's been wiped off the face of the earth. With each passing second, worry carves a pattern into my chest. I miss her from the bottom of my soul, it feels like my heart has been ripped from my body. All I've done for seventy-two hours is conjure up every horrific possibility of what's happened to her. Each one claws at my brain with unrelenting ferocity.

What if she was in an accident? What if she's hurt? Abducted? *Dead*.

The darkness of my thoughts is a black hole, pulling me under.

Why didn't I insist on getting her address? I know she's not on socials, but why don't I know her parents' first names? Why don't I know what fucking school she went to? We've spent nearly every waking minute together for the past few weeks. I can tell you the location of every freckle on her body.

How do I not know how to track her down?

The thought of Ivy scared and alone is a dagger to my soul.

As I wait for coffee to brew, the empty bottle taunts me. Evidence of my failed attempt to cope. For all my talk of integrity, I'm a fucking fraud.

The thing is, her absence is suffocating. The silence in my loft is a stark contrast to our conversations and the sounds of our passion. Her laughter, once a beautiful melody filling my loft, now echoes like a ghostly reminder. Will I ever hear it again?

Dragging my weary body to the shower, I let cold water shock my system. Wash away the stench of alcohol and despair. I resolve to find her, no matter the cost. The fear I'm already too late is crushing.

When I find her—and I will—I'll never let her go again.

I can't believe the most important meeting of my career is in an hour. I have no idea how I'm supposed to get through it, let alone make a presentation. Yet, after nearly canceling two dozen times, something compelled me to keep it on the books.

The reality is, Ivy is probably fine. Safe with her family. It doesn't explain why she won't text me back, but it's possible she doesn't want to talk to me after I rejected her idea of eloping. Maybe she's ashamed about lying to me about her virginity. Maybe her dad has her on lockdown. Who knows.

Fuck. Fuck. Fuck. Fuck. Fuck.

I've dedicated my entire adult life to McGloughlin Construction. Today is crucial, a potentially career-defining day. I have to suck it up for an hour. *One goddamn hour.* Surely, I can push my personal shit aside and manage.

Once I've scrubbed myself clean, I get dressed. Rather than my usual work clothes, I put on a pair of dark jeans and a button-up shirt. I keep my steel-toed work boots on, though. I don't have the energy for pretense. I am who I am. A blue collar worker who's made something of himself.

Shit. Was I enough for her? Her family is rich enough for a full house staff. It's possible our story was always going to end this way.

I *think* her feelings for me were real. Mine certainly are. I love her. She says she loves me. It felt sincere. But, could I have been her summer fling? A walk on the wild side? I mean, the girl was a twenty-four-year-old virgin, for God's sake. Who could blame her for wanting to sow some wild oats. I sure did at her age.

The fucking age difference. It's always worried me.

Every moment we shared was precious to me and the thought of it being over like this twists a knife in my gut.

The thought of her fucking someone else makes me feel murderous.

Fuck it.

I grab my keys and head out.

The way this organization disclosed the meeting location to me was nuts. Enshrouded in layers of secrecy I've never experienced in my life. Yesterday, I was required to sign a new stack of NDAs. The address was finally sent to me in an encrypted email message a hour ago.

I guess it underscores the high stakes and confidentiality of the project, but it didn't make planning easy. Luckily, the drive to the meeting isn't far and I find myself at a compound close to the Port of Seattle with plenty of time to spare.

Trying to push thoughts of Ivy to the side for a moment, I sit in the car to visualize my presentation. It's useless. Ivy invades my thoughts instead. Her laugh. Cuddling on the couch. Making love whenever and however the mood strikes.

Shaking the memories off, I decide to head inside. There's no shame in arriving early. I'm shown to the designated conference room—a stark, modern space. Very cold and impersonal. Setting up my materials, I attempt to anchor myself in the moment, but my hands tremble when I lay out the sample blueprints on the polished glass table. The words and diagrams blur before my eyes.

Then the door opens.

Stanley Bright, titan of the shipping industry, steps into the room with a presence demanding attention. He's a tall, imposing figure with a broad, sturdy frame. His hair is silver and neatly trimmed. His beard is impeccably groomed, which adds to his distinguished appearance.

His unusual blue eyes are sharp and assessing—yet familiar—as he scans me from head to toe before extending a hand. "Stanley Bright. Thank you for coming today."

"Cillian McGloughlin, sir. It's my pleasure." I grip his hand tightly as we shake. There's something about this man. I've never met him, but it's like we know each other. I can't seem to place him, though.

A few minutes later, a string of executives wearing dark suits whose faces are a blur, follow him in. The last woman to enter the room stops my heart.

Dressed in a sharp black suit, her blonde hair pulled back in a sleek knot, Ivy Davies takes a seat next to Stanley. She flicks her gaze to my surprised face and everything becomes clear. Those beautiful turquoise orbs I've gazed into for hours on end—are her father's eyes.

Ivy Davies isn't her real name. She's Ivy Bright, and looks every inch the business prodigy her father is training her to be.

What. The. Actual. Fuck.

More lies. Am I in the twilight zone?

She flicks those eyes to mine with a message. A plea for discretion, perhaps? I see the flash of the pain and confusion I'm feeling mirrored in her hollow, haunted expression.

Leaving me in a surreal fog as the meeting commences.

Stan introduces his team, ending with Ivy. As if the day couldn't get worse, he drops another bombshell eviscerating my entire being. "Cillian, this is my daughter, Ivy. She just turned eighteen, but finished both high school and her undergraduate business degree this year. I'm proud to say, she'll start her master's program at Stanford Business School this fall before she takes her executive role at Bright Shipping."

Every drop of blood freezes in my veins.

I feel like I'm about to pass out. The room spins. The walls close in.

Eighteen.

Every moment with her, every conversation, every discussion about the future crashes down around me. Lies. All summer long. About her age. Her virginity. About who she is.

Everything.

And yet, as Stanley continues to describe the project and the impending timeline, the only thing I can think of is the raw, undeniable pain etched into her features.

Why does she look like a ghost? What's happened to her in the days we've been apart?

Stan stands up. "Cillian, I'm looking forward to discussing our new vision and how McGloughlin Construction's capabilities line up."

How I manage to nod and begin the presentation, I do not know. Probably muscle memory, at this point. I've never been more discombobulated in all my life. "As you can see from the plans on my most recent project..." I project detailed blueprints on the screen behind me, "...we're prepared to not only meet but exceed the current standards for environmental efficiency and safety in construction."

I continue answering the questions tossed in my direction. Stan seems oblivious to the glances Ivy and I steal. It seems like she's trying to get a message across. Maybe an apology. Or, warning me not to say anything. I also could be making this shit up in my head. What the fuck do I know?

As the meeting wraps up, against all odds, Stan seems pleased. "Impressive, Mr. McGloughlin. We'll be in touch shortly with our decision."

My plan was to stay behind and talk to Ivy, but I'm ushered out and my pass is taken away. Back in my truck, I stare at the building. Wonder if I should sit here and wait until she comes out. I'm sure there are security cameras everywhere, though. At some point, someone's going to ask questions.

She's okay. Alive. Out of harm's way.

Which means? *Fuck.*

Gripping the steering wheel tightly, my thoughts are still a chaotic swirl. Now, with new emotions. Anger, betrayal, and confusion wrestle for dominance in my mind.

Eighteen. I fucked Ivy on her eighteenth birthday. She was a virgin.

Holy. Fucking. Hell.

Thank Christ we kept to ourselves. If my friends or family knew, I'd be a laughingstock.

Oh, Jesus.

Fuck. Fuck. Fuck. Fuck. Fuck.

If her father finds out I stole his precious daughter's innocence, he'll kill me. Literally kill me.

I feel like a disgusting creeper. I can't even count about how many times my cock's been inside her body. Her pussy. Her mouth. Her ass. How many times did I make her come? How many times did I fill her with my seed?

She's *fourteen* years younger than me, not eight.

I'm wrecked. I'm *done.*

I hope the deception was worth it for her.

Because I'll never recover from this betrayal.

Seventeen

Same Day Different Perspective

MY ENTIRE WORLD HAS fallen apart.

Exploded into sharp, piercing shards of agony.

I can barely breathe from my heartache. My eyes are puffy from crying for three solid days. Every muscle in my body is tense and sore.

The morning I got his texts, I prepared myself for my dad's disappointment. Anger, even. All of it a given. Oh, I really had no comprehension of his wrath. For the past seventy-two hours, give or take, he's screamed and yelled at me and called me every name in the book.

I know I fucked up. I've lied to my parents. I've lied to Cillian. I'm not proud of it. I know I deserve for everyone I care about to be furious with me.

I also understand how scared he was when he called Emma's parents to find out I hadn't spent even one night there. Then I didn't answer his texts or calls for twelve hours.

But...did it give him the right to cut me to the bone? I can't take any more.

This morning, I thought it was finally over when he asked me to go into the office with him.

But, no. Today, it's the silent treatment.

The engine of his two-tone silver Maybach Sedan purrs quietly as we glide through the city streets. My father's presence looms beside me, a towering figure of authority. Emotionally drained, I'm sitting as far from him as possible in the backseat, pressing my forehead against the cool glass window. Trying to be invisible. The last thing I need is to trigger him, so it's best I keep a low profile.

For now he's quiet, but the silence is thick and suffocating. I'm scared he'll come at me any minute now. It's been relentless.

Like the loyal employee he is, our driver, Louis, says nothing. His eyes remain fixed on the road ahead. He's paid to remain oblivious. Discreet.

Fifteen minutes in, it begins.

"Ivy." My dad's voice is a low growl. "This is getting ridiculous. You're going to tell me everything. I demand it. Where the *fuck* were you?"

As stubborn and determined as my father is? I'm tenfold. I keep my gaze fixed on the passing scenery and my mouth shut. I won't tell him anything about the past few perfect weeks. The happiest of my life.

And, I won't *ever* betray Cillian.

"*Answer* me!" He slams his hand against the leather seat. "I'm fucking *serious*."

The sudden noise makes me flinch but I refuse to look at him. No way. He's not getting the satisfaction. "I told you I was with a friend. The rest isn't your business. You treat me like I'm your slave. You call me names and try to break my spirit. It's bullshit."

"*Bullshit*?" he scoffs. "Do you think I'm a fucking idiot? I trusted you to follow the rules and you didn't stay at home one goddamn night. You're behaving like a low-class whore. Who is he? *Who were you fucking all summer?*"

Tears sting my eyes. What kind of father slut-shames his daughter, who's always been perfect and obedient? My heart pounds like thunder in my chest. I never wanted to hurt my dad, but he's been hurting me for years. Cillian is my everything. If my dad finds out who he is, he'll destroy the man I love more than anything in this world.

I'll do everything in my power to protect him, even if means being on the brunt end of horrific verbal abuse.

My voice trembles despite my efforts to keep my cool. "I told you the truth. I needed to do my own thing and make my own decisions. I was always safe."

"*Safe*?" His voice drips with sarcasm. "You were off doing God knows what with God knows who. Were you on drugs? Drinking? I know you were fucking someone, Hilde showed me his fucking *underwear*."

Shit. I forgot I wore Cillian's T-shirt and boxers home after our first night together. Rookie mistake.

"No. Of course not." I dig my nails into my thigh. "You can't control me forever. I'm an adult. Do not treat me like a child."

"I'll be the judge of how to treat you as long as you're living under my roof." His bitter laugh is harsh. Cruel. "You're treated like a child because you're acting like a child. And I can and will take back control. For your own good."

It's no use. He doesn't understand and doesn't care about what I want or need. He never has. All he cares about is keeping me under his thumb.

"I've told you I'm sorry. I didn't mean to worry you." My words are hollow because I feel hollow.

"But you *did*." He punches his fist. "For the next five weeks, you're coming to work with me every day. You're not leaving the house without my permission. And, I'll have someone watching you 24/7 at Stanford. You cannot be trusted."

"*What*?" Panic permeates every pore. I whirl around to see if he's serious. "No. You wouldn't go that far."

He picks up the old-school *Wall Street Journal* newspaper from the seat. "You bet your fucking ass I will. You'll thank me one day."

"I'll never thank you for this." I can't stop the tears this time. "You're ruining my life. Taking away everything that matters to me."

He glares at me, his expression hard. "Why don't you tell me *who* the guy is. What kid had the audacity to touch my little girl? Defile her innocence. You're so naïve. You're being used. ."

"How can you jump to such a crass conclusion? And even if it were true—which it isn't—if you'd let me live my own life, I wouldn't be so fucking naïve." My hands clench into fists. "You'd trust me."

"Oh, that's rich. I gave you my trust and you pissed all over it." He points at me. "Tell me, did you take the pregnancy test I left for you?"

I stare at him, unable to comprehend the invasion of my privacy. Has our relationship come to this? "You're unbelievable. Do you hear yourself?"

He glowers at me but doesn't utter a word. I know this tactic, he's taught me all of his negotiation skills. Stay mute until the enemy breaks. The silence between us stretches, a chasm which is rapidly becoming too wide to bridge.

"Dad, *please*." I finally crack, no match for his years of honed experience. "You can't keep me in a cage. I deserve to live my own life out from under your thumb. To make my own mistakes."

"You've made enough mistakes in seven weeks to last a lifetime." He lowers his reading glasses to peer at me through slitted eyes. "I know you better than you know yourself. You might as well settle in, the restrictions are the consequences of your own actions."

"*Know me?*" I dab the tears from my cheeks. "You've *never* known me. You don't even *see* me. You see Forrest. You're trying to protect a fucking *ghost*."

My cruel words hang in the air, a sharp but painful truth. I hate myself for sinking to my father's level, but I swear I see a flicker of something. Pain. Regret. Who knows, but it's gone as quickly as it came. My dad's face hardens, and he looks away.

Lying back against the seat, I squeeze my eyes shut. I need Cillian. I have to find a way back to him. To the beautiful life we were creating. He's the only thing that makes sense anymore. Our relationship is the only thing I care about. God, the thought of him worrying about me. Wondering where I am. It rips my heart out.

He'll probably never be able to find me, I realize. He might know the house is in Medina but he doesn't know my real name. I destroyed my phone so my dad couldn't track our conversations. What must he think? I disappeared. Does he think I didn't care enough to say goodbye?

God, maybe my dad has me pegged. I'm immature. Selfish. Impulsive.

A liar.

Before this summer, I'd never been untruthful, at least not deliberately. In the past few weeks, I've lied to everyone who's important in my life. My lies are the reason I'm living in this hellish reality of isolation, heartbreak and emotional abuse.

No matter what my reasoning, what I did was wrong.

The car pulls up to the headquarters of Bright Shipping, a well-worn building my grandfather built seventy years ago. I've loved coming here from the time I was a girl. Today hits different. I don't want to be trapped anymore. Controlled. Monitored.

Dread settles in my stomach.

Then, I make a silent vow to myself. I'm breaking free from my father's control. I have to, even if it means giving up everything I've ever known.

My father turns to me. "This is an important meeting. I expect you to behave like a professional in there, Ivy. It's time to table this immature bullshit. No more trouble."

I nod numbly, unable to find the words to argue. What's the point? Regardless of the situation I've put myself in, I wouldn't do anything to jeopardize our family business. My father strides ahead, his presence commanding respect and attention from the hustling, bustling employees. I trail behind, feeling small and insignificant in the shadow of his power.

The elevator up to the top floor is filled with cold, silent tension. Once again, I follow Dad toward his office. Before we step inside, he turns to me. "The contractor we choose today will be responsible for transforming this space into a modern, green technology port, increasing our profits by thirty percent. I need you to be focused. I want your opinion on this company."

It's ironic how much he trusts my business acumen but not anything relating to my own life choices.

At this point, we're running a few minutes late, but my dad never rushes. Everyone adjusts to his schedule, and he knows it. We reach the conference room, he hands me a presentation folder and opens the door. I glance down and freeze.

This can't be true. It's *impossible*.

The McGloughlin Construction logo is embossed at the top of the proposal.

Cillian's company.

My mind reels as I take my place next to my dad. Instinctively, I glance up and see the man I love looking at me in shock, though he's trying to keep his composure. I try to communicate to him with my eyes. Tell him not to give himself away. He stares back at me, processing. A myriad of emotions flash in his eyes. Surprise followed by hope. Then pain. Confusion.

Devastation. Utter and total devastation.

Because of me.

"Cillian, this is my daughter, Ivy." Dad places his hand on my back and I can't help but flinch. I fix some sort of smile on my face until I hear him say, "She's only eighteen, but finished high school and her business degree this year. I'm proud to say, she'll attend Stanford Business School this fall to further her education before she takes her executive role at Bright Shipping."

I didn't think my life could get worse. I was wrong.

I stare at Cillian, horrified he's finding out my biggest secret this way.

The look on his face might be unreadable to the room, but I've stared into those hazel eyes for hours. I know this man. He looks away, trying to hide his disgust for me after he learns the truth. I know what I've done is irreparable. He finally realizes how completely I've deceived him.

There's no going back to the way things were.

I feel like I'm going to faint.

Eighteen

Later That Night

I'M DRUNK AS FUCK.

I'm holed up at my favorite low-key drinking hideout. The Central Tavern is steeped in 90s band nostalgia, with exposed brick walls lined with old concert posters from the grunge era. When I need a stiff drink, this is where I park my ass.

Nursing my fifth—maybe sixth—whiskey and savoring the burn as each sip goes down, I'm vaguely aware of a rock band on stage, though I have no clue who it is. Around me, there's a soft hum of conversation and clinking glasses.

None of it registers completely. All I can think about is Ivy and what a fucking mess I'm in.

Brock slides into the seat next to me, concern etched on his face. He's a big guy, all muscle and gruff exterior, but he's got a heart of gold. He's been my best friend since we were kids, and he knows me better than anyone.

"Jesus, Cillian." He takes in my disheveled appearance. "You look like shit. How long have you been here?"

"Fuck off." I take a swig of my drink.

Undaunted, Brock signals the bartender and orders a beer before turning his attention back to me. "What's going on? You've dodged my calls for two days."

"It's Ivy." I run a hand through my hair, exhaling deeply. "She's...*fuck*, Brock, she's barely eighteen. The night I met her was her birthday."

Brock's eyes widen in shock. "Eighteen? You've got to be kidding me."

"She lied about her age. Hell, she lied about everything." I finish my whiskey and signal for another. "She was a virgin and didn't tell me. I feel like such a dirty fucker. I can never tell my family about this."

He leans back and lets out a low whistle. "*Rough*. How did you find out?"

"Oh, in front of about a dozen people at Bright Shipping where I was making my final presentation," I say bitterly. "Imagine my shock. She showed up at the meeting and sat next to Stanley-fucking-Bright and he introduced her as his daughter. I nearly shit my pants."

Brock shakes his head, running a hand over his face. "Fuck. A hell of a way to find out."

"Yeah." I can't stop my voice from cracking. "But, I got the contract." I hold up my fresh glass. "*Yay?*"

He winces. "Whoa."

"I thought she was fucking dead. After her text, I hadn't heard from her. Didn't have a goddamn clue what happened. For three days I was out of my fucking mind with worry. Then I see her there. An entirely different person than who she said she was. How can I take this job and spend the next few years around her father knowing I fucked his eighteen-year-old daughter's virginity away? It's unbearable." I take a big swig.

Brock takes a long pull of his beer. "Have you talked to her?"

"How?" I shake my head, the thought of Ivy twisting the knife in my heart. "I have no way to reach her."

Swirling his chair to face me, Brock grips my wrist. "Kill, don't beat yourself up."

"I feel like a goddamn fool." I slide the empty glass away. "She's a kid. I'm fourteen years older than her. I've never felt this strongly about someone and I feel like a pervert for..."

It's the sex. I can't stop the visions of her beautiful, wondrous face every time I made her come. How incredible it felt, lying in my bed, entwined and naked with Ivy after fucking all night. Washing her hair in the shower while she rode my cock. Licking whipped cream from her nipples.

Everything we did now seems...tainted. I feel disgusting. Like I inadvertently groomed her, or something.

"You didn't know," Brock says gently. "You can't feel bad about something you didn't know about."

"Yeah, but why did she lie? Was I some summer fling to her? A way to rebel against her dad? It felt like so much more." I shake my head, the confusion and anger bubbling up inside me. "I'd have never touched her had I known. It's unfathomable. I can't wrap my head around it."

"What are you going to do?" Brock takes another sip of his beer.

"I have no idea." I bury my face in my hands. "She's the daughter of a billionaire. She told me her father was controlling. Maybe I'm just a pawn in some strange family dynamic. Or, maybe she really loved me. I don't know anymore."

"And now you've got this contract." Brock leans forward. "It's a huge opportunity, Kill. But I get it. It's complicated as hell."

An understatement if I've ever heard one. "Yeah. I don't know if I can do it. But, I don't know if I can't. This job will catapult the company to a new level. It's everything I've been working toward."

"You've got to figure out what's more important to you. The job or your sanity." Brock slugs me in the arm, trying to lighten the mood.

We sit in silence for a moment, the noise of the bar fading into the background. Brock's correct. I can't figure out what matters more. It's not an easy choice.

"I wish I knew why," I say finally, my voice breaking. "Why she lied to me. What she really wanted. I was in love with her. *Am* in love with her."

Brock grips my shoulder. "You may never get those answers. Don't let it eat you alive, she was with you willingly. You didn't do anything wrong, she's a consenting adult. No matter what happens, you've got to find a way to move forward."

As the night wears on and the bar starts to empty, the alcohol and mental exhaustion catches up with me. "I'm fucked."

If only I could talk to Ivy. Get some closure. I know it's unlikely, she's leaving for Stanford soon, and as far as I'm concerned, I'm not initiating contact. She's off-limits. It's too dangerous. We can't continue whatever this fucked-up relationship is, anyway.

As we leave the bar, the cool night air hits my face, a stark contrast to the warmth inside. "Thanks, Brock. I don't know what I'd do without you."

"You'd probably be face down in a ditch somewhere." He whacks me on the back. "Seriously, Kill. You're going to get through this."

I nod, unconvinced. "I hope so."

My Uber ride home is quiet, the city lights blur past as I replay the night's conversation in my mind. I realize, the faster I get over Ivy, the better. I need to forget the past few weeks. Forget about her. She's leaving for a new life soon. One without me.

A case or two of Jamison 15 should help. No, Red Breast. Fuck it, I'll get both.

Ten minutes later, I crawl into my bed, which still smells like her. The room spins. Squeezing my eyes shut, I know what I must do. For the first time in days I fall into a dreamless sleep.

A loud pounding on my bedroom door wakes me up the next morning.

Rubbing the sleep from my eyes, I stagger to my feet. There are only a few options of who it could be. My brothers or Brock.

Or Ivy.

I let out a heavy sigh and fling the door open. "What the fuck?"

"Uh, can you put some fucking pants on, man? I don't need to see your morning wood." While I pull on some joggers, Brock grabs a chair, spins it around, and sits down, leaning his arms on the backrest. "I've decided. You can't let this Ivy bullshit ruin you, Kill. You've got to sign the contract with Bright Shipping. It's a huge opportunity."

"I know," I mutter, running a hand through my hair. "The only thing keeping me from signing is how am I supposed to work with Stanley Bright knowing what happened with Ivy? How am I supposed to look him in the eye?"

Brock's gaze is steady. "You do what you've always done. You get the job done. You're a professional, Cillian. You can't let your personal feelings screw this up. Remember. *You. Did. Nothing. Wrong.*"

The impact of my best friend's words resonate. He's right. This contract is too important to let go because of my tangled emotions. I'll focus on the business and making McGloughlin Construction the success I've always dreamed it would be.

"I'm signing the contract." My voice is firm. "I'll do the best damn job I can. I'll make sure Stanley sees me as an asset."

Brock smiles. "I like your spirit. Don't let a summer fling ruin everything you've worked for."

My heart aches at the term "summer fling," but I push the pain aside. Ivy might have lied to me, but I won't let her deceit define me. I have to be stronger.

"Yeah. I'll do what I've done for years." I grab a T-shirt from my dresser. "I'll keep things professional. Pretend like nothing ever happened. I've got Stanley Bright's trust and I'm the man for this job, there's no need to do anything to fuck it up."

Brock stands up and heads for the door. "Awesome. Glad to hear it. You've got this. Don't let anything stand in your way."

Though my head is pounding, after a shower, a couple Tylenol and a bottle of water, I'm as good as new. The road ahead won't be easy, and the ghost of my love for Ivy will haunt me, but I can't let it break me. I have to keep moving forward, for the sake of the business and for my own sanity.

I may not have all the answers, and the pain of Ivy's betrayal will linger for a long fucking time, but I won't let it destroy me.

I'll turn this into a victory, no matter what it takes.

Nineteen

IVY

A Few Days Later

I HAVEN'T BEEN ABLE to get out of bed.

Not since I saw Cillian at the office earlier this week.

My heart aches for him, but what started as a way for me to break free from my father's control has mushroomed into a disaster.

Seeing Cillian at the meeting shocked me to the core. I knew he had some big project in the works, but had no clue it was building my father's new headquarters. Coming face to face with him before I could explain what happened was mortifying.

But nothing could have prepared me for my dad's oblivious introduction. I watched Cillian's face morph from surprise, to confusion, to devastation and finally horror when he found out who I really am. And how old I am.

Watching his reaction, I fully comprehended how my lies hurt the people I love the most.

I'm ruined.

Despite every one of my dad's threats, for the past few days I've been buried under my comforter, trying to block out the world. The memory of Cillian's pained face haunts me. It's unbearable. I can't believe how badly I've messed my life up.

A gentle knock on the door barely registers until my mom's voice cuts through the fog of my despair. "Ivy, can I come in?"

Fuck her. What's she doing back? The woman's barely acknowledged my existence for over five years. I don't respond, hoping she'll take the hint and leave me alone. But she doesn't. I hear her footsteps as she approaches the bed.

"I brought you something from Paris." She approaches and I hear her place something on the floor. "A few items from Givenchy's new collection."

I peek out from under the covers. "When did you get home?"

"A few minutes ago." She sits on the edge of the bed. "I came back as soon as your dad told me what's going on."

We used to be close, but her presence isn't a comfort anymore. More like another source of anxiety. I haven't really talk-talked to her in years. She's been lost in her grief over my brother, leaving me to fend for myself in the gilded cage my father calls protection.

Turning away from her, I pull the covers around me. I'm not ready to face her or anyone else. I'm surprised she doesn't give up, instead placing a comforting hand on my shoulder. "Ivy, please talk to me," she pleads. "I know things have been hard, but shutting yourself off from the world isn't the answer."

Oh really? Her words infuriate me. I fling the covers off and flip over to face her. Show her my red, puffy eyes from crying for a solid week.

"Hard?" I spit out. "Try *impossible*. I apologized. I know I was wrong, there's no justifying lying. I get it. On the other hand, the way Dad controls my life, the way he keeps me in this protective bubble wrap, it broke me. Instead of compassion he's verbally attacked me every single day. Did you know he forced me to take a pregnancy test? I'm done, Mom. I don't want to go to Stanford. I won't work with him. I need something else. I can't keep doing this."

My mom's face falls. She nods slowly. "Oh, my darling girl. Your father loves you more than life itself. He can't bear for anything to happen to you. He thinks he's protecting you but doesn't realize how much it's hurting you. I didn't either."

"He's called me horrible names, Mom." My voice is wobbly.

She shakes her head. "I'll talk to him. Will you tell me where you were??"

"He's not wrong. I met someone and spent the past seven weeks with him. Now it's over and I'm utterly heartbroken. For many reasons." Tears pool in the corners of my eyes. "For a short time, I felt alive. Like before Forrest died. Now my life is ruined and there's nothing I can do but protect the man I love. Dad will destroy him if he finds out his identify. I won't do that to him."

My mom's eyes widen slightly. She takes my hands in hers. "Oh, Ivy. You're in love?"

"Yes. So much." My tears fall freely now. "I can't tell you who because I don't trust you won't tell Dad."

She grimaces and shakes her head. "Okay. I understand our trust is broken . For the past few years I've been lost in my grief and it's been hard for me to function, let alone be a mother. You've suffered and I should have been there for you. I wish... I'm so sorry, my baby girl."

We sit in silence for a moment, our shared pain hangs heavy in the air.

"You know, when your father and I first met, things were complicated too." She scoots back, leans on the headboard and wraps her arm around me. Just like she used to before everything went to shit.

"What do you mean?" I look up at her sniffling.

She smiles wistfully. "Your father wasn't always the serious, powerful man he is now. Your grandfather built the company, but he wasn't sure he wanted to follow in his footsteps. My family was on the wrong side of the tracks and I was a wild, wild child. His parents didn't approve of me, we had to sneak around to see each other."

"What happened?" I'm intrigued. I've never heard this story before.

"We found ways to be together." Her eyes grow distant with the memory. "Those stolen moments were some of the best of my life. I knew, deep down, he was the one for me, no matter what anyone else thought."

"I'm glad he's your person, Mom, but do you realize how hard he is on me? Or that neither of you wished me happy birthday? You haven't in five years. You left on your trip without even saying goodbye. I really didn't think either of you cared what I did." I know she's trying to draw parallels, but my own situation is very different. "I wanted to have some fun. And I did. Then I met him."

"We've both failed you," she admits. "I completely understand why you were looking for something—someone—to make you feel wanted. Loved. We drove you to it."

"Thank you for saying that." Tears well up in my eyes again. "I know how much losing Forrest broke you. It's not the same, but being without my guy is killing me."

She leans her head on my shoulder. "It doesn't have to be ruined. Your father left for Hong Kong this morning, he's gone for a week. I'm lifting your restriction. Get yourself together and go to him. Talk to him. Explain everything. Then you and I will have a long talk about what you want to do with your life. I'll make it happen. Whatever it takes."

"You mean it? You'll help me?" Fragile hope flickers in my chest. "This isn't a trick?"

My mom kisses my temple. "You're wise beyond your years, always have been. You also know your own mind. It's not like we can take back what's already happened, can we?"

"No." My face pinkens.

"You're still on birth control?" She scoots off the bed and stands.

I nod.

Tears glisten in her eyes. "You're an adult now. Legal. Able to vote. Make your own decisions, including being intimate with a man you love. I'll set your dad straight. You're under no obligation to work for Bright Shipping if that's not your path.

Leave it with me. I promise I'll be here for you no matter what happens. Now go. Find him and explain what happened."

"Please don't have me followed. I mean it. I can't let dad know who he is," I plead. As elated as I feel to go find Cillian, I can't risk my actions causing him to lose this job with my dad. I've taken too much from him already.

I'm not sure how he and I will navigate what comes next, but first things first. I owe him an apology. It's time to make amends.

Mom lingers in the door. "Take my car. In case your dad air-tagged you. By the time he gets home from his trip, things will be different. I promise."

With a renewed sense of purpose, I get out of bed. The room spins slightly as I stand. Too much crying. Not enough sustenance. Steadying myself, I shower quickly and get dressed and pack a small bag with essentials. My heart pounds in my chest thinking about seeing Cillian again.

I have no idea how he'll react to me, but hopefully I can explain everything to him. Make him see what we have is real.

Despite my mom's assurances, I take extra precautions to avoid being followed, parking the car in a hotel lot and taking an Uber to Cillian's loft, even though it's only a few blocks away. My hands shake as I enter the code to the elevator and it starts going up. I step into his living room, it's quiet. His familiar scent fills the space, but he isn't here. I feel a pang of anguish.

Sitting on the couch for hours, waiting for him to return, my mind races with a thousand thoughts. Is he out on a date? Did he go away for the weekend? Where is he?

My heart aches when I think about how betrayed he must feel. I practice what I'll say over and over. As it gets closer to midnight, I start to feel stupid. Stalkerish. Maybe he's not as devastated as I've been.

I'm about to leave when I hear the elevator whirr. A few minutes later, Cillian stumbles in, so drunk he's barely able to stand up on his own. His eyes widen in shock as he sees me. Tries to focus. For a moment, time seems to stand still.

Then we run to each other and I jump into his arms. Our lips smash together and the world melts away. In this kiss, all my pain, confusion, and heartache seem to disappear.

He holds me against him tightly, whispering my name over and over as we kiss.

Nothing matters but him. Us.

Our love burns with the heat of a million fireballs as he walks us back to his bedroom.

Twenty

Earlier That Same Night

IT SHOULD BE THE best fucking time of my life.

Yesterday, I received the news McGloughlin Construction was awarded the Bright Shipping contract. The equivalent of winning the lottery—hundreds of millions of dollars in fees for the next three years. I'd like to celebrate with my Da, but all I feel is a hollow ache in my chest and the gnawing torment of memories I can't escape.

Ivy.

Sitting at the polished bar at the Metropolitan Grill, I toss back another whiskey just as I've done for the past few evenings. The amber liquid burns a trail down my throat. I've been sitting here for hours, lost in the haze of alcohol, once again trying to get drunk enough so I can sleep without dreaming about her. The bartender shoots me a concerned look but knows better than to ask questions. He's getting used to me nursing my heartbreak one glass at a time.

It's unfathomable to me how I've fallen hard for an eighteen-year-old. No matter how mature she seems, loving Ivy makes me feel like a complete idiot. Then I think about all the lies she told me and it's like a knife constantly stabbing me in my junk. In any given moment, my mood shifts from anger to longing to betrayal...always ending up at desire. I want her so fucking much. I'd give anything to bury myself inside her one more time.

The whiskey might blur the edges, but it'll never fully erase the images of her from my mind.

I down my drink and stagger out of the bar. Stumbling toward home, my vision sways with each step. The sidewalk morphs into two, then three pathways. Somewhere in the back of my mind a voice tells me, *"knock this shit off,"* but I know I'm not going to. The only time the pain dulls is after a few wee sweeties, as my da used to call them. I finally make it home, the elevator ride up to my loft feels endless and I'm not looking forward to going to bed alone.

The door opens, and through the fog of my inebriation, I see her.

Ivy.

Is this a fucking mirage? My angel is sitting on my couch in a pink sundress, her turquoise eyes are wide and filled with emotions I can't quite decipher in my drunken state. This has got to be a cruel trick of my mind. Then she stands and everything about her becomes startlingly real.

"*Cillian.*" Ivy's voice trembles.

In an instant, the world narrows to the two of us. I don't think—I react. I bolt toward her and she jumps into my arms. Everything feels right again. Our connection is immediate and all-consuming. I slam my lips against hers and kiss her like there's no tomorrow and everything feels possible again.

Ivy wraps her legs around my waist and her arms around my neck. Her touch is fire against my skin. Gripping her ass, I yank her against my cock, needing to feel her core heat against me. I whisper her name, over and over, like a prayer. She's here, and nothing—not her age, not the lies—*nothing* else matters but sinking my needy cock into her.

I carry her to my bedroom and we fall onto my comforter, our bodies entwined, grasping and clawing each other's clothes off. Each of us driven by a desperation bordering on madness. We're a whirlwind of limbs and breathless kisses. Every touch, every movement is a plea for understanding. For grace.

For *forgiveness*.

My hands trace the contours of her body. Ivy's skin is so fucking soft. She smells like flowers warming in the sun. As I kiss down the hollow of her throat to her chest, I tug her white bra cups aside and fasten my lips to a rosy nipple. My fingers work their way down the front of her panties and I plunge them into her velvety heat. Ivy's palms span my ass and she pulls me closer. Even though I'm wasted, I try to memorize this moment. Hold on to the sensation of our bodies pressed together again.

"I'm gonna lick your sweet little pussy until you're screaming," I growl, kissing my way to her stomach. I rip her panties off in one motion. Hoist her leg so it's resting on my shoulder, run a finger through her drenched folds and bury my face into her wet heat. She smells and tastes delicious. I lap up her arousal and suck on her lower lips. Fuck her with my tongue. Tease her until she's shuddering around me.

"*Ohmygod*," Ivy screams through her first orgasm. "Don't stop. *Please*, baby."

Oh, I'm never going to stop. I latch on to her clit. Curve my fingers into her and massage the spot exactly the way I know will drive her insane. Her hips rotate and gyrate against me and then Ivy's breath hitches and she moans so loud, the sound seems to reverberate in my bedroom. I don't let up, I've got her on a roll. I manage to coax out two more intense orgasms until she grabs my wrist. "Cillian, I need a break."

I'm willing to oblige for a second. I pull my fingers out and take a long suck of her delicious juices. Rub her belly until her pussy finally stops contracting. Then, I kneel between her legs and press her thighs apart. My cock is flush against my belly, aching like mad to be inside her.

"I'm gonna fuck you hard, baby. Are you ready for me?" I grip her ankles and angle my cock to align with her opening which, I realize, is not easy given my state of intoxication. Undeterred, my dick glides up and down her slit until I'm able to push in roughly. "Oh, *yeah*. You're soaking. Are you going to cream all over my cock, Ivy?"

"*Yessssss...*" she cries out. I slam into her and pull nearly all the way out before plunging in again.

Her thighs tremble as our bodies move in unison. I can't look away from where my cock pumps in and out of her pussy. It's *everything*. My fantasy. My reality. My eyes lock on to hers. I lean over to kiss her plump lips, back down her collarbone, across her neck and chest. Once again, I suck her distended nipple between my lips and she arches into me, whispering my name like I'm the only person who matters to her.

My head is spinning, but I don't care. My focus is on Ivy and being connected to her again. My hips roll into hers, driving deeper and deeper until I feel her clamp around my cock. Her entire body shudders beneath me with yet another orgasm.

Flipping her over, I nudge her legs open with my knees and ram into her from behind. Ivy looks at me fucking her through the full-length mirror on the wall. Her gorgeous eyes never leave mine when I band my arm around her stomach and tease her clit as I fuck her. "Do you have any fucking idea how sexy you are, Ivy? You're taking my cock like such a good girl."

"I *love* watching you fuck me. I love *you*." Ivy holds herself up on her forearms, her tits swinging with the force of my thrusts. "*Ohhhhh*, Cillian, *yessss*. Right there."

Circling her hard little nub as fast as I can, I buck into her harder. Cruder. Push her to the edge. Ivy's low, keening moans grow urgent. Intense. "Do you know what those sounds do to me? You're so fucking sexy, *Mo shíorghrá*. Come for me. Give me another."

Ivy throws her head back and I hold her upright against me, watching my fingers strum her when she gushes all over them. Her eyes close in pure bliss and her pussy tightens around me so fucking hard, I have no choice but to fill her with my come.

"Fuck, Ivy." I pull her head back and kiss her, not wanting to pull out of her yet.

We fall to the bed. I'm exhausted and still drunk as fuck, but I hold her close, and trace patterns on her back. Kiss the knuckles on her dainty hand. I want to stay like this forever. Pretend nothing's changed, but it's impossible. Morning will come soon and we'll have to face the harsh light of reality.

I press my forehead against hers. "Why, Ivy?" I murmur, my voice slurring from the booze. "Why did you lie to me?"

"I didn't mean to. Not really. It started out innocently. I had a fake ID." She combs her fingers through my hair. Then her eyes fill with tears, and she cups my face in her hands. "I was into you. No one ever made me feel the way you did and I already knew you thought I was too young. I *wanted* to have sex with you that night, so I let you think I was older. It was wrong. I'm sorry. It's no excuse, but I didn't realize we'd fall in love..."

I stop her from saying any more with a kiss. I pull her closer, needing to feel her tits pressed against my chest. "All of this is fucked up. *You* really fucked me up."

"I know, I'll never forgive myself." Her voice breaks. "What started out innocently kept snowballing."

I cup her head with my palm. "I thought it was strange when you wouldn't let me see where you lived. In retrospect, it was a huge red flag, and I fucking ignored it because I trusted you. I feel like an absolute idiot."

"I didn't lie about that. I didn't want to risk you showing up on the security cameras. My dad would have—"

"Jesus, Ivy," I interrupt. "Did you know I was pitching your dad? Seeing you there destroyed me."

She leans up and shakes her head. "I had no idea. I promise I mostly told you the truth."

"Except your name, your age, and your fucking identity." I snort out of frustration.

"Davies is my mom's maiden name and my middle name." Her brow furrows. "I didn't tell you who my dad was because he's…"

"Stanley-fucking-Bright." I shut my eyes. My head is starting to pound, but I'm not willing to let her go.

"*Yeah*." She lays back down on my chest. "He came home early from his business trip and threatened to call the cops. I texted you and then smashed my phone so he couldn't find out who you are. Then, he wouldn't let me out of his sight. He made me go to work with him. I never expected to see you in that conference room."

"How are you here, then? Sneaking around again?" I sigh.

She traces my nipple with her finger and my traitorous cock twitches. "No, he's away on business. My mom came home and we had a talk. I told my mom everything except your name—I don't want to do anything to mess up your chances with my dad." She glances back up at me. "Cillian, she told me to come. She knows we're in love. Please say we can figure it out. Get back to where we were. We have to. I can't lose you."

"I...dunno." I slam my head back against the pillow.

Ivy climbs on top of me, straddling my torso. "You *do* know. We belong to each other."

She guides me into her and my eyes nearly roll back in my head. For the next couple hours, I allow myself to believe her. Envision waking up to her every day as I watch her ride my cock. Dream about building a house for our kids when I fuck her from behind. Picture us growing old as we suck each other off.

The truth is, as amazing as it feels to get lost in her words and her body, there's no future for me and Ivy. I already feel remorseful for having sex with her tonight. I know this can't last. She's still only eighteen. Reality will come crashing down in the morning. For now, I allow myself one last time to hold her.

Love her.

Tonight, in this fragile bubble of time, nothing else matters. It's Ivy and me.

She's real. This is real. We're all we need.

Tomorrow, however, I know what must be done.

Twenty-One

IVY

The Next Morning

I'M TRULY HOME.

Sunlight filters through the blinds, casting a soft glow across the room. I wake up in Cillian's arms, his warmth enveloping me. I'm fucking happy. Everything feels perfect, like we've found our way back to each other. I smile, nuzzling closer, inhaling his familiar, woodsy scent. Reaching down between us, I grip his semi-hard cock and stroke him lovingly.

Cillian's lips curve into my favorite expression, a pleasurable smile. His hips swivel as he bucks into my hand. Then, as if a bolt of lightning zaps him, his eyes fly open and he sees me grinning up at him. The atmosphere abruptly shifts. His body tenses and he quickly disentangles himself, sitting up and throwing his legs over the side of the bed.

He rubs his temples, muttering, *"Fuck."*

"Morning." I reach out and touch his arm.

He flinches, but doesn't turn around. "Morning."

My heart lodges in my throat. I'm not sure what's happening. Last night, he fucked me until dawn. Usually, no matter how many times we do it, we're unable to keep our hands off each other when we wake up. I thought everything was fine. Why is he being weird?

It's awkward. Uncomfortable.

I've got to get things back on track. My life depends on it.

"Cillian, about last night." My voice trembles. "Thank you for letting me explain. I meant every word. I love you and I know we can figure this out."

He finally flicks his gaze toward me, his hazel eyes filled with sorrow. Guilt. "Ivy, this is no excuse, but I was loaded drunk. Not thinking straight. We shouldn't have... Look, I don't want to hurt you."

"What do you mean?" I tilt my head as dread settles like a boiling vat of acid into my gut.

He pinches his nose with his fingers. "I *can't* be with you. I didn't mean for, *uh*...anything to happen."

I hold up my hand as tears spill down my cheeks. "*No.* Don't say that. You wanted it too. We both did. Please, Cillian, it'll be okay. It doesn't matter how old I am, I know I want to be with you."

"You don't know shit, Ivy. You're eighteen.." He stands and pulls on his jeans. Then runs a hand through his hair. "You have your whole life ahead of you. You're infatuated. I was your first. But, you're going to Stanford. You should not be focusing on me. And I, most definitely, should not be focusing on you."

His words cut me to the core, but I'm not a quitter.

Wrapping the sheet around me, I approach him, placing a hand on his chest. "I'm *not* some little girl who's infatuated. Please don't diminish my feelings. I've essentially been an adult since my brother died and I'm a legal adult who can make my own decisions. I love *you*, Cillian. Age doesn't matter. What we have is *real*."

He steps back, recoiling from my touch. "Stop. It *does* matter. It matters a lot. I promised myself I wouldn't let this happen again and yet..." He shakes his head, agonized. "I'm a weak man. I can't resist you. No, that's fucked up. This is *not* your fault. I'm the one who's taken advantage of you. *Again*."

"Taken advantage?" My voice rises in frustration. "I was the one who pursued *you*! I lied about my age because I knew you'd never give us a chance if you knew the truth. I *wanted* you, Cillian. I still do. I showed up here last night to make sure you knew you did nothing wrong."

"You tricked me into taking your virginity on the day you turned eighteen. Can't you understand it makes me feel like a fucking creep? A thirty-two-year-old man fucking an eighteen-year-old girl? *God*." His voice cracks, like he's as anguished as me. "And seeing you at your father's office. It was mortifying for both of us, listening to the truth—knowing what we did all summer while your father stood there *oblivious*."

Crying harder, I try to take his hand but he yanks it away. "I'm sorry, I know I messed up. You have to know lying to you killed me. I agonized over it every single day. I wanted to tell you, I *did*. But, you thought twenty-four was too young, what was I supposed to do? After everything we meant to each other, I was scared of losing you."

"*What were you supposed to do*? Try telling the truth. How can I *ever* believe you now? About anything?" His shoulders sag. "I've taken the job with your dad, Ivy. Try to understand, whatever we have—*had*—it's over. You need to live your life and let me move on. You're beautiful. Smart. Funny. Sweet. You've got everything going for you. Learn from this and your next boyfriend will be the luckiest man in the world."

My heart shatters into a zillion pieces. I'm desperate. Without thinking, I drop my sheet and stand naked and vulnerable before him. "*Please*, Cillian. Look at me. My face. My tits. My pussy. I'm *yours*. Don't do this. You're the only one who's ever really known me. Don't throw me away. I don't want anyone else but you to *ever* touch me."

"I *can't*, Ivy." His eyes fill with tears as he picks up the sheet and wraps it around me. "I don't want to touch you. *I don't want you*. Being with you makes me feel like I'm doing something wrong. I can't keep feeling this way. It's too much."

Undeterred, I grab his hand and press it to my breast. "Stop. Look at *me*. Look at who I *am*, not my age. We can make this work. *Please*, Cillian. Don't give up on us."

"*Stop*!" He pulls his hand away, his voice breaking with emotion. "*Please*. I do not want to hurt you any more than necessary, but I need you to get dressed and go. *I. Don't. Want. You*."

Stunned, I stumble back. His words finally register and hit me like a physical blow. Sobbing and humiliated, I gather my clothes, hastily dress and run for the door. Cillian watches me from the kitchen, but he makes no move to stop me.

I reach the elevator and glance back one last time, hoping for a miracle, but his back is turned.

Then I know. It's over. My lies have ruined the best thing I'll ever have.

Bawling my eyes out in the elevator on the way down, my heart aches with the finality of it all. The door closes, cutting off my view of him, and I collapse against the wall. The love we shared, the future we could have shared…it's all gone. I have no idea how I'll move on. I will *never* forget him. How could I? I'll always carry a piece of him with me. Losing him will haunt me forever because I can't imagine loving anyone like I love Cillian.

Now, I'm left with nothing but the pain of what could have been.

What am I going to do?

The ride down feels like an eternity. Once I reach the lobby, though, my upbringing kicks in. I force myself to stand tall and wipe away my tears. It's time to be strong. For myself. For the future I must face without the man I love.

As I step outside, the noise and bustle of people around me barely registers. On my way back to the car, I replay our emotional breakup over and over in my mind. Each word slices me to the bone. I try to push the memories of our summer to the recesses of my mind and nearly run into a guy who cuts me off on the way into his office building. God, how can he be having a normal day? I'm stuck in an endless loop of heartbreak and regret.

Then it hits me. I can't stay here. Not in Seattle. Not surrounded by all these memories. I have to get away from everything that reminds me of him.

I'm not going to Stanford. I'm not running Bright Shipping because I certainly can't risk running into Cillian during the building process.

The only thing I can do is take control. Make big changes in my life.

I'm getting the fuck out of town.

No one, not even my father, is going to force me do anything I don't want to do.

Ever again.

Twenty-Two

Six Months Later

BURYING MYSELF IN WORK hasn't made me forget her.

It's quite the opposite, actually. Especially because I see her father every goddamn day. A constant reminder of my loss and my shame.

Six months have crawled by since I told her to leave, but Ivy's reaction is seared into my memory. Her turquoise eyes wide with shock, gorgeous face twisted in utter devastation. I can still hear her wracking sobs. Feel the weight of her heartbreak.

I crushed the only woman I've ever loved into dust. The guilt gnaws at me relentlessly, which makes me drink myself to sleep at night. Each morning, I wake up hating myself more.

Familiar sounds of construction echo around me—jack-hammers, cranes, the chatter of workers. It's been a long fucking day in the freezing cold, but there's much work to be done and a deadline looming. Bright Shipping's head-quarters is slated for demolition soon, and the endless last-minute bullshit red tape to handle drives me crazy.

Peter Vander approaches with a clipboard in hand. "Here are the latest environmental reports. We've got a meeting with the city inspector early tomorrow morning to, hopefully, finalize everything."

"Thanks. I'm ready. The last thing we need is a delay." I skim through the documents feeling confident we'll work through the issue.

As we stroll around the building, which has been cleared out, Peter and I discuss the demolition schedule when we run into Stanley Bright. He's a daunting figure, always impeccably groomed and dressed in a tailored suit. For obvious reasons, I'm never fully comfortable around the man, but I try to hide it.

"Good morning, gentlemen." Stanley's booming voice commands attention. "I'm ready for the progress report."

I purposely meet his gaze. "We're on track for the demolition, Mr. Bright. Just finalizing a few environmental concerns."

"Excellent." Stanley nods, his piercing blue eyes assessing me. "I trust there won't be any issues?"

"No, sir," Peter replies confidently. "We've got everything under control."

Stanley turns his attention back to me. "Cillian, I hope I can trust this project is in capable hands. You were late this morning."

"Uh...sorry, Mr. Bright, I had a family matter," I lie, feeling mortified he noticed. The truth of the matter is, I slept through my alarm.

He squints, then points at me. "Don't make a habit of it."

Stanley walks away and Peter and I exchange a glance. "He's a hard man to please," Peter mutters.

"Yeah," I agree, my mind drifting to Ivy growing up under his tough scrutiny. I wonder how she's doing at Stanford, but quickly push those thoughts aside. I have a job to do.

Thirty minutes later, I'm in my truck on the way home to shower before I head out for the evening. Before I can stop myself, I'm parked at BevMo, where I pick up four bottles of Red Breast. Every time, I tell myself my drinking is under control—I only drink to silence my mind long enough to fall asleep.

I know it's a lie.

I'm terrified I can't stop.

Tonight, I have dinner plans with my brothers, Seamus and Brennan. I'm not looking forward to it. I've avoided family dinners ever since I ended things with Ivy because I don't want to talk about it. Everything is too raw and painful. It's easier to try to get through each day alone.

Once I'm home, rather than shower, I sit at the counter, pour myself a drink and stare out into the space. The ache in my chest intensifies picturing Ivy and me cuddled up on the sofa watching a movie. I miss her beyond words. Taking a long sip, I wish the whiskey would numb the wound. I know better, though. It won't heal. It never does.

Let's be real, no amount of alcohol will ever fill the void Ivy left behind.

My phone buzzes with a text from Brennan.

Where are you? We're waiting at O'Malley's.

Fuck.

Feeling a pang of guilt, I pick up the phone. The truth is, I don't want to see my brothers tonight. I text back.

Not feeling well. Can't make it. Catch you later.

Moving to the sofa, I sit down with a fresh glass and savor the whiskey burning a familiar path down my throat. I'm lost in thought, but vaguely hear the elevator churning its way up. I'm not surprised to see Brennan and Seamus emerge, concern etched on their faces.

"Cillian, what the hell?" Brennan demands, holding up the half-empty bottle. "You said you weren't feeling well. Seems like you're fine here drinking by yourself."

"Fuck off." I shake my head.

Seamus, my youngest brother sits beside me. "We're worried about you, Kill. This isn't normal."

"Seriously, guys." I glare at them, the alcohol fueling my irritation. "What's it to you if I have a few drinks at home? I'm not hurting anyone."

Brennan's expression softens. "We're worried you're going down a path. It's a slippery slope when you start hiding your drinking."

"I'm not, Dad," I snap. "I've got everything under control."

"Do you?" Seamus asks quietly. My softspoken brother is different from the rest of us. "Because it doesn't seem like you do. You have the world at your feet. The business is doing better than ever, this should be the best time of your life. Don't let everything you've worked for slip away because you're drowning in a bottle."

I look away. The truth of their words stings but they have no idea the Bright Shipping project doesn't come close to being the best time of my life. The seven weeks Ivy and I spent... "Stop making such a big fucking deal. I have a lot on my mind. A couple of drinks before bed helps me sleep."

"We get it." Brennan sits on the other side of me and places a hand on my shoulder. "Can't you find another way to relax? Drinking yourself into oblivion isn't the answer. You *know* this."

I scoff and take another swig. "You two think you know everything, huh? You think you understand what my life is like?"

"We saw what Da's drinking did to him." Brennan's voice is steady but pained. "And we're worried about you following in his footsteps. You missed his fucking birthday party. We know it wasn't work-related, you were here on your own getting drunk. You should know, it tore Mom apart."

Seamus pleads, "Don't go down the same path, Kill. We don't want to lose you to this."

My childhood memories flood back. Connor's resentment. The fights. The tears. The way Ma would cry herself to sleep. I shake my head, trying to block it out.

"I'm *not* Da." My voice rises. "I'm not going to end up like him because I don't have a wife or kids. *Who the fuck cares?*"

"I do. Seamus does. Your family cares." Brennan claps my back. "We can't stand by and watch it happen."

"Get the fuck out," I snap. My anger boils over. "Both of you. Leave me alone. Neither of you know what it's like to live with this...*emptiness*."

Seamus reaches for me "Kill, please..."

"Leave!" I shout at the top of my lungs. "I don't want your pity. I don't need your help. *Get. The. Fuck. Out.*"

My brothers hesitate for a moment and I have a flashback to the moment I told Ivy to leave. Jesus, the looks on their faces. Helplessness. Sorrow. I'm pushing everyone I care about away.

As the door closes behind them, the silence in the loft is deafening. I finish my drink and pour another one. My guilt, shame, and anger has turned into quite a toxic cocktail. Now it's bleeding into my relationships with my brothers.

"I'm not Da," I whisper to myself, trying to believe it.

Except, the more I drink, the more I feel like I'm slipping into some unknown oblivion. The whiskey burns, but it's a familiar pain. One I've grown accustomed to. Seamus and Brennan have a valid point. I should stop but, truthfully, I don't want to.

A while later, I finish the bottle and stumble to bed. As I collapse onto the mattress, Ivy's face haunts my thoughts.

I think back to our last moments. The desperate passion. The intense breakup. I replay it over and over, wondering if

I made the right decision. Every time, I come to the same conclusion.

Yes.

I've spent a lot of time around her domineering father, I've come to understand why she lied about her age and rebelled. Truth be told, she could have had anyone, I happened to be at Kells the night she set off on her mission. Which meant I was the lucky one to share those blissful weeks with her.

Ivy deserves better than me. A man fourteen years her senior who greedily took every part of her innocence. The fucking idiot who tossed her aside like she was trash instead of treating her with empathy and care.

"I'm sorry, *mo shíorghrá,*" I whisper into the darkness. "I miss you so fucking much."

My words are empty. An echo of my endless, consuming remorse. No amount of whiskey can ever erase her memory or fill the void she left behind.

My love for her was real.

I wish I could find a way to move forward, but it's impossible.

The memories are a bittersweet reminder of what could have been.

Ivy haunts my every waking moment.

Twenty-Three

One Year Later

Sometimes I pinch myself to see if my life is real.

I can't believe it's been a year since I moved to Florence. At first it was rough, but eventually I found a sense of peace and purpose I never thought would be possible after Cillian broke things off. It doesn't hurt that the restrictive rules my dad used to make me follow are a distant memory.

Now, I'm sitting at my bistro table in my flat, sketching out ideas for my next painting. Mom hums softly as she pours steaming liquid into two cups, sets out fresh pastries and fruit, then sits next to me.

"What are you working on?" She takes a bit of a marmalade cornetti and groans. "God, this is fantastic."

I take a sip of rich, dark coffee. "Ideas for a new piece. We're going into a week on portraiture. I'll probably force you to be one of my subjects, be forewarned."

"I'd be honored. You're very talented." Her smile is filled with pride. "You've come such a long way, Ivy. I'm proud of you for following your passion."

It's true. For past year and a half, I've lived life on my own terms. First, traveling to Europe with mom. Then, putting down roots in Italy. I'm in my third semester of intensive courses at the Florence Academy of Art, where I've immersed myself into everything they offer—from drawing and painting to sculpture. I've made a ton of friends and feel like the Ivy I used to be before my brother died.

"I couldn't have done it without your support." I sink my teeth into a custard bomboloni, the greatest pastry in the history of the earth.

She and I settle into our usual comfortable routine, eating and planning out our upcoming travels. This time, my mom is only here for a couple of weeks so we're sticking close and heading to Siena. I look forward to exploring the medieval city and drawing inspiration from its historic architecture.

"I booked us a room at a charming bed and breakfast in the heart of town." Mom turns her phone so I can see the modern decor. "We'll be able to walk everywhere."

Excitement bubbles. "It's hard to believe I haven't been there yet. I can't wait to see the *Piazza del Campo* and the cathedral."

"I love seeing you happy." Mom stirs her coffee. "Last year broke my heart…"

I nod, the memory still raw. I try not to think about the events leading up to meeting Cillian and the demise of our relationship. "My world fell apart. But you stood up for me with Dad. If you hadn't whisked me off to Europe, who knows where I'd be."

Mom's eyes glisten. "Your father was caught up protecting you, he couldn't understand how his words would affect you. It didn't take much convincing, we both want the best for you."

"We're a work in progress." My dad and I aren't fully on track, but the distance helps. "At least you made him see we needed to be a family again."

She clears our plates. "Well, spending six months traveling while he was tied up at work, it was exactly what you and I needed."

"Yeah. It helped us get to know each other again." My voice is thick with emotion.

From Paris to Rome, London to Ireland, Prague, Hungary, Amsterdam, Munich and Spain, my mom took care of me during the worst of my heartbreak.

Mom puts her hands on my shoulders. "I'm grateful for our travels, Ivy. I feel closer to you than ever."

"You helped me so much." I stand and envelop her in a hug. "It's freeing to finally open up."

"Are you ready to share his name with me?" she asks gently.

I shake my head. "No. Maybe someday. He knows who Dad is and since he didn't ask to be brought into our family dynamic, I don't want to add to his humiliation by outing him for something that wasn't his fault."

"You're showing maturity and compassion beyond your years." Mom squeezes me tightly. "I'm curious, obviously. But protecting someone you care for is admirable."

I lean in to her. "I know it hasn't been easy, but your support means the world to me."

"Speaking of which, isn't it time for your dad to call?" Mom looks at her watch.

My phone starts buzzing. "ESP, much?" I show my mom, then hit the speaker button.

"Girls?" My dad's voice booms through the speaker. He's always loud, but sounds more relaxed than usual.

"Hi, Dad." I keep my voice steady. "We're here."

He hits the video connect and his face fills the screen. "There they are. How's Florence treating you both?"

"It's wonderful, Stan." Mom smiles at him. "The school is superb. We've been exploring the city and are planning a trip to Siena this weekend."

His smile is tight. "I miss you both, but I'm glad you're enjoying yourselves."

"How's the build going?" I can't help myself. Any news of Cillian is like food, and I've only had the most minuscule of crumbs.

"We're ahead of schedule. I had to deal with a bit of a mess at the jobsite today." He rolls his eyes. "McGloughlin Construction has been excellent, but Cillian missed a critical meeting with the city. It's sorted now, but I won't hesitate to replace him if it happens again."

My heart sinks. It's not like Cillian to be unprofessional, I hope he's okay. Then, I push the thought aside. It's none of my business. He doesn't want anything to do with me. My focus has got to be on the progress we're making as a family.

The three of us talk for easily an hour about school, our upcoming travel and where we'll spend Christmas this year. None of this would have been possible without dozens of virtual family therapy sessions. I don't completely trust him yet, but I can see the effort my dad's making to allow me to live my own life.

It's a far cry from the distant, controlling man I grew up with.

"I'm really proud of you, Ivy." Dad's voice cracks. "You're special. I'm sorry you felt forced into a life you didn't want."

I'm surprised at his show of emotion. A lump forms in my throat. "It means a lot to hear your apology, Dad."

"I'm truly sorry for everything. I know I can't change the past, but I'm committed to being better." He sucks in a breath.

Tears well up in my eyes. "I know you are, Dad, I appreciate it. We're all healing, one step at a time."

I hope he means it.

After the call, Mom and I gaze out at the golden glow cast by the morning sun over the Arno river. The peaceful atmosphere has helped me cope and I feel a sense of calm. All of us are moving forward. Rebuilding our lives.

"Your father's made progress." Mom wraps an arm around my shoulder. "He's devastated about how his actions—and his harsh words—affected you."

She isn't aware I know she threatened to leave him if he didn't get help. I overheard the conversation before she told me we were going to Europe for six months. "I know. It's hard to let go of the past, but I'm glad we're working through it."

I don't express my hope for Cillian to forgive me somewhere down the line. Maybe we can work things out. Of course, he could be seeing someone—a woman closer to his age. The thought claws at my guts. I can't bear anyone else touching me. The thought of him making love to someone else kills me, though I have no right to feel this way.

"Do you ever think about going back to Seattle?" Mom smooths my hair. She knows I'm thinking about Cillian. We're in tune with each other again.

"No." I shake my head. "I'm taking things one day at a time. My life is here for now. I'm truly happy with how things are going and I want to see it through."

Mom moves away to clean up our breakfast remnants. "I'm glad you've found your place. I'll always be here to support you, wherever you end up."

"I still think about him all the time," I blurt out, needing to confide in her. "Especially after all the discussions with my therapist."

Mom turns to me. "Of course you do, sweetheart. He was your first love. Your first sexual experience. He'll always be a big part of your life."

"And yet, he was ashamed of me. I wanted to be as important to him as he was to me. Everything about our relationship has been the most profound thing in my life." Tears pool in my eyes. "Maybe we could have gotten past it if I hadn't lied."

She guides me to the sofa. "Most couples with significant age differences genuinely fall in love without any hidden motives. Eighteen is tough—you're technically legal, but he probably was worried you didn't know your own mind. I think it speaks to his character that he took this so hard—he was worried about taking advantage of you. I'll admit, I was concerned when I heard about what you'd done. But, I didn't want you to feel like you had to sneak around. I let you go to him because I trusted *you*."

"Thank you." I'm relieved to finally have a conversation we've deliberately avoided. "For me, it was more than being attracted to each other. Our sense of humor is the same. We have lots of shared interests. The way we listened to each other and really learned about our values and dreams for the future. None of these things have anything to do with age."

She smiles softly. "The shock of finding out how old you really were probably made him question all of it."

I sigh. The familiar pang of regret hits me in the gut. "Yeah. I can't blame him for how he felt. I've learned a lot about honesty and trust through all of this."

"You've grown up so much." Mom squeezes my hand. "I'm proud of you for facing these issues head-on and learning from them."

As we sit in silence listening to the sound of the river, memories of Cillian flood my mind. Despite everything, I'm still in love with him. He was the first person who truly saw me. Who understood the pain and longing I kept hidden from the world. If he knew I was here pursuing art, my guess is he'd be happy for me.

I think back to one rainy afternoon. We were curled up on his couch, talking about our dreams and fears. I confessed I didn't want to take over my dad's company. How I'd much rather spend my days painting.

Rather than discourage me, Cillian wrapped me in his arms, kissed my entire face and told me I deserved to be happy. I deserved to follow my dreams.

"I love you, Ivy, You're the most beautiful soul." He pressed his cheek against mine. *"You're stronger than you know. Be honest with him. He'll understand."*

Fighting back tears because I miss him desperately, I know we're an impossible dream. My focus must remain on the life I'm living here in Florence.

Losing him is still unimaginably painful.

And there's nothing I can do about it.

Twenty-Four

Same Day, Different Perspective

God, I fucked up.

For months, I was able to stay on top of things before anyone was the wiser, but this time…

Unacceptable.

I'm spiraling, but I can't seem to get off the ride.

The crisp morning air does little to clear my head as I approach the Bright Shipping construction site. The familiar clang of metal and shouts of the workers used to fill me with pride. A sense of purpose. Not anymore. I'm oppressed with my own personal turmoil.

Today's meeting with Stanley Bright isn't going to be our usual discussion about timelines and budgets. It's a come-to-Jesus reckoning—a confrontation. In all likelihood, I'm going to lose this job. If I do, I'll never recover. Not just as a CEO, but as a man.

How have allowed myself to sink so low?

Trudging across the site, my every step is heavy. Each breath a labor. Passing the vast array of cranes and scaffolding, I'm reminded what's at stake. The success of this project is critical, not just for Bright Shipping but for the future of McGloughlin Construction, the company my father nearly ran into the ground because of his own battles with alcohol.

Battles that now seem to be mine as well.

Stanley Bright waits for me in the office trailer, his silhouette imposing against the morning light. He doesn't waste time on pleasantries.

"Cillian, I'm not beating around the bush." His voice is stern and cold. "I hired you because of your reputation in the industry and the nearly unanimous opinion about your ability to lead. This project is crucial to Bright Shipping, and I've been hearing things about your presence. Or, lack thereof more precisely."

The accusation hits hard, and I stiffen. "Mr. Bright, I assure you—"

"Save it," he cuts me off sharply. "I'm not here to listen to excuses. I've invested a lot in this partnership, and your recent behavior is concerning. Missing a crucial meeting with the city? *No*."

His words are like a slap, jolting me to the core. I can feel my face redden with shame. "I'm handling it."

The truth is, the rumors he's heard are not unfounded. My reliance on alcohol has grown and I'm often not able to get going until late in the morning. My crutch for dealing with the heartbreak and guilt over Ivy has morphed into an addiction. I know it, but I can't seem to stop.

"Handling it?" Stanley's gaze is unrelenting. "How? This is not just your reputation on the line. It's your entire company."

"Please accept my apology. I take full responsibility. I won't let you down, Mr. Bright. I'm committed to this project, I'm meeting with the city this afternoon." The assurance sounds hollow, even to my own ears.

I don't tell him I had to pull every favor in the book to get back on the schedule. Rabbit tricks will only go so far, though.

To my surprise, Stanley's expression softens slightly, but his next words are no less severe. "I'm giving you one last chance. Something is going on with you and I don't like it.

Be a fucking professional. One more fuck up and I'll pull the plug. Trust me, I'll make sure no one in this industry touches McGloughlin Construction with a ten-foot pole."

The threat is clear and the gravity of the situation settles in. I'm not just risking my job or my company; I'm risking everything my da and my brother, Connor, sacrificed to keep the business going. I'm risking what I built, growing McLoughlin Construction into a legacy business. One I hope to pass down to my kids. I'm risking the jobs of hundreds of employees at McGloughlin Construction.

You're such a piece of shit.

The meeting with Stanley Bright leaves me reeling. As I walk away from the office trailer, the pressure is crushing. After I walk the jobsite and check in with my project leads, I head back to my truck. The tension coils tighter with each passing minute.

My drive to DPD is a blur. I take a moment to collect myself. Hating my first thought is to stop and get a drink before the meeting. I glance at my reflection in the rearview mirror, noting the dark circles under my eyes and the strain etched into my features.

Get it together, Cillian. This is your last shot.

Inside, the hallways are a maze of bureaucracy. I navigate them with practiced ease, reaching the meeting room where the city inspector, Jon Billings is waiting. I've worked with him for years. Hung out at his house. Now, my heart pounds as I step inside. My hands tremble as I arrange the blueprints on the table.

"Cillian." Jon's tone is formal and unforgiving. "What the fuck? I've never known you to miss a meeting. Is everything okay?"

"Yeah…" I try to hide the turmoil churning in the pit of my stomach. "I apologize for any inconvenience. I don't really have an excuse, other than I wrote down the wrong day."

The ensuing discussion is intense. I field questions about environmental impacts, safety protocols, and budget allocations. Luckily, I know this project backward and forward, and I'm able to respond with a level of precision that belies the chaos in my mind. As the minutes tick by, I feel a semblance of control returning.

I've pulled it off. For now.

Finally, Jon pushes away from the table, signaling the end of the interrogation. "Approved. Now, don't ever stand me up again."

"Understood." Relief floods through me and I vow never to drink again.

Two hours later, I'm back at my loft staring at the half-full bottle of Red Breast.

I manage to resist for a while, until the familiar self-loathing creeps into my head. Whispers of how I'm not good enough. How I'm bound to fail. The next thing I know, the bottle is empty.

Through my alcohol-infused haze, I hear the whir of the elevator.

Fuck. It's bound to be Seamus. Or Brennan. Maybe even Connor. My brothers have been taking turns surprising me with "visits" to keep me from drinking. It doesn't work, because I'm a stubborn motherfucker, but something about tonight feels different.

I want them to stop me because, God knows, I can't seem to stop myself.

"Cillian!" Brennan's voice booms as he storms into the living room.

Dragging myself to my feet, I stumble and knock the coffee table over. I manage to right myself to be shocked to my core. Da is here, standing next to my brother. Both of them look at me like I'm an alien.

"What the fuck do you want?" I slur, trying to push past them into the kitchen where a fresh bottle is waiting in the cupboard.

"Nope. We're not doing this, Cillian." Brennan follows me. "We're here to end this once and for all."

I roll my eyes. "Great. A family intervention."

Da joins us. His presence is commanding, as always. My father's been sober for a decade now and it's clear he's not here to play nice. "Sit down, Cillian."

Ignoring him, I stagger to the cupboard to grab my last bottle. Brennan snatches it away, opens it and pours it down the sink.

"What the hell, Bren?" I snarl.

"We know. You missed an important meeting with the city." Brennan's voice is tight with frustration. "You've got a real problem. Do you understand how serious this is?"

"Of course I do." I collapse onto the floor, my head pounding. I can't go on. I know it. I have no control.

Da steps forward, his eyes bore into mine. "I know how you feel, son. It's time to get help. It's gone too far. It's affecting everything. Your work, your relationships, your life."

"I'll stop," I insist, but my voice lacks conviction.

"No, you won't. Not on your own," Brennan says. "This isn't normal or healthy."

"I don't need your help." I try to stand up but fall on my ass. "I can handle this."

Da crouches down. "You're not handling it, Cillian. You're drowning. You've been home alone drinking a bottle of whisky every night. It's time to face facts. I did and you can too."

I look into his eyes, seeing the pain and concern there. It's hard to argue with him, I know he's right.

"I'm scared." My voice breaks. "I don't know how I got here."

My father grips my shoulder. "It doesn't matter. We're here to help you before it's too late."

"We're going to figure this out." Brennan sits next to me. "We'll find professional help."

"No, I can't go anywhere. The Bright Shipping job..." Panic rises in my chest. "Stan will never trust me again if he finds out."

Da takes my hand in his. "We've got it covered. I'll step in and take over while you're gone. We'll tell Stan you're dealing with a medical issue and need some time off. He doesn't need to know the details. I'm more than capable of filling in for as long as it takes. You're more important to me than any job."

I stare at them, my mind racing. The thought of rehab terrifies me, but the alternative is losing everything. I try to steady myself. "No, it's too much trouble. I'm not going, I can handle this on my own."

"No, you can't." Brennan is adamant. "You're scared and you're hurting. It'll be okay. It's time to focus your stubbornness and drive on yourself."

The fight drains out of me. I bury my face in my hands. "I'm ashamed. I don't know what to do."

"You start by admitting you need help." Da helps me up. "Then you let us support you. It worked for me and it will work for you. You're not alone."

For the first time since I broke it off with Ivy, I don't feel alone. My family's words and genuine concern permeate my defenses. I break down, sobbing as all the fear, shame, and pain I've been bottling up pours out.

"I'm sorry." My words are barely audible through my sobs. "I'm so sorry."

"You're grand." Brennan pats my back.

My da nods. "Don't worry. We're going to help you get through this. I'll drive you tomorrow. Tonight, we'll stay with you to make sure you don't drink. I'll go to the jobsite tomorrow and let Stan know I'm filling in. You need to focus on getting better."

"Okay." All I feel is relief. I'm exhausted.

Brennan squeezes my shoulder. "Let's get you cleaned up and to bed."

For the first time in over a year, I feel a flicker of hope.

I'm facing a long road ahead, but I'm not alone.

Maybe I'll find my way back to the man I used to be.

Twenty-Five

IVY

Six Months Later

IT'S HARD TO PUT my finger on why I feel tense.

It doesn't make sense. I can't recall the last time my life felt this steady and serene. It's almost surreal how much has changed since I moved here for school.

The peace is almost unsettling, making me nervous. Is something big is about to happen? It's too quiet, and that worries me.

The cobblestones in the piazza are warm from the late-afternoon sun. Lively chatter fills the air. I'm sitting at a small table near the Duomo with three of my friends from the Academy. Pierlo, with his dark, curly hair, startling green eyes and infectious laugh, is directly across from me, while Matteo and Lucia flank us on either side. The scent of strong espresso and a hot margherita pizza make for a perfect evening out.

Gazing at the beautiful architecture all around us, sketchbook in hand, I can't believe I'm studying art here. The city is a vibrant classroom, with inspiration and masterpieces around every corner. From the grandeur of the Duomo, where we're sitting tonight, to the timeless works at the *Uffizi*, the *Galleria dell 'Accademia*, and the *Palazzo Pitti*, Florence is a living gallery. It fuels my creativity every day.

"I'm telling you, Matteo, the new exhibit is going to blow your mind." Lucia bats her eyes at her boyfriend. "The use of light and shadow is revolutionary."

"I'll believe it when I see it. I'm more interested in what Ivy's working on. We're supposed to be hanging out and she has her book." He leans over and peers into my sketchbook. His eyes widen. "Well done. These are incredible. Who's the model?"

Lucia points to a drawing of Cillian laughing. "He's dreamy. *Uomo di bell'aspetto*. He looks so alive in this one. You've really captured his spirit."

"This one is cool. There's a lot of depth in his expression." Pierlo studies another sketch where Cillian is gazing out the window, lost in thought.

Lucia flips to the next page and smiles. *"Che bello.* And these... so many of him in bed. Was he sleeping next to you? They're intimate and tender."

Recalling the warmth of Cillian's touch. The way his fingers used to gently trace patterns on my skin. His lips kissing every part of me. God, the way his embrace made me feel safe and cherished. I still miss him. I'd give anything...

Closing the sketchbook, I try to hide my blush. "Thank you. He was once very special to me."

"Maybe he still is." Lucia elbows me. "Nothing wrong with a hot older man to rev up the engine, eh?"

I laugh, taking a sip of my cappuccino. "Yeah. It was a couple of years ago. I'm sketching out ideas for our portrait week."

"*You* would make a beautiful portrait." Pierlo' s voice is softer than usual.

A new blush creeps up my cheeks. Pierlo has always been kind and complimentary, but tonight there's something different in his tone, a hint of something deeper. "Thanks, Pierlo. The compliment means a lot coming from you."

Maybe it's time for me to try to move past Cillian. Pierlo is very easy on the eyes. He's kind, sweet, and an accomplished sculptor. He's also my age.

Lucia exchanges a knowing glance with Matteo and suddenly stands up. "Well, I think it's time for us to go check out the exhibit, don't you, Matteo?"

"Absolutely. Ivy, Pierlo, enjoy the rest of your evening. *Ciao*." Matteo waves as he follows her down a side street.

Before I can say goodbye, they're gone, leaving us alone. An awkward silence falls over us, broken only by the clinking of cups and murmured conversations from nearby tables.

"Ivy, there's something I've been wanting to tell you for a while now." Pierlo leans forward and takes my hand.

My heart skips a beat. "Oh? What is it?"

"I've admired you for a long time. Not only as an artist, but as a person. You're talented, and beautiful." He takes a deep breath. "I've been too shy to say anything, but I would love to take you out. Would you consider it?"

The sincerity in his eyes is touching, I appreciate his courage in speaking up. "Pierlo, how nice of you."

"But?" he prompts gently.

"I moved to Florence after my heart was broken. I don't know if I'm ready for anything serious." I choose my words carefully because I don't want to hurt his feelings. "I'm still figuring things out."

He smiles and shrugs his shoulders. "I understand. I only wanted you to know how I feel. No pressure."

"I appreciate it more than you know." I squeeze his fingers.

We finish the pizza and our drinks, chatting comfortably about our classes. Pierlo holds my hand as he walks me back to my flat. It's nice. I like him. As we reach my door, he leans in and kisses me softly. I close my eyes, waiting for a spark, the feeling of soul connection.

But there's nothing. No attraction. No magic.

He pulls back and I muster a smile. "Goodnight, Pierlo. Thank you for tonight."

"Goodnight, Ivy." His eyes search mine for something more. But I turn and head inside, closing the door gently behind me.

I kick off my shoes and head to the bathroom to wash up and put my pajamas on. As I brush my teeth, I can't shake the emptiness I felt during Pierlo's kiss. He's wonderful, but he's not Cillian. No one ever will be.

Why can't I be a normal twenty-year-old and hook up with different people without a second thought for the fun of it? I crave the freedom to move on, to let myself be swept away by someone new, but my heart stubbornly clings to Cillian with a grip I can't seem to loosen.

I'm being ridiculous, holding on to these feelings. It's not like he'll give me another chance. He said so himself. Cillian has probably been with a million women since me. I can picture him now, effortlessly charming. Drawing attention to him like moths to a flame.

The thought of Cillian with someone else twists a knife in my gut, making me feel foolish and naïve. The problem is, no matter how much I convince myself to let go, memories of how we were are seared into my soul. I miss *everything* about him.

Even though I *should* move on, my heart isn't ready to let go.

It's early, but I decide to go to bed and watch a movie. Halfway through, my phone buzzes—my parents are Face-Timing me from Seattle.

"Hi, Mom. Hi, Dad." I angle the phone so they can see I'm safe at home.

"Hi, sweetheart." I see they're sitting in my dad's home office. "How was your day?"

I shift to my side and prop my phone up on my nightstand. "It was fine. I was out with some friends from school. We had coffee and pizza near the Duomo."

"Sounds wonderful." My dad has lost a bit of weight and he looks tired.

Rather than bring up his appearance, I use my father's patented vague question tactic to shift subjects. "How are things going with the build?"

"Eh—I've got to say, construction is going well." His face brightens. "We're ahead of schedule. Cillian's father took over for a bit during his health scare. He's stayed on to help. We're not only back on track, Rory's stayed on. He's a hoot."

Every cell in my body freezes at the mention of Cillian, but I have to keep my composure. "Sounds terrible. What kind of health scare?"

"Eh—it's fine now." Dad waves his hand in front of his face. "The project is moving along faster than expected."

"Good to hear," I mumble, though my mind is whirling. I want to call Cillian to check on him, but I don't have his number anymore. I manage to remember I'm on a call with my parents and reengage without missing too many beats. "And how are you, Dad?"

There's a pause. My mom glances at my dad and back at me. "Actually, Ivy, your dad is experiencing a bit of a health scare himself. They found some polyps during his colon screening."

"What? Is he okay? Are you okay?" Blood whooshes to my ears.

"They were cancerous but we caught it early." Dad leans in. "It's a minor operation. I'll be down for about a week. There's no need to worry."

My voice shakes. "No need to worry? I'm coming home. I want to be there with you."

"No, Ivy," he insists. "Please stay and finish your classes. I'll be fine. Don't disrupt your schedule."

I try to process what I want to do. "Are you sure?"

"We're sure." My mom takes his hand. "It's minor surgery. Really. The reason we called is I'm postponing my next visit by a few weeks to help your dad through recovery."

I nod vigorously. "Of course. It makes perfect sense."

After we hang up, I lie in bed and stare at the ceiling. Life is fragile. One minute everything seems fine, and the next, it's all hanging by a thread.

At first, moving to Florence helped me escape the isolation I'd felt in Seattle. It took my mind off my broken heart. Lately, though, it feels like I'm just as alone here as I ever was at home.

Don't get me wrong, I enjoy my friends and love focusing on my art, but everything—my dad's health, my future, and even my unresolved feelings for Cillian—bears down on me.

I'll be twenty-one next year. I need to figure out what my path is and what, if any, role I want to play in my family's legacy.

I'm grateful for my time here—it helped me figure out who I am. It's given me the opportunity to live a regular life. Buy groceries. Cook and clean for myself. Do what I want when I want to do it.

And, let's be honest, it allowed me to avoid running into Cillian after he rejected me.

I'm stronger now, though. Maybe it's time to think about what comes next. Maybe I *should* go home and help my dad with the business and let him take a step back.

Maybe it's time to stop hiding.

Twenty-Six

Six Months Later

TODAY'S A BIG MILESTONE for me.

I'm celebrating it with my family.

As I walk up the familiar steps to my parents' house, the scent of blooming spring flowers fills the air. Tonight is my one-year sobriety anniversary. I've never been prouder of any accomplishment. It's funny, I feel the weight of the past year lift slightly as I approach the front door.

"Cillian, there you are!" Ma is waiting for me the second I step inside. Her eyes are filled with pride.

I kiss her cheek. "I'm sorry I'm late, I ran into traffic. You look beautiful and it smells great in here."

"Ach—you silver-tongued devil. Come on in, everyone's sitting down already." She swats my arm.

The house is filled with the sounds of laughter and clinking dishes. The aroma of roast beef and buttery mashed potatoes wafts through the air, making my stomach rumble. I follow her into the dining room, where my da and my brothers are already eating.

"There he is!" Da's booming voice fills the room. He stands up and claps. "Proud of you, son. One year is no small feat."

"Thanks, Da.." I take my seat.

How is it possible it's been an entire year since that dark night when I accepted help? The day I decided to stop hiding. Including my entire family in my recovery has been healing for all of us. Above all, I don't ever want to slip. Knowing the people who love me will hold me accountable has been motivating. I wouldn't be here without them.

"Uncle Cillian!" Tristan and Toran, Connor and Ronni's twin boys, come barreling toward me, nearly knocking me over.

"Hey, you two!" I laugh and gather them to me. "Been behaving for your parents?"

Connor chuckles, shaking his head. "Define 'behaving.'"

"They're a handful, as always. But we wouldn't have it any other way." Ronni cradles wee Teagan who's nestled in her arms.

I catch Brennan's eye across the table. He nods, but is quieter than I thought he'd be considering his role in getting me here. I make a mental note to check in with him later.

Liam and Padraig are bickering about something, their low-level jabs are laced with an unusual snark. Something seems to be causing tension between them.

Ma holds up a glass of sparkling apple juice. "I'd like to make a toast." Her eyes brim with tears. "To my husband and my son. It's not easy for a man to make a change and turn his life around from addiction. It takes a special kind of fortitude, and both of you have shown such strength. I'm proud of you, Rory, for the man you've become. And Cillian, your journey is just beginning, but you're on the right path. I love you both."

We raise our glasses, the clinking sound echoes in the dining room.

"To family." My voice is thick with gratitude. "Thank you all for being my support. I went to a dark place and it's a relief to be on the other side."

"Cillian, do you want to share what's next for McGloughlin Construction?" Da passes me the mashed potatoes.

"Yeah, we're in the bidding process for a big shipping project in Long Beach." I can't help the excitement creeping into my voice. "Peter Vander and I are finalizing the proposal. We have a few new buildings on the slate and Stan wants us to build another office by the Port of Tacoma."

"Busy times." Connor, who is currently on a break from touring with his band, LTZ, raises his glass. "*Slante.*"

We clink glasses again and I take a moment to soak in the easy camaraderie. Our family has gone through tumultuous times. It's nice to have moments like these. It keeps me grounded.

As dinner winds down and the dishes are cleared, I see Brennan furiously texting in the living room.

"Everything alright, Bren?" I approach cautiously.

He sighs, then pastes a smile on his face. "Investor bullshit. I'm also dealing with some news from an old classmate. It's nothing, really. I'll be fine."

"You've been my rock, Bren. Let me be yours. Whatever it is, I'd like to help." I recognize the same guarded look I used to have. I'm not worried about his drinking, but we McGloughlins all tend to hold our problems close to the vest.

"Yeah, I appreciate it." He looks around. "I'll talk to you about it later. I promise."

Liam and Padraig's banter continues, their playful insults carrying an undercurrent of tension. Without warning, the situation escalates and before anyone can intervene, Liam storms out, slamming the door behind him. Seamus and Padraig are now huddled in the corner, deep in conversation.

There's never a dull moment in a family of six brothers. Despite the chaos—and the occasional fight—there's a warmth in the air. A sense of belonging I wouldn't trade for anything. Especially after I lost many of these nights to the bottle.

Eventually, everyone but me heads home. Ma settles on the couch to watch a *Real Housewives* show and my da and I find ourselves on the wraparound porch.

"You've done well, son. I'm proud of you, so I am." He claps me on the back. "One year sober. That's something to be proud of, so it is."

"Thanks, Da. It hasn't been easy, but it's worth it."

We stand in comfortable silence for a moment, the sounds of the night enveloping us.

A few years back, Da took a step back because he trusted me. The processes I implemented helped increase revenue and helped manage staff accountability. He knew McGloughlin Construction was in good hands.

After I hit rock bottom, he was back in full force, showing me that facing your demons and coming out stronger on the other side is something to be proud of. He stepped up and seamlessly took the lead on the Bright Shipping project and our other jobs. When I came out of rehab, I was able to ease back in.

Yeah. Working regularly with my da again has been special. His support and guidance have taught me a lot about business, resilience, and commitment. It's brought us closer in ways I never expected.

"I'm going to sell the loft," I admit, breaking the quiet. "It doesn't serve my needs anymore. In thinking about my future, I'd like to build a house. I'm considering moving into my townhouse for the time being."

Da glances over. "Well, it's important to move on if the time is right. You deserve happiness, Cillian."

"I'll never forget the day we learned you built them for us." I recall my parents distributing a deed to each of us almost a decade ago. "I didn't understand it then, but now I realize it was your apology for the trouble you'd put the family through during your battle with alcohol. It was such a cool gesture."

My da's eyes glisten. "Aye, it was important to me. Mostly, I wanted to repay Connor for putting his life on hold to get yous all through high school. He rents his place out these days, as does Brennan. Liam and Padraig stay at their places when they're home. Seamus is the only one of you who lives there as his primary residence. I'm sure he'll love to have you closer."

"Yeah, me too. Plus, it's the perfect space to plan my future." I lean against the rail. "I'm coming up on thirty-five, if you can believe it. I'd like to settle down. Have my own family. I'm feeling a renewed sense of purpose."

He squints at me and nods. More than anyone, my da has a unique insight into my struggles. "It's tough to confront your demons, but it's also important to move on. You deserve happiness, Cillian. What would make you happiest?"

Ivy.

Her name flickers through my mind, unbidden. As it always does when I allow myself to tap into my deepest desire. The truth is, she's not part of my world anymore.

I wish I could accept it.

Our relationship was a whirlwind—passionate and all-consuming. It burned brightly. *Fiercely.* She and I were drawn together with an irresistible pull. Emotions ran high. Every moment felt heightened. I loved her deeply and thought she was my future.

Once I learned how young she was, my mind went to a dark place and stayed there for too long. I discounted her decision-making capabilities outright, believing I'd taken advantage of a young, impressionable woman. I didn't trust what we had was real.

Now I know it *was* real. The realest, truest feeling I've ever had.

Perspective has a funny way of rectifying things. Intense counseling during rehab helped me cut through my own bullshit. At the end of the day, our timing was wrong. The situation was fucked up. Rather than berate myself—or her—for how we handled things, I've embraced the truth. My time with Ivy was a brief but powerful chapter in my life.

I'm sad it ended the way it did but now it's time to focus on the future. On the family I want to have. The legacy I want to leave behind. I take a deep breath and look back at my da. "Building something new would make me happy. Creating a place where I can start fresh."

"Are you thinking about the woman in your life? The one who got away?" He cocks his head. "She's Bright's daughter?"

My words nearly get caught in my throat. "*What*? Why would you say that?"

Da squints at me. "Oh, I picked up on a few conversations about some young girl you were dating on the down low a few years ago. While you were in rehab, Stan and I often talked about our kids. He mentioned his brilliant, eighteen year-old daughter who was supposed to go to Stanford Business School and run his business and, instead, was in Europe with her mother. She moved to Italy after a bad breakup with a boyfriend she kept hidden from the family. Seemed coincidental your alcohol abuse took on a life of its own around then."

"How in the fuck did you put two and two together?" I swallow hard, processing his words.

I'd gleaned a lot about Ivy's whereabouts from Stan over the years, but obviously never asked for specifics. So much of my drinking stemmed from envisioning her fucking some young, Italian boyfriend. The thought was unbearable. Still is. Though I'm not naïve enough to believe she hasn't moved on after all this time.

"Guessed." My da takes a seat on the porch swing. "Even though you didn't tell me anything, the timing and details—it clicked for me. He had a lot of guilt around driving her away. Blamed himself for expecting too much. He said it was a real wake-up call when she stopped speaking to him. They've made some progress, I think. Obviously, I didn't let on what I suspected."

Taking everything he says in, I'm able to exhale for the first time in a few minutes. "I thought she was older when we met. I found out who she was at my presentation at Bright Shipping. Ivy never told her parents who I am—there's no way Stan would have kept us on as contractors if he knew I was the guy."

"Cillian, did you fall in love with her?." He pats the seat next to him and I sit.

"Yeah." I squeeze my eyes shut. "She wanted us to be together and I refused to consider it because she lied to me about her age and who she really was. I wasn't sure which way was up and now I don't think I'll ever love someone like that again."

Da clasps my shoulder. "You kept all of this to yourself. How's that worked out for you?"

"What could I have done?" I look up at him. "At first, I thought she was in her mid-twenties, which was young, but acceptable. We were only together a few weeks and I figured things would work themselves out. We talked about introducing each other to our families, but we never got the chance." I punch my fist into my hand. "I had no idea she was living a secret life. That she was only eighteen."

His eyebrows knit together. "Doesn't seem like the timing was ideal."

I rub my hands together. "No. It wasn't. After getting to know Stan and how goddamn intense the man is, I understood more about her upbringing. The pressure. The expectations. Grief brings out the worst in people. I'm not mad anymore and I certainly don't blame her for trying to take control of her destiny. I feel lucky to have ever meant something to her because she meant the world to me. It wouldn't have worked, though, and I knew it. She's fourteen years younger. In a completely different place in her life than I am."

"Aye." Da thunks me on the back a few times. "I'm sorry it didn't work out."

"The sucky thing is, I haven't been able to look at another woman in three years, and believe me I've tried to move on." I'm not proud of my drunken—and ultimately aborted—attempts to get over Ivy by getting another woman under me. Since I've been sober, I downloaded and deleted dating apps. Hated them. None of the women hold a candle to Ivy. It's depressing.

Da stands. "Well, at the end of the day, if you're patient the right woman will come around." He moves toward the door. "Time for bed."

"I'll head back home. See you tomorrow." Da and I say our good nights and I bound down the stairs to my truck.

On the way home I picture Ivy in a sunlit studio in Florence painting in a big, white shirt. She turns when I walk in the door, illuminated by the glow of creativity. I bend to kiss her sweet lips...

No.

What we had will never come again. She's gone. Forever.

A year ago, the thought would have sent me straight for a bottle of whiskey.

Today, I don't even have a craving.

I'm ready to face whatever comes next.

Twenty-Seven

Three Months Later - Present Day

GOD, IT'S STRANGE TO be back home.

Florence, with its cobblestone streets and Renaissance art, already feels like a distant memory.

We crest the hill past Boeing Field and the familiar skyline of Seattle comes into view, stirring up a maelstrom of emotions. I left almost three years ago. Broken. Unable to function. I never thought I'd return.

Now I'm back. A far cry from the scared, desperate girl who was willing to do anything to escape my father. I'm almost twenty-one, a woman who's come into her own.

"How are you feeling?" My mom's voice is tinged with worry as she takes the exit to our neighborhood. "You've built a nice life in Florence. You don't have to give it up."

I gaze out the window at the new construction all around me. So much has changed in my city that holds so many memories. "I'm worried about Dad, of course, but I was ready to come home. Honestly."

"He's been holding strong, but the chemo is really taking its toll." Her grip tightens on the steering wheel. "Having you here means the world to him."

Mom pulls through the gate into the driveway and the sweeping grounds come into view.

It's funny how I never paid much attention to the plush, green lawns, elegant flower beds, and towering trees. With my newfound appreciation of architecture, I take in the tall white columns, large arched windows and the rich, dark wood double doors. It's stunning. I can't believe I grew up here and I'm only admiring it now.

We step inside and I breathe in the familiar scent of fresh lilies and lavender, which is piped through the central air system. The grand entryway, with its marble floors and sweeping staircase, is adorned with exquisite paintings of my family, from my great grandparents to me and Forrest. Every surface is impeccably polished and dozens of vibrant floral arrangements are positioned around the room.

This was my prison. Viewed through new eyes, it's gorgeous. Welcoming, even.

Huh.

"He's back here." Mom leads me down the expansive hallway to the great room, a vast, inviting space with high ceilings and plush furnishings. My dad is set up comfortably in his favorite armchair, watching the news on a massive flat-screen TV.

Seeing him frail and tired leaves me momentarily breathless and I know coming back was the right decision. It's been a long time since I've hugged my dad.

A lump forms in my throat. "*Dad.*"

"Ivy!" His face lights up. "It's nice to see you, sweetheart."

I rush over and hug him. "I missed you. How are you feeling?"

"Meh." He pats the cushion beside him. "I've had better days, but knowing you're here makes it a lot easier. How was your flight?"

"Easy." I plop down and lean on his shoulder. "I caught up on all the project documents, but there are still some gaps. I was hoping you could get me the files before I head to the site tomorrow."

He smiles. "Diving in, I see. Look, we're in the final stages of the buildout, it's mostly about overseeing the finishing touches. For the Tacoma contract, we're still in negotiations, waiting for their proposal." He points to a binder on the table. "It's all in there, but I've also sent you a link to the electronic documents. I've marked the key points you'll need to address."

"Thanks, Dad. I want to make sure I do you proud." I grab the binder and flip through it.

"You will." He squeezes my hand. "You've got this, Ivy. And remember, Cillian from McGloughlin Construction has everything under control. He's been handling things exceptionally well, you won't be on your own."

I try to tamp down the jolt running through my body at the sound of his name. My stomach twists into knots. I knew going into this I'd have to work with him. Seeing him again will be...God. I dunno. I'm nervous.

No, I'm freaking the fuck out.

"Yeah. Thanks for the reminder, it helps." I keep my emotions in check out of habit.

At some point, do I tell Mom and Dad the man who broke my heart was Cillian? I've been protecting him for all this time, but maybe the past is water under the bridge. Dad seems to like him, everything he's told me over the years has been positive.

Ugh. This secret is the only remnant from our summer, it would be nice to have it out in the open.

The three of us eat dinner as a family for the first time in, gosh, nearly a decade. It's nice. After dinner, my jet lag catches up with me, and I excuse myself to head to bed early.

My bedroom is exactly how I left it and I'm surprised at how comforting it feels. Once I'm snuggled under the expensive sheets and cushioned by the memory foam mattress, exhaustion quickly pulls me into a deep sleep.

The low-level panic begins the second my alarm goes off.

Cillian has no idea I'll be meeting with him today. Dad didn't tell him I was taking over.

"I didn't want him to worry," he said, unaware of the personal history between us.

In many ways I'm glad he doesn't know. I'm still mortified by the last time I saw him—standing before him naked and crying, begging him to love me...cringeworthy.

Today, I'm approaching my role as a pure professional. Fully prepared to handle anything related to the Bright Shipping business. As I wound my life down in Italy, Dad and I spent many hours preparing for these responsibilities. I may not have pursued my MBA, but I do have a business degree and Dad trained me relentlessly for years before I left.

Besides, immersing myself in the world of art had an unexpected benefit. I was able to clear my mind. Have balance and focus. Painting and drawing will always be my favorite way to spend time, but I'm fine stepping in for as long as my dad needs me. In the meantime, it's crucial Cillian sees me as capable and confident, not as the lovesick girl he once knew.

Starting with my appearance. Most of my clothes are in transit, but I find a tailored, navy-blue pantsuit in my closet. A little snug, the result of one too many pasta dinners, but it'll do. I apply minimal makeup and, since it's raining, I pull my hair back into a sleek ponytail. Professional and composed is the look I'm going for.

Every nerve ending is on high alert when I pull into the designated parking next to the newly erected structure. It's a gorgeous building, even more impressive in real life than the renderings and photos. Despite the steady downpour, windows are being installed today and the construction site is buzzing with activity. Workers in hard hats hustle back and forth. Cranes hoist two-thousand-pound glass panels into place.

I spot Cillian almost immediately, standing under an umbrella by the lineup of office trailers, engrossed in conversation with one of the foremen. Wearing a fitted white Mc-

Gloughlin Construction Henley with the sleeves rolled up to show off his muscular forearms, he's only gotten more handsome. Dark jeans hug his legs in all the right places. *Wow.* He's definitely put on muscle since I last saw him.

Though I try to tamp it down, my reaction is visceral. Powerful. My nipples tighten. My pussy clenches at the memory of his perfect cock.

I honestly don't know what to do. Every plan to be professional feels out of reach—I want to run to him, jump in his arms, and tear his clothes off.

Because he's your man.

Except...he's *not*.

After a few calming breaths, I compose myself and walk toward him. I know the *exact* moment he sees me—his eyes lock on to mine and time seems to stand still as it did the first time I saw him. The noise of the construction fades into the background, leaving the two of us in this charged moment.

He visibly pales and a myriad of emotions pass across his face. Surprise. Confusion. Fear. Anguish.

Love.

"Hi, Cillian." I shake off my stupid imaginary thoughts and manage to keep my voice steady, despite the storm of emotions whirling inside me.

"*Ivy?*" There's a beat of silence, thick with tension. He looks around and then back at me. He shifts his weight from leg to leg. "I, uh, didn't expect to see you here today."

"I know." I tack on a smile. "My dad needs a few weeks off for a medical procedure. I'm stepping in to help until he's back on his feet."

He give me a strange look as he absorbs the news. "I'm sorry to hear."

"Thank you." My voice catches slightly. "He's undergoing chemotherapy."

I didn't mean to tell him, it's just...he and I always had such easy conversations. Two minutes in and I'm confiding family secrets like we're still a couple.

It's important for me to remember how I felt the day he rejected me. When he told me, under no uncertain terms, he didn't want me. As much as my heart yearns for Cillian, I can't be vulnerable with him ever again.

Tamping down my emotions, I jut my chin out and look him in the eye.

Cillian's expression softens. "I'm really sorry, Ivy. Pass on my good wishes. If there's anything I can do..."

"Thank you, I appreciate it." I clear my throat. "Actually, I could use a briefing on the current status of the project. I'm fairly caught up but there are still some gaps."

"Of course." He, too, slips back into a professional demeanor. "Let's get out of the rain. We can go over everything in the office."

I follow him, my eyes lingering on his muscular ass and confident stride. Somehow, Cillian seems more grounded. More assured. A pang of longing permeates my belly. I wonder if I'm affecting him the way he still affects me.

Inside the trailer, Cillian spreads out a series of blueprints and permitting documents on the table, his focus entirely on the task at hand.

"We're in the final stages." He points to various sections of the plans. "The structural framework is complete after the windows go in. Next, we'll begin the interior finishing. The electrical and plumbing systems are about eighty percent done, and we've scheduled the final inspections for November."

I nod, taking notes on my e-tablet. "And the Tacoma project?"

"We're in the negotiation phase for the contract," he explains. "We've submitted our proposal, and we're waiting for their response. I have a meeting with their representatives in a couple weeks to discuss the details."

"Great." I open my phone. "I'll need to attend that meeting. I have a new number, could you text me the date?"

Cillian raises an eyebrow but doesn't comment. Instead, he takes down my number, sends me the calendar invite and continues with the briefing, providing detailed updates on the project's progress, challenges, and upcoming milestones. I'm impressed by his thoroughness and the clear passion he has for his work.

As we wrap up, I hear myself blurt out, "How have you been?"

Good God, I'm an idiot.

"I'm okay. Busy. And you?" He pauses, his hazel eyes meeting mine. "How was Florence?"

I didn't realize he knew where I was. "Incredible. I learned so much and made lifelong friendships. But, being back here feels great. Especially now."

We stare at each other. It's like we're suspended in time. I can practically feel the tether between our hearts going taut.

Finally, Cillian breaks another awkward silence. "I meant what I said. I'm really sorry about your dad. It's tough when someone you love goes through cancer."

"Thank you." My voice is barely a whisper. "It means a lot to hear you say."

He squeezes his eyes shut and sighs. "Ivy..."

"No, *don't*." I press my palm to my chest. "Not now."

Despite the undeniable chemistry crackling between us, we haven't spoken in three years. He could be married or in a relationship. Hell, he could have kids. Besides, I've moved on...

Liar.

I must stay focused. Professional. I have a job to do.

No matter how strong my feelings are, Cillian is my past.

He needs to stay there.

Twenty-Eight

CILLIAN

Two Weeks Later

Two weeks have flown by since Ivy returned.

Fears about fucking up my sobriety aside, I haven't felt the urge to drink since the day I first saw her and ended up at the Metropolitan Grill. That night scared me. Thank God for Brennan.

I've made a point to go to a meeting every day since, to keep myself on track.

The truth is, the shock of our first encounter has settled into a strange new normal. Working alongside her—*shit*. I'm the happiest I've been in three years.

It's fascinating seeing a different side of Ivy. Before, she was trying to escape her structured life—and I was part of her rebellion. Now, she seems to be embracing her legacy. Watching her seamlessly and gracefully navigate the complexities of this construction project, I often forget she's not even twenty-one yet.

She's brilliant. Her intensity and focus are nothing short of inspiring. It's easy to see why she graduated high school with a college degree and got into an MBA program at eighteen.

And her class and grace are undeniable. Despite how poorly I treated her the day I broke things off, she's given me nothing but respect—which, let's face it, I don't deserve. Her maturity and kindness cements in my mind how extraordinary she is.

I'm lucky to have once been loved by Ivy Bright.

I wish I'd have been more careful with her.

Today, she and I are traveling to Tacoma for a preliminary intake meeting. It's a crucial step in the process for the next build, where city officials review our application to ensure its complete and meets all requirements. We're prepared to go through the blueprints, application forms, reports, and other documents. If we do our job, it can speed up the review process by reducing the number of correction letters and re-submittals we'll have to deal with.

By the time Ivy pulls up in her sleek black Mercedes coupe, I'm waiting outside the office trailer. She rolls down the window and smiles, a familiar spark in her eyes. "Ready to go?"

"Yep." I climb into the passenger seat. The car smells faintly of her perfume, a delicate floral scent so intoxicating, if I could, I'd bury my face in her neck.

She looks incredible, with her blonde hair loose and curled around her face. Turquoise eyes rimmed with black eyeliner, glowing with determination and a touch of nervousness. Her simple black dress is professional, yet the way it hugs her figure makes it hard for me to keep my eyes off her. Her curves are mouthwatering.

Ivy is perfect. Being with her is a constant reminder of what I lost. What I still long for.

She's still off-limits, though.

As we merge onto I-5, she flicks her eyes to me then back on the road. "I've gone through the checklist again. I think I'm prepared, but this is my first meeting with a city official. I'm nervous about missing something important."

"You'll be great." I resist the urge to grip her knee to reassure her. "The plans are solid, and we've covered all the bases. The city's intake meeting is a formality at this point.

Plus, Peter Vander is meeting us there, he'll answer all of the structural stuff."

She nods but keeps her eyes focused on the road ahead. "Thanks, Cillian. It helps to know how these things work ahead of time. Makes me less nervous."

The road stretches ahead of us and we pass the time with basic small talk, touching on the latest Netflix documentaries to the quirks of Seattle weather. It's easy, like it always was. I have to constantly remind myself not to lean in and kiss her. Or to brush a stray hair from her forehead.

I don't resist the urge to steal glances at her, though, even if my heart aches with every look. Being with her makes it easy to forget the pain of the past, but I find myself yearning to have a real conversation. I want to apologize to her. How I treated her weighs heavy on my mind.

"Do you spend much time in Tacoma?" Ivy follows the GPS directions, taking the exit past the Tacoma Dome to down-town.

"Not often," I admit. "Mostly passing through. It's really coming into its own. I think there's lots of potential for Bright Shipping here."

Her eyes light up. "Yeah. I think we can do something great."

"Absolutely." I look over at her. "And with you leading the charge, I have no doubt it'll be a success."

Ivy blushes and I feel a tug on my heart. I'm not imagining it—the attraction between us is still there. Like an ancient melody only we can hear. Despite the years between us and the heartache of our past, it's a subtle yet relentless tune playing whenever we're in proximity.

Fuck. I need to stop reading into shit. Ivy isn't mine. She's here to help her father, to take her position as an executive at Bright Shipping. There's no room for old flames or rekindled romances.

We pull into the parking lot of the city planning office. "Ready?"

"Yeah. Let's do this." I get out of the car and we head inside.

Inside, the office is a hive of activity. We're directed to a conference room where Peter is waiting. We sit down, and I spread our documents on the large conference table.

As the meeting progresses, it becomes clear Ivy has left no stone unturned. The official nods approvingly, making notes on his clipboard. "Everything seems to be in order," he says finally. "We'll review the documents in more detail, but I don't foresee any major issues. You should receive your first set of review comments within the next two weeks."

Ivy, Peter, and I exchange relieved glances. "Thank you." She holds her hand out. "We appreciate your time and attention to detail."

The three of us gather in the hallway and Ivy points to Peter's tattooed arm. "I've been thinking about getting a tattoo of some of my art, but I have no idea where to start. Your piece is stunning."

"My wife." Peter beams. "She owns the Salty Siren, a killer tattoo shop."

"Jordan is my brother's bandmate's sister," I tell her on the way back to the car. "She has a year waiting list, but I'm sure Peter can at least introduce you. She has a fine art background, I think you'd like her."

"Really?" Ivy's genuine, radiant smile lights up her entire face.

I nod, unable to speak for a minute. God, I'd do anything to see her look happy every day of my life. "You were amazing in there."

"Thanks." She starts the car. "I couldn't have done it without you."

"Sure you could have. You're a natural. Your dad must be incredibly proud." I clamp my palms on my knees to keep them safe.

Her expression softens, and she nods. "He is. And it means the world to me. I disappointed him so badly."

Yeah...*fuck*.

"Has your relationship with your dad improved?" My curiosity gets the better of me. I've got to know more.

Her jaw sets and she barely gives me an answer. "Yeah. It seems better. My time away really helped."

We settle into the drive back to Seattle, but there's no more playful banter. Somehow, with my comment about her dad, I've walked into a land mine. The air suddenly feels tense. *Fuck.* Maybe I should get everything out there so we can close the door on our past baggage.

"Your birthday is in a couple of days." I break the silence.

She turns to me, surprised. "You remembered?"

"*Ivy.* Of course I did. How could I ever forget?" I don't restrain myself and reach up and touch her cheek.

Her breathing intensifies but she doesn't say anything.

I remove my hand.

"Your dad and mom are throwing a party. They've invited me, my parents, and a few others." I swallow hard. "Do you think I should come? I don't want to do anything to make you feel..."

"Cillian, I..." Her hands start to shake as she grips the steering wheel tighter.

"Ivy, please. I regret so much." I press my fists to my eyes. "For making you feel less than, for doubting what we had. Seeing you now, the woman you've become. I wasn't worthy of your love. Not in the slightest."

Her eyes shimmer with unshed tears. "Oh, God...you don't have to—"

"I do," I interrupt and proceed to unload it all. "You need to know how impressed I am with you. You've handled our breakup with such grace and strength. You spent time doing what you loved. I went to a very dark place. Started drinking too much. It nearly ruined everything. My dad even took over the project for a while because I couldn't function. I ended up in rehab. I've been sober for over a year. Your dad doesn't know."

Her eyes widen in shock. "Cillian. Ohmygod. I'm so, so sorry. Are you okay?"

"You have nothing to apologize for." I shake my head. "The day it ended, I didn't give you enough respect. You were owning your freedom. Exploring your sexuality. And I made you feel bad about it. Like our beautiful love for each other was wrong. I'm sorry for ruining what was special between us."

She takes a deep breath, her voice trembling. "It wasn't your fault. I lied to you. It was wrong. You had every right to—"

"No!" I touch her shoulder. "The image of you standing in front of me... Ivy, it haunts me. I loved you with all my heart and couldn't handle it. I never deserved you."

Ivy shakes her head and wipes tears from her eyes with her thumb. "That's not true. I'm the one who didn't deserve you."

A heavy silence settles between us as we process our confessions. She exits the freeway and instead of going back to the site, pulls into a diner parking lot.

"Come to the party." She caresses my wrist tenderly. "It would be weird if you didn't show up."

"Are you sure? I know you never told your parents about us, or I'd have been fired. I've never said a word to your dad either. But, there's this huge secret we have. What if he finds out now?" I place my hand over hers to keep her in place.

"Cillian. Relax. You coming to the party isn't some big outing." Ivy disentangles herself from me. "It's not like we're getting back together."

Her words are a knife in my kidney. Of course we're not. I'm a thirty-five-year-old recovering alcoholic who, until Ivy, was a fuck boy for most of my adult life.

I'm misinterpreting her kindness for chemistry. "No. It's best to leave the past in the past."

Seconds then minutes tick by with us staring at each other. Searching for...I dunno. Hope?

"I've got to get back." Abruptly, Ivy starts the car and we drive the rest of the way to the jobsite in silence.

A missed moment of reconnection. Or, a bittersweet closure.

Seeing her again brought back all the feelings I thought I'd buried.

I've said what I wanted to say, there's nothing left.

It's done.

Twenty-Nine

Two Weeks Later

WELL, I'M FINALLY TWENTY-ONE today.

This year, my parents have gone all out. We're in the Palisade Orchid Room, a stunning old-school Seattle venue with handblown artisan glass chandeliers and sweeping views of the downtown skyline, Mt. Rainier, Bainbridge Island, and the Olympic Mountains.

Huge floral arrangements adorn the room and the smell of fresh lilies mingles with the sea breeze wafting up from the open deck area. The long buffet table features a feast of Northwest specialties, including towers of King crab legs, oysters, and prawns. In the corner, there's even a social media station where my name and age are displayed in big lighted letters, surrounded by balloons.

I bet there's easily a hundred guests in attendance ranging from family friends, classmates from boarding school, and my BFFs from Italy—Elena, Javier, and Lucia. There's quite a few people from Bright Shipping too.

Despite the festive atmosphere, I'm not used to this much attention. My folks insisted on throwing a big party to make up for all the years they didn't acknowledge me. I hope turning my birthday back into a joyful occasion rather than a tragic memory of how we lost Forrest helps them heal.

I get why they're doing this—but I've moved past needing their validation. I took charge of my own destiny three years ago. The day I met Cillian.

God. *Cillian*.

Since our intense conversation on the drive back from Tacoma, Cillian's kept a polite distance. Our easy banter has been replaced by awkward formality. Every word we exchanged that day plays on a loop in my mind, making it hard to focus on anything else.

I'm blown away by Cillian's confession of regretting his behavior the morning we broke up. But the revelation of his downward spiral into alcoholism—because of the demise of our relationship—has left me completely reeling.

I'd always figured he'd moved on. Knowing how much he suffered breaks my heart all over again. We took two wildly different paths to forget each other. Both spectacular failures it seems. We're embedded in each other's souls.

And yet, despite our lingering feelings for each other, both of our walls remain impossibly high. I doubt either of us have the fortitude to scale them again. The risk of failure is too devastating to contemplate.

Speaking of which, my eyes are drawn across the room where Cillian chats with his parents, Rory and Maureen. When he introduced me earlier, he barely looked me in the eye. They were both lovely, and charmed me with their to-die-for Irish brogue.

My God, will I ever get over him? I have no idea what to do. He agreed with me—there is no future for us. Why am I faced with such a huge undercurrent of unresolved emotions? He's all I think about.

I want him. Crave him. Ache for him.

"Happy Birthday, Ivy!" Lucia runs toward me. "You look amazing."

"*Grazie, amica mia.*" I twirl in my knee-length turquoise dress that perfectly matches my eyes. "I'm glad you could make it."

Pierlo and Matteo join us and Pierlo hands me a beautifully wrapped gift. "*Buon compleanno*, Ivy!"

"We wouldn't miss this for the world." Matteo grins. "It's from both of us."

It's heavy and I tear the wrapping off to reveal a striking glass sculpture in silvery tones, full of graceful movement and light. "*Grazie mille*. It's gorgeous"

Lucia looks around the room. "This place is incredible. Your parents really know how to throw a party."

"Yeah, they do." I follow her gaze at the beautiful setup. "It's been a long time since we celebrated my birthday like this."

As we chat, I can't help it, my eyes keep drifting to Cillian.

He's moved to the patio, where my parents are laughing at something he's saying. My God, the man is effortlessly handsome in a black tailored suit. I've never seen him in formal wear before and he's absolutely jaw-dropping. The jacket hugs his broad shoulders and muscular frame perfectly. His dark hair is slicked back with a few loose waves that frame his chiseled, clean-shaven jaw.

His intense hazel eyes seem to always find mine, but his expression remains unreadable.

"Ivy, bella, are you okay?" Lucia touches my arm. "You seem distracted."

I snap back to the conversation, forcing a smile. "Yeah. As cool as this party is, I'm a bit overwhelmed by how many people are here. Truthfully, I'm more comfortable with a more intimate gathering. I wish it were just the four of us."

Matteo squeezes my hand. "It's understandable. But remember, everyone is here to wish you well and you only turn twenty-one once. Enjoy it."

"You're right. Let's get some food." I clap my hands.

We make our way to the buffet, piling our plates high. "Everything tastes amazing." Pierlo pops a mini crab cake in his mouth.

"They really outdid themselves. Flying the three of you here is my favorite part." I lean my head on his shoulder, but find myself glancing around the room again to find him.

Sure enough, I catch Cillian looking at me. Then at Pierlo. Then back at me. His eyes are narrowed and his jaw is set.

He's jealous.

My heart skips a beat, but I quickly look away. Even though he once had a crush on me, Pierlo and I never had a romantic connection. I'm not going to adjust my behavior around my dear friends for anyone, including my ex.

The party continues with laughter, music, and lively conversations. A couple of my classmates from boarding school come over to reminisce about old times. Madison, seems genuinely happy to see me.

"Happy Birthday, Ivy!" Madison says, giving me a hug. "It's been ages. You look fantastic!"

"Thanks, Maddy. You too." I clink my champagne glass to hers.

Emma cocks her head. "What have you been up to? I heard you've been living in Florence after ditching grad school."

Awwwkkkwwaard.

"Yeah...well." I'm not sure what to say.

"C'mon Ivy, it's time to spill. Who were you spending the night with that summer if it wasn't me?" Emma takes a sip on her cocktail and turns to Maddy. "Remember when her dad called my dad looking for her? Apparently, miss goody-two shoes had a secret boyfriend after we graduated high school. She lied to her parents and said she was going to stay at my house."

Maddy giggles. "Oh *yeah*. I remember being mad impressed. If you'd have let us know, we could have covered for you."

"It wasn't like that." I try to seem nonchalant but my eyes flick to Cillian, who's talking to my dad. "Mostly, I was sick of following the rules and didn't want to be stuck at home alone all summer."

"Ooooh. So there was *more* than one guy. Nice work." Emma clinks her glass to mine.

Maddy squeals. "Ivy Bright, you *sorceress*."

"Seriously, you guys." I know my face is as red as a beet. "It wasn't that big a deal. It was three years ago, can we drop it?"

Emma shakes her head, tsking me. "You're no fun. Now tell us about the hot dudes in Italy. Does that guy Pierlo have a girlfriend?"

I fill them in on my travels. They tell me about life at Wazzu. It's nice to catch up, even if for a short while.

For the next couple of hours, I make my way around the room, greeting guests and thanking them for celebrating my birthday with me. As an introvert who can fake for a while, I feel more and more overwhelmed by the attention as the evening wears on. The constant smiles and well-wishes are starting to feel suffocating.

I need some solitude. And quiet. After I wrap up a conversation with our neighbor, I manage to slip out to the deck unnoticed and continue all the way to the dock where I take a huge, deep breath of sea air. It's a welcome relief. I stroll to the end of the pier and gaze out at Puget Sound. The city lights reflect off the surface, creating a mesmerizing and calming pattern.

My entire body relaxes now that I'm away from the noise.

"Ivy," a familiar voice calls out softly from behind me.

I turn to see Cillian walking toward me. He stops a few feet away. "Are you okay?"

"I needed some space." I try to sound casual. "I'm a bit peopled out."

His eyes scan my face. He knows this about me. Few do because I'm adept at putting on a pleasant public face. "Yeah. It's a beautiful party, though. Your parents did it up."

"Yeah, they did. It's their way of trying to make up for all the years we didn't celebrate." I can't take my eyes off him. I long to feel his arms around me.

Cillian steps closer, his gaze intense. "About our conversation the other day…"

"Cillian, it's okay." I hold up a hand, stopping him. "We don't need to keep hashing it out."

He shakes his head. "No, um…it's not, um. Look, I've been struggling. I didn't like how we left things. I'm not as skilled with words as you are—I wasn't able to articulate what I wanted to say."

"I've been struggling too." My heart begins to race. "I knew being around you would bring back old feelings, which you clearly don't reciprocate. If I've made you uncomfortable in any way, I'm sorry. I wish I knew how to turn them off."

He shuts his eyes and sighs. "Are you seeing the guy you were with upstairs?"

"Pierlo?" I ask, though I know exactly who he means. "No, he's my dear friend from Italy."

"Thank Christ." Cillian closes the distance between us, grips my face with both palms and angles my head back. We look into each other's souls before he lowers his mouth to mine and gives me a long, slow, openmouthed kiss that makes my toes curl. I kiss him back, pouring all of my confusion, longing, and love for him into this moment.

All of a sudden, it's like no time has passed—and yet everything has changed in an instant.

We finally pull away, breathless. Our foreheads remain pressed together.

"Ivy," he whispers, his voice ragged. He grabs my hands and brings them to his lips, kissing my knuckles. My heart melts.

My heart aches with the intensity of my feelings for him. "Cillian, I'm scared. I don't want to confuse what you want with how I'm feeling. I couldn't bear getting hurt again."

"Are you serious? You're *all* I want. My every fantasy. I tried to fight it, but it's useless. You're it for me." He kisses me again.

Tears well up in my eyes. I blink them back. "Except, it's not only about us. My parents, the company—it's even more complicated. I'm not running away from my life anymore."

"I don't want you to. I'm willing to face anything if it means being with you." His thumbs wipe the tears from my eyes. "I promise, I'll do everything in my power to make this work. I'll never hurt you again."

I lean into his touch, the warmth of his hands soothes my fears. "I want to say yes, but we need to talk more and tonight's not the time. Dad gets pretty tired, they'll probably head home soon. I should get back up there."

"One more minute." Cillian envelops me in his arms. "I don't want to let you go."

After a long embrace, I clutch his forearms. "Um…my mom put my friends and I up at the Edgewater Inn for the weekend. I'm in the Presidential Suite. Stay with me tonight?"

He doesn't hesitate. "Fuck, yes."

"I've missed you so much," I whisper.

Cillian inhales sharply. He runs his hands over my hair. "*Show me.*"

His fingers wind around the back of my neck as he lowers his lips to mine again. He kisses me gently, swiping his tongue along my lips. I snake my arms around his waist and press myself tightly against him. His hard cock presses against my belly, causing a shiver to run through my body in anticipation of our night. A groan I can't control escapes. As our kiss deepens, I feel a very familiar pulse start to throb between my legs.

My God, am I going to come from kissing him?

"Let's go inside." I pull back slightly. "I'm about to climb you like a tree, but someone's bound to come looking."

The sound of laughter and music comes back into focus, reminding us of the world we've momentarily stepped away from.

Cillian nods and smiles sheepishly. "You go. I'm gonna need a minute. Maybe two."

"Here." I locate the card key to my hotel room in my bejeweled crossbody bag. "Room 523. Just go in. I'll be there soon."

After a quick kiss goodbye, I practically skip back up to the party. The other day, when he said we should leave things in the past, I was forced to give up hope. His kiss, though. Holy shit. For the first time in a long while, I feel complete.

On my way back to the restaurant, the otherworldly feeling I've kept suppressed, but felt the first time I saw him, permeates my body—Cillian and I are meant for each other. I believed it at eighteen and I believe it today. Later tonight, we'll reunite and now nothing stands in our way.

Except, maybe, my dad.

Inside, people are dancing, laughing, and celebrating. I'm chatting with my Italian friends, my parents, and a few random people when I see Cillian slip back in. Neither of us can take our eyes off each other for a minute, but I compel myself to look away and focus on the conversations I'm engaged in.

A few minutes later, Lucia teases me on our way to the dessert table. "Where did you disappear to?"

"I needed some air." I can't help but flick my eyes to Cillian, who's watching me intently.

Matteo follows my gaze and smirks. "Well, while you were getting some 'air,' you missed out on boogieing with us. Come on!"

I laugh, letting them pull me onto the dance floor. The music is loud, and the room is filled with joy. I get lost in the moment, dancing with my friends. I feel happy. Free. I'm surrounded by people who love me. It's the perfect day.

Cillian watches from the sidelines, his gaze never leaving me. There's a new understanding between us. A promise of something more.

Whatever it means, I can't wait for us to get naked.

And for tonight, that's enough.

Thirty

CILLIAN

An Hour Later

THREE YEARS AGO SHE utterly and completely captivated me.

Not one goddamn thing has changed.

As I watch Ivy dance with her friends, every sway of her hips makes my heart ache with longing. I can't take my eyes off her, but it's time for me to go. We're going to celebrate her birthday alone later and I need to make this night one she'll never forget.

A night that'll set the tone for the rest of our lives.

I slip out of the party quietly, leaving behind the noise and lights. It's late, but I manage to find a high-end grocery store where I buy a bottle of sparkling cider and clean them out of roses and candles. My heart races with anticipation as I drive to The Edgewater so I can get Ivy's room ready for us.

The suite is magnificent, with a master bedroom featuring a four-poster king bed, a full panoramic view of Elliott Bay, and a private deck with Adirondack chairs and a chaise lounge. There's a dining area and a wet bar, a loft-style living room with a gas fireplace, and a glass surround shower with waterfall and handheld shower heads.

Oh, we're gonna have some fun here.

Quickly, I take off my jacket and tie to get comfortable. Then I set things up. First, I sprinkle rose petals from the door to the bed and all over the duvet cover. Then I light the candles and take out the cider and glasses. Finally, I compile a quick playlist of soft music and pipe it through the sound system.

As I survey the scene, the door opens and I spin around.

Ivy steps into the room and her eyes widen in surprise. She's breathtaking. Her dress shimmers in the candlelight, silky blonde hair falls in loose waves around her shoulders. Her cheeks are flushed from dancing and her lips still slightly plump from our kisses.

I've never wanted her more than I do in this moment.

"Cillian." She sets her purse on the table.

"Ivy." I'm so taken by her, my voice is barely a whisper.

The past three years—the pain, the heartache, the shame—all melt into the background and we move toward each other.

Before I say another word, Ivy's in my arms. Her lips crash against mine in a kiss that's both desperate and passionate. Her hands tangle in my hair, and I pull her closer, pouring all my love, longing, and regret into the kiss.

"I've missed you." She presses herself against me.

"I've missed you too, baby. More than you can imagine." My words come out garbled, thick with emotion.

Ivy winds her arms tightly around my neck. I grip her waist as if letting go will mean losing her all over again. Our bodies press together, hearts pound in unison, the intensity of our connection is palpable and undeniable.

The gas fireplace casts a warm glow all over the living room as we move toward the couch and recline in front of the flames. Entwined on the cushions, we fit together perfectly. Our hands explore each other with a hunger that's been building for three long years.

"I was such a fool," I say between kisses, my heart aching with the need to make her understand. "I regretted pushing you away. I've never stopped loving you, Ivy."

Ivy massages my temples with her thumbs. "I've never stopped loving you either, baby. Every day without you has been agony."

We continue to kiss, gently caressing each other. The feel of her skin against mine, the taste of her lips—it's all familiar and yet new. We're both different people now. I'm bigger. Stronger. Working out has replaced drinking in my life. She's leaner, more self-assured. Confident. Our lives have changed. Circumstances are different but my feelings for her haven't changed..

Tonight is about reconnecting with the only woman I've ever loved.

Ivy moans against my mouth and climbs onto my lap, rolling her body against mine. Her fingers skim down the back of my neck, raising goosebumps. In one swift motion, I stand, lifting her effortlessly. As we have done many times before, Ivy wraps her legs around my waist and I carry her to our inevitable destination. Each step is filled with anticipation.

The bedroom is filled with only the warm glow of candle-light, which casts a romantic aura across her face. We reach the four-poster bed, where I lay Ivy down on top of the rose petals. She looks up at me with a mix of longing and love, and I lean down to kiss her again, savoring this moment we've both waited so long for.

My cock twitches in excitement when she reaches between us, unbuttons my shirt and slides it down my arms. Deliberately she traces her fingers along my pecs, around my nipples and finally down my stomach to my pants. She unbuckles my belt, but I grasp her wrist.

"You're first, baby." I reach under her and unzip her dress. "I need this off of you."

"No problem." Ivy rolls out from under me and shimmies out of her dress, revealing a lacy black thong and matching bra, which pushes her tits up perfectly.

I pull her back down on the bed and run my hands along her back to her ass while I press my face to the swell of her breasts. "You're out of my league."

She traces my eyebrow. "I'm not."

"You are, but if memory serves, my superpower is making you come. You'll never want to leave me after tonight." I nip her bottom lip and kiss across her throat before fastening my lips to her neck.

Her body arches against mine and her breathy pants test my control. "Ohmygod, Cillian."

"How the hell do I work this?" I fumble with the fancy clasp on her bra. It's sexy as hell, but it's going to look better on the floor.

"Here, let me help." Ivy laughs and effortlessly pops it open, freeing her succulent tits.

I toss it behind me and cup them, licking and sucking her nipples until she's a moaning mess. My fingers slide between her legs and I push her panties to the side, she's slick with desire. Pressing my thumb to her clit, I circle it lightly—teasing her.

"Please," she pants as she drags her nails over my back and her body cants up against mine. I push two fingers into her and immediately locate her bundle of nerves. I know her body so well, I want to make her fly apart and then take my time. Ivy's fingers dig into my arms as she whimpers, "*Yesssssss.*"

"You feel incredible, baby. Tight. Wet for me." I fasten my lips on her perky nipple and suck hard. My thumb continues to pet Ivy's clit as I curl my fingers inside her and press and wiggle. Panting and moaning, she writhes against me as I fuck her with my fingers. Her legs splay open, revealing every beautiful fold of her creamy, responsive pussy. Her toes curl and her thighs shake as Ivy comes apart with a hoarse yell.

"*Ahhhhhhh.*" Ivy shudders, clamping around my fingers.

She watches, glassy eyed, as I withdraw them and suck and savor her juices. "Still my favorite taste. I hope you're ready for more, because I'm gonna fuck you until morning."

"I'm soooo ready," she rasps, dragging her palm up and down my shaft, which threatens to burst through my slacks.

"Before we, uh…will you…" Ivy wince-smiles and throws her forearm over her eyes.

"What baby?" I lie next to her, move her arm and kiss her so she can taste herself on my tongue. "What do you need?"

"I'm ready for…" She blinks at me then swallows and takes a slow breath. "Will you go down on me? I've missed your magic tongue."

My heart beats ten times faster and swells in my chest every time Ivy asserts what she wants sexually. I dig it so fucking much. Groaning, I press my face to her throat. "Of course. Whatever you want. Tonight is all about you."

"About *us*." She drapes her calf over my hip and slides her hand between her legs. With two fingers, she spreads her lips apart, flashing her pussy. My eyes flick back up her body to take in her wild turquoise eyes, raw lips, and the blush spreading over her cheeks and down her chest. Her nipples are puckered and distended. "I'm yours, Cillian. All of me. My body. My heart. My soul. *Everything*. I *love* you.

The certainty in Ivy's words makes my heart feel like it's about to explode. Any doubt, fear, or insecurity I've ever had about our age difference, the pain of losing her or the years spent apart disappears. Everything snaps into place.

This is where I'm meant to be. With her. She's always been mine, and I've always been hers. This is our second chance, and I'm never letting her go again.

"*Mo shíorghrá*, I loved you from the minute I laid eyes on you, Ivy. I'll love you until the day I die and beyond." I take my time kissing and worshipping her body until I reach her stomach. Pressing her legs apart, I kiss her upper thigh and roll her panties down and off.

She smells fucking *amazing*. God, I missed this so much.

Ivy squirms and fists my hair when I tease her, licking, kissing, and tasting her everywhere. Her clit pokes out from under its hood, begging for attention. I flatten my tongue and lap at it, sucking and swirling until she gasps and clutches my head, holding me in place. Lazily, I circle her pleasure point again and again. Her hips roll and buck against my lips as I keep her on edge with different angles, paces, and combinations.

I jerk her tighter against my mouth and devour her. I've been starving for Ivy for years and I savor every ounce of her cream. The sounds coming out of her mouth are incoherent. I wrap my lips around her clit and suck hard, flicking my tongue back and forth until she cries and begs and moans for me to keep going.

I don't stop. Pressing her shuddering thighs wider, I look up to find her watching me as she plucks and twists her nipples. Her eyes burn hot with lust and unspoken promises, but her breathing sounds somewhat close to a sob. I swipe my tongue furiously back and forth across her clit then suck, keeping up the combination until she writhes and digs her heels into the mattress.

Ivy's orgasm hits us both like a tidal wave. Her thighs nearly squish my head from the force of her release, which drenches my entire face. As I drink every ounce, my balls start to tingle and I'm forced to reach down and grip the base of my cock to stop myself from coming in my pants.

"Are you ready for me, baby?" I press myself up and shed my slacks and briefs in an instant. My cock weeps from the tip and points stiffly toward her opening, as if it knows where it belongs. "I want you badly."

"*Yes*. Fuck me, Cillian. Fuck me so hard I'll feel you tomorrow."

I enter her slowly. She's fucking tight, I take my time stretching her pussy until I'm fully embedded.

"Is this what you missed, baby?" I nip her throat. "Me, buried deep inside you, making you come over and over again?"

"I missed all of you. Every part." She clutches my ass as I pick up the pace.

Before long, I'm thrusting into her hard and I barely notice the bed squeaking or the headboard thudding against the wall. I can't make myself care, not when Ivy moans when every cant of my hips pushes my cock deeper into her velvety heat. "Mine," I pant. "*Mo shíorghrá. You're mine.*"

"All yours, Cillian. *Forever*." Ivy clenches around me as she comes for the third time.

I flip her over and ram into her from behind, stroking my hands along her spine to her hips. "I'm not done, are you still with me, baby?"

"I never want you to be done." She pushes back against me and my eyes roll back from the ecstasy.

Glancing to the side I see the wall is actually a mirror and the vision of Ivy splayed out with me impaling her pussy nearly sends me over. I band my arm around her stomach and pull her up, never breaking contact. Swinging my legs over the side of the bed, I sit us both up until she's straddling me reverse cowgirl-style.

I rest my chin on her shoulder, cup her breast with one hand and circle her clit with the fingers of my other one. "Look at us"

Ivy's eyes meet mine in the mirror and she looks down to where we're joined, her thighs draped over mine. My cock buried deep inside her. "*Ohhhhh*. Wow."

It's us, doing what we're best at. Loving each other.

"Watch yourself come." I lean over her shoulder to get a better look.

"We're beautiful." Ivy's hand joins mine and we rub her clit in unison. "I'll never get this picture out of my head."

Neither will I.

Our bodies swivel and grind until we're both panting and moaning with abandon. Picking up the pace, I grip her hips and move her back and forth before bouncing her on my cock while she continues to work her clit.

Heightened by the visual of our fucking, neither of can help the sounds we make. Groaning, shouting, keening, swearing, crying out—chasing the ultimate release, and then I feel the ripple of Ivy's pussy clamping around me. With a feral roar, I ejaculate what feels like three years' worth of come inside her.

"Fucking hell," I whimper as my eyes roll back and Ivy slumps back against me.

Our bodies keep moving through aftershocks. I pump into her over and over again as my whole body shakes like an earthquake. I caress her sides and belly. "I want to be inside you all night."

"*Mmmmmmm.*" Ivy's eyes are half-mast. "Sounds like heaven."

I tilt her head back to look directly into her eyes. She needs to know we're back together now. I meant it. She's mine.

"Nothing will keep us apart this time," I promise, my voice filled with conviction. "We've been through too much. I'll never let anything come between us again."

And I mean it. With all of my heart.

Thirty-One

IVY

Three Hours Later

"Show me how much you missed me."

Cillian presses kisses down the length of my neck. His cock presses against the crease of my ass.

"Again?" I turn to find his eyes dark with desire. My eyes drop to his chiseled chest and eight-pack abs. My God, his body is ridiculous. "Isn't he supposed to hibernate for a bit?"

It's four in the morning. We're in the walk-in shower to clean up after round four—or is it five? Apparently, neither of us has any intention of sleeping tonight. I run my fingertips down the length of his body then crouch down until I'm eye level with his shaft and look up at him.

"Nah, he won't let us down." Cillian chuckles.

He gently runs his fingers through my hair as I grip his engorged length in my fist and swirl my tongue around the tip. He still tastes of both of us, I suck and lick him ravenously.

"*Fuck*," he hisses and leans back against the tile. "You have no idea how much I love your mouth on me."

His response urges me on, and I take the full length of him to the back of my throat. Holding his hips for balance, I find my rhythm, taking him deeper with every pass, sucking him harder each time he lurches his hips into my mouth.

Cillian's breathing grows labored. "Fuck, Ivy, you're blowing my mind.."

He pushes the wet hair from my forehead and runs his fingers down my cheeks, feeling them hollow around his cock as I suck. I look up at him to find him watching me.

"Stand up, baby." He pulls himself free of my mouth and bends to kiss me, slow and gentle. "I need to fuck you again, precious girl."

"I need it too." I wind my arms around his neck.

Cillian helps me to my feet and trails his hands up my sides to cup my breasts. My nipples immediately pucker under his fingers, which pinch them into tight peaks. His breath quivers when he slips his fingers into my slickness and kisses my neck with an open mouth. With him, I'm perpetually aroused, as if my body is liquifying from the inside out.

How is it possible to want someone this much?

Cillian's fingertips circle my overly-sensitive clit, causing me to shudder. "You're still dripping wet for me."

I clutch at the back of his head as he moves faster. I can't even speak, let alone answer. A low moan escapes and the tingles start. Every time he touches me, my body goes into overdrive on a one-way race track to orgasm. I widen my stance and he plunges his fingers inside me, scissoring them over my G-spot.

"Oh. *Ohhhhh.*" I grab on to his forearms to hold myself up.

Before I know what's happening, Cillian hoists me over his shoulder and walks back into the master suite where he tosses me onto the bed. Before I have a chance to move, he crawls over me and settles his hips between my legs. Reaching down, he grips his cock and rubs it up and down through my swollen flesh, while holding his weight up on one straightened arm.

"Are you too sore?" he chokes out. "Is all of this too much?"

"Never." I grip his face.

Cillian runs his hand down my thigh, then underneath my knee to bring my leg up around his hip. Slowly he kisses down my throat to my breasts, sucking my nipple hard between his teeth. My back arches off the bed as he moves lower and his tongue swipes through my folds.

Reaching up, he links his fingers with mine and our eyes lock. The intimacy of the moment nearly overwhelms me. My eyes begin to water when his tongue lashes deep, long licks on my clit. My thighs begin to shake and tears spill down my cheeks.

"Ahhh, baby." He stills to calm me. "I *know*."

I nod and squeeze his hand, unable to articulate words. Cillian moves back up and cages my head with his arms, and with one hard lunge he's buried inside me to the hilt. He sucks in a breath, closes his eyes and remains still for a while. His eyelids twitch and blink open, I see a depth of love that permeates my entire soul.

"*Mo shíorghrá*—I love you, baby." Cillian's voice breaks and his eyes mist over a bit too.

I thread my fingers through his hair and bring his lips to mine. "I love you too. *Everything* about you. I love everything about *us*."

He nods and circles his hips, then pulls out and pushes back in. He repeats the motion and increases the pace in slow increments until I can't take it anymore. I grab his ass and purr, "Faster. Harder."

"Like this?" Cillian nips my neck and slams back into me.

He rolls his hips into me hard, the bed sounds like it's going to break as it hits the wall. "*Yesssss*," I groan as I run my hands over his muscled body.

Our kisses turn aggressive. We claw and grope and fuck with every last ounce of energy.

Thrashing my head from side to side, I scream at the top of my lungs as my orgasm rips from my body. Cillian reaches around and grips my ass hard, pulling me up to meet him every time he thrust against me. One, two, three hard lunges later and I feel his hot release fill me.

"*Fuuuuuuuuuck.*" He holds me against him.

I'm a noodle. Completely spent.

He rolls us over and positions me on top of him as his cock pulses inside me. Our breathing is labored for a while, but eventually we both settle down and he slips from my body.

At some point, I'm somewhat coherent again and I notice the room is bathed in the soft glow of morning light filtering through the curtains. The world outside is waking up but here in this suite, time seems to have stopped. Cillian and I lie tangled in each other's arms, our bodies still humming from the intensity of our reunion.

He did, indeed, fuck me until morning.

Cillian's fingers trace lazy patterns on my back. "Ivy," he whispers, his voice husky with emotion. "I truly never thought we'd have this again."

"Neither did I." I look up at him, my heart swelling with love. "But here we are. It feels...right."

He presses a kiss to my forehead. "I missed you so much. Every day without you felt like a piece of me was missing."

"*Yeah.*" Tears prick at the corners of my eyes. "I always thought about you and wondered if you were okay. If you were happy."

He tightens his hold on me, his eyes reflecting the depth of his feelings. "I wasn't. Not in the least. I hit rock bottom, truth be told and I'm not proud of how far I sunk. I meant what I said the other day. My drinking got bad. *Really* bad. I nearly made the same mistakes as my father."

"You told me in the car. I was shocked and not sure what to say. I've wondered if the way things ended between us pushed you over the edge." I slide down to the mattress and face him.

He turns to his side, shaking his head firmly. "Before we met I was on a slippery slope. A shot here. A few drinks there. For a long time I told myself it took the edge off. We split up and it evolved into taking the pain away. Then I couldn't function without it. A fucked-up natural progression. Losing you gave me the excuse to drink more until I was downing a bottle every night alone in my loft. I missed family events. Missed a crucial planning meeting. Your dad nearly fired me."

"Is that how you realized you needed help?" I search his eyes, recalling my dad mentioning Cillian messing up.

"It should have been." He looks away and winces. "Later that night after your dad threatened my job I was falling-down drunk when my da and brother, Brennan, found me and intervened. They convinced me to go to rehab. I was there for a month. Da took over the job for a bit. He told your father I had a minor health issue."

"Oh, baby." I feather kisses along his jaw. "I can't even picture you like that. It never occurred to me you'd be susceptible to alcoholism. It seems out of character. Aside from our night at Kells and a glass of whiskey here and there, I don't remember you drinking much at all."

"I never drank around you because, except on the night we met, you didn't really indulge. Besides, we were naked most of the time we were together. After you left, though, I more than made up for it. Doubled then tripled down." He swallows hard and traces my eyebrow with his finger. "I've been sober for a year now. I'm serious about my sobriety—I go to meetings, have a sponsor, and I take things one day at a time. Before we get too deep, you need to know what you're getting into. I won't drink again, I can't. Not with my family history."

My heart aches for his struggle and strength. "I'm proud of you for facing it and getting help."

"It doesn't make you want to run screaming?" His eyes search mine. "You're a beautiful twenty-one-year-old woman with the world at your feet. I'm a thirty-five-year-old recovering alcoholic. It doesn't paper out."

I absorb the vulnerability and fear in his expression. "No, Cillian, it doesn't make me want to run screaming." I cup his face gently. "I *know* you. From my own experience and everything my father's told me over the years, you're a stand-up guy You've fought your demons and have come out stronger. You're a guy who's turned a successful business into a formidable company. You love your family and treat your workers with respect and kindness. You always make me feel seen and understood like no one else ever has. Our age difference, your past—none of it matters to me. It never did. What matters is who you are as a person and how much we love each other."

"I know I've already apologized, but I'll say it again. It haunts me how I pushed you away so cruelly. Made you feel like you weren't enough." He lets out a deep breath. "It was wrong and if you'll let me, I'll spend the rest of my life making it up to you."

"And I'll never lie to you again." I press closer and wedge my leg between his. "We've both made mistakes and it's time to let them go. Let's focus on our future."

We bask in each other's arms, lost in our own thoughts. The seriousness of what we've discussed settles over us, but there's a sense of peace too. I feel his heartbeat against my cheek, steady and reassuring, and I know we're ready to face whatever comes next.

"Cillian, I'd like to tell my parents about us soon." I trace "*I love you*" on his chest. "I don't want to start this new chapter with secrets."

He nods thoughtfully, his hand gently caressing my shoulder. "Yeah, I don't want to hide anything either. I'm worried about how they'll react, though. Especially since your dad's my biggest client. If he finds out I'm the man from back then...it'll be a blow. He may never accept me."

"True," I admit, feeling the tension. My dad and I have come far but I've only been home for a few weeks. "At the same time, my mom and I are closer than ever. Maybe I should tell her and see what she thinks."

Cillian kisses the side of my face. "Let's do it sooner rather than later. I've been jealous as hell at the idea of you loving another man. Seeing you cuddled up with Pierlo at the party—it nearly drove me insane. I want us to be exclusive. Hopefully I'm not going to freak you out when I say...this is forever."

"It doesn't freak me out because I feel the same way. And, don't think I haven't felt the same. The thought of the other women you've been with after me…I cried myself to sleep too many times to count." I look up into his eyes. "I haven't been with anyone else. I *couldn't*."

His eyes widen in surprise and relief. "It's probably selfish of me to say, 'thank God.'" He kisses me. "You need to know, I haven't been with anyone either. There's no way I could get it up for anyone else. I knew you were the one the second I saw you."

We sit in silence for a moment, processing the revelations. I'm shocked and happy.

"Maybe I should tell my parents everything. Lay it all out from start to finish so they know how serious we are. This isn't some fling—it's real and I don't want to spend another night without you." I sit up and lean into him.

He cups my breast and thumbs my nipple. "If that's the plan, we should do it together. They need to see how committed I am to you."

"About the future…" I swing my leg over his waist to straddle him and grip his half-hard cock. "I know what I want." I stroke up and down his length until he's fully erect. "I want a family. A life with you." I guide him inside me.

He grins and rests his hands on my hips as I gyrate against him until my clit hits his pelvic bone. His eyes shine with love. Determination. "That's it, baby. Find your spot."

"Can we do this every day?" I gasp as he thrusts up from under me and pinches my nipples. "I'm addicted to your cock."

Cillian laughs. "Sure, first you need to move in with me, then I want to marry you." He reaches between us and presses a palm against my flat stomach. "And someday, I want to watch our babies grow in here."

"If you're serious." I flatten my palms against his abs and rock against him. "We'll have it all. And a lifetime of this." I squeeze around his cock. "I'm insatiable for you."

As our bodies meld, I know what we have is rare. Worth nurturing. I'll do anything to protect our love.

Ivy Bright isn't a naïve teenage girl anymore. I'm a grown woman who can make my own decisions and stand by them with conviction.

My dad might be angry about our past deception, but I'm not going to hide from my truth.

Cillian and I know we belong to each other and nothing—and no one—will keep us apart ever again.

Thirty-Two

CILLIAN

The Next Morning

IT'S STILL EARLY. I'M alone in the suite, exhausted, and surrounded by the remnants of my passionate night with Ivy.

Squished rose petals are scattered across the floor. The champagne glasses are still half-full of sparkling cider. Soft music continues to play on a loop in the background. The room smells of sex, sweat, my cologne and her perfume. I breathe in deeply.

Us.

A few minutes ago, Ivy went downstairs to have breakfast with her parents and the Italian friends. They'd planned the day long before our reunion last night and while she was reluctant to go, it's her only day to play tourist.

While I miss her already, it gives me time to collect my thoughts. Come up with a plan.

I sit on the bed and memories of our night play vividly in my mind. The way we spent hours exploring each other. The way her pussy responded to me as if no time had passed at all. How our bodies moved as one. We were up all night reconnecting.

Every kiss, every touch, every breath was a reminder of the love we share and the future we'll have together.

The images of Ivy and I fucking take over and before I know it, my cock stands at attention. *Jesus*. It's possessed by the mere thought of her. I jack it gingerly because I'm sore. Facts are facts, though, nothing will satiate my burning desire for her. I need release.

I close my eyes and picture myself pushing into Ivy's tight opening. Her swollen clit quivers under my thumb. She plucks her puckered nipples as my cock fills her and re-treats. Fills and retreats. Fills and retreats. *Fuuuuuck*. My hand moves faster. In my mind, Ivy tells me to fuck her harder. To fill her with my come. To make her pregnant.

Holy *shit*...with a loud groan I spurt all over my fingers and stomach.

God, the effect she has on me.

It's not just sex with us. Like I told her, I want to marry her. Have kids. Build a future.

With our crazy chemistry, we're gonna fuck like rabbits for the rest of our lives.

After a quick shower to wash the spunk off, I decide to tidy up the room in case Ivy and her friends decide to come back up here before housekeeping arrives. My mind is a whirlwind of thoughts and emotions. She and I have a lot to discuss. Things to figure out. I'm stressed about how her parents will feel about us being in a relationship.

Looking her dad in the eye after he finds out I'm the secret lover Ivy lost her innocence to will be tough. On both of us.

Once the suite is back in order, I leave the hotel and head straight to my parents' house. I park in the driveway and head inside, the familiar scent of my mom's cooking greets me as I step through the door.

My mom pokes her head around the corner. "Cillian?"

"Hi, Ma." I give her a kiss on the cheek.

We step into the kitchen where my dad is sitting at the table with a steaming mug in hand. He looks up as I enter. "I didn't expect to see you today. Want some breakfast and a coffee?"

"Sure, thanks, Da." I take a seat across from him. He pours me a cup, I take a sip and wait for a blessed jolt of caffeine.

He raises an eyebrow. "Something on your mind?"

"I need some advice. From both of you." I take a deep breath, deciding to come out with it. "Ivy Bright and I… Um…*err*…"

Da leans back in his chair. "Aye. Go on, then."

His acknowledgement doesn't surprise me because of what I've previously confided, but I dive in. "I've never stopped loving her. Not for a second."

"Well, you certainly didn't hide your admiration at the party last night." He rests his chin on his hand. "What's the problem?"

I bury my face in my hands, then look back at him. "We, um, reconnected. She and I want to make it official but I'm not sure her dad, in particular, will be on board with his daughter dating me generally, let alone finding out it's not our first rodeo."

"Are you sure she's the one for you? I'm not impressed with the lying part. She put you in a very precarious position." Ma sounds pissed. She places a traditional Ulster breakfast on the table and returns with plates for her and my da.

I rub my hands nervously, I should have known Da would have told her what was what. "Please don't hold it against her, Ma. Her personal family stuff and why she felt it necessary to lie about her age and identity is not my story to tell. Trust me when I tell you she's taken full responsibility, as have I."

"Sounds like the girl's a bit of drama, so it does." Ma tosses her head, a fierce protector of her sons to the umpteenth degree. In her eyes, I'm pretty sure none of us can do wrong.

"Please quit calling her a 'girl,' Ma." I wince. "It's a sore spot. The age difference is already significant, it's an obstacle we have to deal with."

My mom swishes her hand across her face. "Get over it, she was legal then and she's legal now. I don't give two shites about your age or hers. It's the deceiving part I have a real problem with."

My da watches our back and forth unbothered. "You want my advice, son?"

"Of course." My heart pounds in anticipation.

He takes Ma's hand. "Maureen, trust me on this. Anyone can see how Cillian feels about Ivy and how she feels about him. On the jobsite, neither of them go for more than a minute without putting eyes on each other. And last night? Jay-sus." He turns to me. "You're not as covert as you think, Casanova."

A flush of embarrassment creeps up my neck. "Do you think Stan has picked up on it?"

"Stanley Bright is a perceptive man, but with his cancer treatment, he hasn't been around the two of you much." He sops up some beans with his soda bread. "Ripping off the band-aid might give you and Ivy some relief, but he's going through a rough time. Be patient. Make sure his health is your first consideration."

Ma smacks the table. "Bullshit, Rory. They have a business relationship where honesty is key." She grasps my shoulder. "Cillian, you need to prepare yourself. If he finds out you deceived him about the true nature of your relationship with his daughter all these years, how do you think he'll feel? How will he be able to trust you?"

"It's the dilemma. It's one thing to say we're dating now. Another to confess to what happened three years ago. We're kind of damned if we do, damned if we don't." I feel nauseous at the choice we have to make. "Because Stan knows there was a guy back then, he just doesn't know it was me. There's a big part of me that thinks what he doesn't know won't hurt him. Maybe it's none of his business, even. What do we gain by hurting him when what matters is how I treat her now."

Da's expression softens. "Stan's been through a lot. Losing his son. Trying to be a parent to Ivy while grieving and running a billion-dollar business. He and I have gotten to know each other over the past few years, as you know. It's funny, I remember him telling me he turned over many rocks trying to find out who the guy was before giving up."

Shit.

"Well, I'm the guy, and I want to marry Ivy with his blessing." I suck in a breath.

Ma raises an eyebrow. "Ach, son. Marriage? Either way, I dunno if you can expect a *blessing*."

"Let me be the voice of reason." Da crosses his arms as he often does when he's about to make some proclamation. "If you and Ivy have worked out your past, it's between you. It doesn't matter what your parents think and you certainly don't need any blessings. Your ma and I had you at nineteen and decided to move here from Belfast. Our parents did not support us but we did it anyway. There was tension for a long time but eventually, it all worked out because we were committed to each other and built our own family."

My mom's expression softens. "Aye, 'tis true."

"What I'm trying to say," Da continues, "is, if you're serious about each other, make these decisions as a couple. Right or wrong, Don't shy away from the hard conversations."

"If Stan objects to our relationship, it could cost the company the Bright business." I glance down at the table and back at my father.

Da presses his hands to the table and stands. "You need to decide what's important to you and what you're willing to risk. McGloughlin Construction is your legacy now, son. I'll stand behind whatever decision you make."

No wiser, but with plenty of input to consider, I help with the dishes, bid cheerio, and head to my townhouse.

Once I'm home, exhaustion overtakes me and I fall asleep. I wake up a few hours later to find I've missed a few texts from Ivy.

2:23 pm Ivy: Dad was tired so my parents went home. Meet us for dinner?

3:44 pm Ivy: I didn't hear from you we're at Pike Place Market

4:06 pm Ivy: Are you okay?

4:15 pm Me: Hey beautiful I was asleep. Someone kept me up all night ;)

4:17 pm Ivy: LOL. Dinner rezzies at 6 at Matt's in the Market. Join us?

4:18 pm Me: *No, you should enjoy your last night with your friends. Sleep-over?*

4:21pm Ivy: *Yes! meet me at the hotel later.*

4:23 pm Me: *I'll be there by 8*

As excited as I am to spend the night with Ivy, the reality of our situation crashes down on me with a jolt. Tonight we have a hotel room, but tomorrow is a different story.

She still lives at home. If we have any hope of being a real couple, we need to tell her parents about us. Right away.

By tomorrow, she and I have to decide how we're going to navigate the complexities of our situation.

Because, I'm not wasting another minute without her by my side.

Thirty-Three

IVY

Later That Day

IT'S BEEN AN INCREDIBLY fun day with my friends.

Pierlo, Matteo, Lucia and I spent all afternoon exploring the city. As disappointed as I was when Cillian didn't join us, it gave the three of us time to catch up.

My friends realized the guy at the party was the same man in my paintings and it turned into a whole thing. They demanded I bring him down to meet them. We're supposed to have a nightcap in the lobby bar an hour from now, but

I convinced them to meet us in the lobby lounge. I want to respect Cillian's boundaries with alcohol.

The way I see it, the faster we integrate our worlds, the better.

By the time we return from dinner to the Edgewater, the sun is setting over the Olympics. I know he's waiting for me and I cannot wait to jump him. We have an hour before we need to be downstairs, plenty of time to take the edge off.

As I enter the suite, I see he's lit the candles again, which flicker gently. There's a bouquet of fresh roses on the table. Cillian stands by the window, looking out at the Olympic Mountains, his silhouette framed by the fading light.

He turns to face me as I close the door and his eyes light up with so much warmth it makes my heart race. *"Mo shíorghrá."*

"Hey." I move toward him. He meets me halfway, pulling me into his arms. The feel of his body against mine, the woodsy scent of his skin—intoxicating.

Cillian leans in, his lips brushing softly against mine. Our kiss deepens, and I feel a rush through my body when his hands cradle my face. Our lips move with heated intensity, each kiss ignites sparks which spread through my entire body, leaving me breathless and yearning for more.

I reach for the buckle on his pants, causing Cillian to pull back slightly. His eyes search mine. "Ivy, can we talk first?"

Dread fills my gut. I hold up my hands in mock surrender. "Oh-kay."

"It's not like that." He leads me to the couch where we sit down, facing each other. Considering the furrow in his brow and the way his eyes flicker with uncertainty, it seems like maybe it is "like that."

"Doesn't make me feel any better." I feel my breath catch.

"Hear me out. Look, I want nothing more than for us to start our life as a couple." Cillian studies me intensely. "Last night, in the heat of passion, we made proclamations and promises. All day, I've struggled to figure out what it means logistically. As a builder, I know the importance of foundation. A strong frame. A leak-proof roof..."

All I hear is him breaking up with me again. I interrupt, angry. "Is this you backtracking? Trying to let me down easy?"

Cillian shakes his head. "No, baby, you've got it all wrong. I believe in us *completely*. What I mean by logistics is...I don't want to spend any nights away from you. I think we have to tell your parents about us and face whatever consequences come our way. I'd like to do it tomorrow."

"I don't want to spend any nights away from you either." I let out a deep breath because I'm relieved, then the rest of what he said catches up with me. "Wait, what? *Tomorrow?* Why?"

"Think about it. I'm obviously not going to stay at your house. Are you going to tell your folks you're sleeping at mine??" He takes my hand between his.

I shake my head. He's got a point. "Um...I don't want to lie to my parents about where I am."

"Okay." Cillian's grip on my hand tightens. "My part is done. I'd filled my dad in about you a while ago and today I told my parents we're back together. We have their support."

It takes me a minute to absorb. "Were they upset?"

"Honestly, my ma took a minute at first but she came around. Da told me anyone with eyes could see we have something going on. Apparently, we're not as subtle as we think we are." He shrugs. "Ivy, we're not fooling anyone. We love each other. It's not a crime. Let's not begin our second chance with lies to your family. My only hope is your folks forgive us for keeping our past from them."

"Hold on, do you think we tell them the *whole* truth?" I can't imagine how my dad is going to react to the current "us" let alone past "us."

"Don't you think it's best? Explain everything—how we met, our past, our plans for the future." A hint of a smile plays on his lips. "We can't assume your parents will react badly. Maybe they'll support us. Maybe your dad has truly changed and will let you live the life you want to live."

I bite my bottom lip, feeling skeptical. "Uh…I'd like to believe you but so far he and I haven't disagreed on anything. If he's backed against a wall, my dad can be pretty intense. He speaks without thinking. Some of the things he's said to me in the past…" Ivy bites her lip. "Sure, he's apologized, but I'm always a bit on edge. I don't want to stress him out."

"Oh, baby. I'll never allow him to hurt you. I'd put a stop to it immediately." Cillian scoots closer.

"I know and I appreciate you wanting to protect me." I sigh. "I guess I've forgiven, but I can't ever forget."

"Look, my da said something that resonated with me: you and I have to be on the same page if we're serious about building a future."

Now I'm confused. "How are we not on the same page?"

"I feel strongly about telling your parents about us, but I'm not going to put pressure on you." He scrubs his hand through his hair.

I look into his eyes, feeling a surge of determination. "I'm not under any pressure. If you asked me to elope tonight, I'd do it. I want all the ickiness to be over. It's time for us to start our life, no matter what it takes."

"If it were up to me, we'd be on the next plane to Vegas. A big part of me regrets not taking you up on it three years ago." A slow smile spreads across his face. "There's an alternative if you're not ready for the fallout. You could get your own place. Then we could see each other whenever we want. You could stay with me, I could stay with you. It would give us more time to ease them into the idea of us being a couple."

Frustrated, I get up and go to the window. "I don't like that option. There's no reason for me to get my own place for optics. Last night we talked about me moving in with you. Getting married. Having babies."

"Of course I want all those things. Why are you upset?" Cillian follows me and touches my arm. "Talk to me."

I turn to him. "I'm not a kid. My dad trusts me to run the company. If he can't trust me to pick my life partner, it's his problem. If you don't want to live together just say…"

"…of course I want to live with you. It's all I want." Cillian pinches his nose.

"Don't overcomplicate it, then. Let me worry about my parents." I grip his elbows and plead, "If I want to spend the night with you while still living at my parents' house, it's my decision. I don't feel any shame about wanting to be with the man I love. If I move in with you, same thing. Telling my parents about our current relationship isn't something I'm shying away from, but slow your roll. We literally reconnected yesterday."

"Point taken. Which is why I wanted us to have options." Cillian takes my hands in his. "Are you opposed to telling your dad about our past?"

"No…" I hesitate.

"Are you sure?" He caresses the backs of my hands with his thumbs. "You said you aren't shying away about telling them about our 'current' relationship. What did you mean?"

I thread my fingers with his and look into his soulful hazel eyes. "I'd like to tell them the whole truth, eventually. But let's start with where we are now. We'll show them how committed we are, how much we mean to each other. Once they see us for who we are, then we explain the rest."

"I don't know." He doesn't look convinced. "I've developed trust with your father over the past three years. I think he might react badly if he finds out later. I'd prefer to be upfront, even if it's difficult."

I can't help but sigh. "But, we've already kept it from him, Cillian. I honestly don't know why, at this point, it's any of his business. I think it's best if we gauge their reaction and if it goes well, we can suss it out from there. I don't want to overwhelm them all at once, especially with everything my dad is going through."

"I don't agree." Cillian squeezes my hands. "But, if you feel strongly, let's roll with it."

Stepping even closer, I wind my arms around his waist. "I understand why you're skeptical." I take his hand and place it on my heart. "But, I've talked with my therapist at length about this. Most children—let alone adult children—don't feel a duty to disclose private details of their sex life to their parents. When we first met, I was under so much of my dad's control, I wasn't acting rationally. Having time away where I learned how to take care of myself in a country I wasn't familiar with has done wonders for my self-confidence. We're *not* going to hide our relationship. We also don't need to be compelled to explain ourselves. I love you. And, I don't need—or care if I have—my dad's approval to be in love with you."

Cillian leans down and kisses me so tenderly it cements what I know. We're in this together, no matter what. "You're a wise woman, Ivy Bright. I'm glad we talked this out. They're your parents. I'll follow your lead."

Our kiss deepens, sending a thrill through my entire body. I pull him closer, my fingers tangling in his hair. "Good," I murmur between kisses, "because we don't have much time before we're supposed to meet my friends, and my pussy is very empty."

"Poor little pussy." He cups my ass and lifts me, and I lock my legs around his waist. "How long do we have to fill her?"

I nip his chin. "Ten minutes, fifteen tops."

He whirls me around and sets me on the back of the couch and flips my skirt up. "Let me see what I can do."

"Aaahhhh!" I moan as he pulls my panties to the side and sucks my clit into his mouth. I buck beneath him, pulling on his hair as he worships me with his tongue.

"You taste like heaven." He inserts two fingers inside me.

He kisses my inner thigh before resuming his feast and curling his fingers against the spot that always makes me shatter into a thousand pieces. Soon, I'm soaring. Floating away on a cloud of ecstasy.

"Mission accomplished," Cillian purrs into my ear. "We even have a minute to spare."

He helps me up and I straighten my clothes. I look in the mirror. It's obvious I'm blissed out. "I'm flushed. My nipples are like bullets. They're gonna know what we were doing."

"Good." He walks over to the burning candles and blows them out. "Let them."

Hand in hand, we get into the elevator to meet my friends.

I feel like a million bucks. We tackled a tough topic, talked it through and worked it out. Cillian really listened, even though he disagreed with me.

And he made me come.

He shouldn't worry though. Telling my parents will be fine.

Mom will, anyway.

As for Dad? Hopefully he's changed. If I'm happy, he should support me.

And no one makes me happier than Cillian.

Thirty-Four

Two Weeks Later

THIRTY-EIGHT MONTHS.

As of today, the Bright Shipping headquarters job is officially my longest, and we have approximately six months to go.

It hasn't been easy. It's taken years to navigate the permitting process, tackle zoning issues with tribal river lands, and managing land use laws, which protect the historically polluted Duwamish River. Working with Peter Vander has been invaluable. I've developed a true passion for conservation.

Ivy is waiting for me to join her at a meeting with subcontractor Zack Fisk, who owns the company we've hired to handle the interior buildout. Last week the sheetrock was completed, which means it's time to finalize selecting finishing materials for the flooring, bathrooms, plumbing, and electric.

I approach from the shipping terminal and enter the building through what will eventually be a functioning loading dock. On my way to the staging area, I breathe in the smell of fresh primer on the newly sheet rocked walls. I love this stage. Everything is clean and pristine, on the cusp of completion.

Up ahead, Ivy, dressed in a simple white blouse and black slacks, is intently focused on Zack, who shows her samples of different tile. As I get nearer, the magnetic pull between us activates and she looks up to see me walking toward her. Our eyes meet, a jolt of electricity zaps me in my balls. A hint of a smile dances across her face.

"What do you think, Cillian?" Ivy holds up two tiles, the first a gray, textured stone, the other an off-white flecked ceramic.

I take them from her, deliberately brushing my fingers over hers. "Bathrooms?"

"Yeah. I love the stone tiles because they have a nice texture." Ivy drags her fingers over the surface and looks up at me longingly. "I think the dark color is a bit too harsh for the overall design, though."

I nod in agreement. "What about this one?" I pick up a lighter, more neutral tile and caress the surface. "It has the texture but might blend better with the rest of the design."

"*Ooooh*." She smiles, her eyes sparkling. "You're right. Great choice."

After we flirt our way through more selections, Zack packs the rest of his samples and leaves, not before waggling his eyes at me on the way out.

Once he's gone, Ivy and I set off on our mission. One we don't even need words for. Side by side, we trek through the building, out the front entrance and make our way to my office. On the way, we keep up the ruse of discussing the best materials for the flooring, but the sexual tension between us is palpable. Each brush of our hands sends my pulse racing.

All of the on-site offices are in converted shipping containers. Vander Architecture has one, Bright Shipping has another designated for the subcontractors, and McGloughlin Construction has the last.

Ivy follows me up the portable stairs and I can feel the anticipation building. The second we step inside and close and lock the door behind us, the floodgates open. Our lips crash together and our hands hungrily tear each other's clothes off. The passion between us is overwhelming, a force of nature we can't resist.

"I've missed you so much," Ivy murmurs between kisses, her fingers tangling in my hair.

"I've missed you too." I pull her closer and pull down her bra to expose her tits. "Every minute feels like an eternity without you."

We collapse on the small couch in the office, our bodies entwined. The world outside ceases to exist as we lose ourselves in each other. It's fast and furious because we don't have much time, but I make sure Ivy comes before I do. Afterward, we lie there, breathless and sated. Not for long, though.

The reality of our situation weighs heavily on both of us.

"Cillian," Ivy says softly, her head resting on my chest. "I hate we still haven't told my parents about us."

I rub her back. "I know. But with your dad's setback and his new treatment, we didn't have much of a choice."

The Monday after Ivy's birthday, a cancer-related complication landed Stan in the hospital. The scare led to a more-aggressive treatment plan, but thankfully, he's nearly recovered and feeling better than before.

"Yeah. His health is most important now, but it doesn't make it any easier. At least his prognosis has improved dramatically." Her voice is tinged with frustration and fear.

"There's no pressure, baby," I say, my heart aching at the thought of causing her more stress. "Obviously, we need to tell them sooner rather than later because you deserve more than a quick fuck in the office. Plus, everyone knows everything around here. We're gonna get caught. Even Zack could tell something's going on with us. We can't hide how we feel."

Ivy sighs and looks down, her fingers tracing circles on my hand resting on her thigh. "Maybe we should talk to my mom. At least then we've told one of my parents. She might understand and help us figure out the best way to approach my dad." She kisses my chest. "We can't keep this up. I want to wake up with you."

"Talking to your mom sounds like a good first step." I brush her hair from her face. "Especially if she helps us navigate this without causing more stress for your dad. I love you so much."

"I love you too," she says softly. "I'm sorry it's..."

Before Ivy can respond, a loud knock echoes through the trailer door. "Cillian! Stanley Bright just pulled up!" Brock's aware what's happening in here between Ivy and me. Thank God he has my back.

My heart races as I realize the urgency of our predicament.

Ivy's eyes widen in panic as she scrambles to grab her clothes. "Hurry, Cillian," she urges, buttoning up her blouse with fumbling fingers. She toes on her shoes and smooths her hair back into a ponytail.

Simultaneously, I hastily pull on my cargo pants and T-shirt, glancing around to make sure we haven't left any obvious signs of our tryst.

"We need to look busy." Her voice trembles as she hands me my beanie.

The situation is a fucking nightmare. We can't go on like this.

"Maybe we should tell him now," I suggest cautiously.

She shakes her head. "Not until I talk to Mom. I don't want to add more stress to his plate."

"I get it." I keep my voice gentle. "But this is crazy. *Look at us*. We're doing exactly what we said we wouldn't do."

A firm knock sounds at the door, making both of us freeze. Stan's voice follows. "Cillian? Why is the door locked?"

Ivy's eyes dart to mine and we share a moment of silent panic.

I take a deep breath and move to the door, unlocking it and pulling it open with what I hope is a casual smile. "Sorry, Stan. We were discussing some sensitive documents and didn't want any interruptions."

Ivy's dad raises an eyebrow, glancing between Ivy and me. "In the middle of the day?" he questions, clearly suspicious.

Ivy and I exchange a quick, nervous look, trying to play it off as best as we can.

Stan steps inside, his gaze sharp as it sweeps over the room. "I hope I'm not interrupting anything too important."

Ivy looks flustered and sick to her stomach. She clutches a stack of papers, which look like payroll sheets. "Yes, we were, um, discussing some sensitive budget adjustments. We didn't want the subcontractors to, uh..." she stammers, her cheeks flushing.

My God, she's terrible at this. Then again, I hate she's in this position in the first place.

"Yeah." I force a chuckle, trying to divert his attention. "We picked out interior finishes today and want to make sure everything is on track."

Stan's eyes narrow slightly as he continues to glance around the room, clearly trying to piece together what he's walked in on. "If you say so."

"You look well, how are you feeling?" I try to change the subject.

"I'm fine." He waves me off. "I wanted to discuss a few changes to the plans. Can we go over them now?"

"Of course." I motion to the table. "Let's get started."

After an intense hour of going over his ideas, Stan finally stands up, stretching his back slightly. "Alright, I think we've covered everything for now."

I get up too, extending my hand. "Thanks for coming by, Stan. We'll implement these changes right away."

"I'll keep you updated on the progress." Ivy's still trying to maintain her composure. I've never seen her rattled quite like this.

Stan shakes my hand firmly before turning to Ivy. "I appreciate it, sweetheart." His gaze lingers a moment longer, as if searching for something.

"Of course." She's unable to keep eye contact and glances away.

"One more thing—maybe keep the door unlocked during the workday." He says as he heads toward the door. "People could talk. I don't want anyone to question Ivy's professionalism."

Shit. Shit. Shit.

Ivy's cheeks slightly flush and I do my best to appear calm and collected.

"Thanks for thinking of me, Dad," Ivy mutters as we follow him to the door, exchanging glances behind his back conveying we're lucky to have narrowly gotten away with it.

Then, Stan's eyes catch something and he squints in the direction of the couch.

In a slow motion, horror-show way, Ivy and I both follow her dad's line of vision. There, on the floor under the couch, is a scrap of pink fabric—unmistakable.

Ivy's panties.

Stan pauses for a fraction of a second, his gaze lingering before he turns back to look at Ivy, then at me, then at her again.

His face hardens to stone. "Ivy, seems like you lost something." He points to the panties. His voice is low and measured, but the icy tension is palpable. "Dinner is at 5:30 sharp. *Do not be late.*"

Ivy's face drains of color, and she quickly retrieves her panties, stuffing them into her pocket with trembling hands. "Yes, Dad."

Stan gives a final, cutting look at both of us before turning on his heel and walking out without another word. The door closes behind him with a soft click, but the silence it leaves is deafening.

Ivy slumps down on the couch, her face flushed with embarrassment. "*Oh my God*, Cillian." Her voice quivers. "When he goes quiet like that...this is bad. *Really* bad."

An understatement, to say the least.

"*Fuck*. We knew this was complicated." I scrub my stubble with my fingers. "I didn't expect it to blow up like this."

"What am I gonna do?" Ivy hugs herself.

"We." I go to her and envelop her in my arms. "What are *we* going to do."

Ivy's not alone in this and I won't let her face her parents without me.

We wanted to stop hiding.

Now we've been outed in the worst possible way.

Thirty-Five

IVY

Moments Later

I'M FROZEN.

What the fuck happened?

The reality of what my dad saw sinks in. He *knows*. *Everything*.

My mortification is overwhelming, making it hard to breathe or think. This is not how I wanted him to find out.

I'm snapped back to reality when Cillian takes my hand. "I'm going with you," he says firmly, his eyes locking on to mine with determination. His support makes me feel slightly less panicked, but no less stressed.

"Um…I'm not sure if it's a good idea for you to be there…" I look down at my fingers fidgeting with the hem of my shirt. "I don't want to make things worse for us. For *you*."

I don't voice my other fears—how my dad can only control his anger so long. How he'll likely lash out and say anything to keep me in line, which will eviscerate all the progress we've made. Still, I'll take it if it means he won't turn this attention on Cillian. I want to protect him from my father's dark, cruel side.

Cillian tilts my chin up until our eyes meet. "Ivy, I'm in love with you. We're in this together. I'm not leaving you to handle this alone. We'll own up to it and face him as a couple." He kisses me tenderly. "You're the most important thing in my life and I won't let him tear us apart."

Tears well up but I manage a small smile. "Okay."

After we gather our things and lock up the office, Cillian and I get into my car. The drive is quiet, both of us lost in thought. The tension is thick, the last time I felt this anxious was three years ago when my dad got home early from his trip.

This is worse, though. Every mile closer, the atmosphere seems heavier.

When we get close to my neighborhood, I glance over at Cillian. His jaw is set with determination. What's about to go down presses on both of us.

I coast through the private gate into Medina, the grand estates and manicured lawns lining the private golf course come into view. My house is secluded on a quiet, tree-lined street abutting the lake, but the tranquil surroundings are in stark contrast to the turmoil churning inside me. Cillian places his hand on my thigh and squeezes, but his sweet gesture does nothing to steady my racing heart.

Being away gave me a false sense of bravado. Until today, my relationship with Dad had improved dramatically. This house even started to feel like home again.

Now, on the long driveway to the parking strip, I'm gripped by the same old dread I used to feel every time I walked through the door. This house, once again, resembles the mausoleum it used to be in the years after my brother's death. A prison my dad held me hostage in.

It's ominous.

"Ivy, it'll be okay. Remember, I've got you." Cillian brings my hand to his lips and kisses it. "No matter what happens."

I gaze at him and try to muster up courage I don't feel. "Okay."

Panic grips me the second we step through the front door, despite the familiar elegance of the house. I try to see it from

Cillian's perspective. The entryway is adorned with fine art and sculptures. French doors allow a ton of natural light to flood in. To the right, the dining room boasts a long, polished table ready for formal gatherings. The living room, with its floor-to-ceiling windows, offers a breathtaking view of the lake and the lush gardens outside. The air is thick with the scent of fresh flowers from the veranda.

Visually, it's peaceful here. A stark contrast to the tension vibrating in the air.

"Dad?" I call out, my voice trembles with anxiety. "I'm here."

"In the great room," his voice booms, sending a shiver down my spine.

Cillian follows me down the hallway to the back of the house where we find him sitting in his favorite chair, a drink in his hand. A complete no-no with his medication, but what can I say?

His eyes are cold and unforgiving as he gives Cillian a contemptuous frown. "I see you had the audacity to show your face," he sneers. "*Sit.*"

Here we go.

We comply, taking a seat on the couch across from him. I feel like I'm suffocating under his stare, which goes on for what feels like ten minutes.

Finally, my dad's eyes narrow on Cillian. "You have a lot of fucking nerve, you predatory piece of shit," he snaps. "Sneaking around like a goddamn coward. Fucking my daughter, who's half your age. You're disgusting. You're a disgrace. And you think it's appropriate to come into my home *uninvited*?"

"Dad, *stop*!" I plead. "You don't know the whole story. Cillian and I are in love. Please, let us explain."

"I don't want to hear it, Ivy. It's fucking ridiculous." He cuts me off, returning his icy gaze on Cillian. "I trusted you with my business. Treated you like a son. And you repay me by screwing my daughter and pretending you give a shit about her? She's only been back for a few weeks. What kind of thirty-something degenerate wants to get his dick wet with a barely twenty-one-year-old girl? You're a pathetic excuse for a man. You *disgust* me."

My stomach drops to the floor. Every word from my dad hits me like a physical blow. My worst nightmare is unfolding before my eyes and the room feels like it's closing in on me. My face burns with shame and embarrassment. I want to speak up, to defend Cillian, but I know how this type of conversation goes with my dad. There's no getting a word in during one of these incidents.

I'm horrified, helpless, and powerless to protect the man I love from a relentless verbal onslaught.

"Mr. Bright, I—" Cillian attempts to speak.

"Shut the fuck up," he barks. "And *you*," he rounds on me, his eyes burning with fury, "fucking one of my contractors like a common whore. Do you know how humiliating this is for me? For *you*?"

Cillian leans forward, his protective stance clear even while seated. "I will not stand by and allow you to speak to Ivy this way." His voice is low and controlled, but filled with conviction. "I love your daughter. No one will tear her down in my presence. Not even you."

"*Love*?" Dad's face contorts with rage. "You're nothing but an alcoholic loser. You think I don't know about your drinking problem? *Think again*. I won't let you corrupt my daughter for one more minute." He leans in closer in an attempt to intimidate Cillian. "You're *fired*, effective immediately. Clear your shit off my jobsite by tomorrow and get the *fuck* out of my house. I *never* want to see your disgusting face again."

Tears stream down my face. This is going off the rails. I try to interject, "No, Dad, *please*—"

"*Shut. The. Fuck. Up*," my dad shouts at the top of his lungs. "I don't want to hear anything from a whore like you. You'll sleep with anyone who gives you the time of day. It's an embarrassment."

Cillian turns to me, devastated. His eyes are filled with a pain that mirrors my own. "Ivy," his voice cracks, "I can't stay if he's asked me to leave. I don't want to make things worse but I won't leave you here with him like this. It's not safe."

His words send a fresh wave of panic through my body. My heart aches at the thought of him leaving, but the vitriol I'll be subjected to without witnesses terrifies me even more.

"*Safe*? Who the fuck are you to tell me how to take care of my own daughter? If you think I'll allow you to waltz out of here with Ivy, you're delusional." My dad's face contorts into a menacing snarl. "She stays *here* with her family."

I stand, my voice wobbly but resolute. "No. I'm not a child anymore. I make my own decisions. I love Cillian and I want to be with him. You can't keep me here like a prisoner anymore. This is my life and I can choose who I want to be with."

"You *slut*," my father spews. "I should have never let your mother take you to Italy on my fucking dime. I *knew* you couldn't be trusted.

My knees buckle and I feel the blood drain from my face. How could my dad speak to me like this? It's like he's saved up three years' worth of pent-up anger and is unleashing it all on me now. Does he really think so little of his own daughter?

The room spins, and I'm on the verge of fainting from the sheer mortification and pain of his words. Cillian's reaction is swift. Protective. He stands and scoops me up into his arms as if I weigh nothing. I cling to him, my tears soaking his shirt. He carries me toward the front door with purposeful strides with my father's hateful words echoing in my ears.

"*Get out*, both of you! You're *dead* to me, Ivy! You hear me? *DEAD*! You won't get a dime from me." His words slice through the air and cut my heart in two as we reach the front door.

I hear a thud behind us and manage to glance over Cillian's shoulder. My father has collapsed to the floor. "*Dad*!"

"Call or text 9-1-1 then call your mom." Cillian flicks his gaze to where my dad lies moaning. "I need to get you away from him after what happened, but we can't let him lie there. He needs help."

His grip tightens and he carries me out of the house to the car where he places me gently in the passenger seat then gets in beside me. My hands are shaking uncontrollably. I manage to pull out my phone and dial 9-1-1, explaining the situation as best as I can. "Please, my father has cancer. He was drinking. I think it interfered with his medication and he collapsed." I give them the address. "Send someone fast."

Once the operator assures me help is on the way, I dial my mom's number. It takes a few rings before she answers. "Mom, where are you? I had a horrible fight with Dad and he fell down. I called for an ambulance, it's on the way."

"I'm next door at my book club, I'll be right over." She sounds frightened and I hear her mumble something to the ladies as she leaves.

Cillian takes the phone from my trembling hand. "Mrs. Bright, this is Cillian McLoughlin." He keeps his voice calm, though his knuckles are white against the steering wheel. "This might come as a shock, but your daughter, Ivy, and I have been seeing each other. Stan found out today. It didn't go well." He takes a deep breath as he listens to whatever my mom is saying before answering. "He got worked up and said some unforgivable things to your daughter. He kicked us out of the house and we were on our way out when he collapsed. Uh-huh. Uh-huh. Yeah, less than a minute ago. No, he's breathing. He's alive." He stops as my mom speaks. "Yeah, that's correct. Ivy called 9-1-1. We're in the driveway and won't leave until you or the ambulance gets here. Then I'm taking Ivy to my place. She can't go back inside after the abuse he hurled at her."

Cillian keeps the phone out until my mom scurries into the house, glancing at us with a quick, frantic wave before disappearing inside.

Everything is blurry. I'm vaguely aware of a siren and Cillian backing up the car and driving away as the ambulance pulls in. I'm more focused on his hand, which rests on my thigh. His touch keeps me from slipping into some sort of fugue state.

All of a sudden, I can't hold it in any longer. I curl into a ball and sob and sob and sob. My body shakes uncontrollably.

The secret about my dad's dark side is out.

And now, I can never go back home.

Thirty-Six

CILLIAN

Half Hour Later

I'VE NEVER BEEN SO scared in my life.

Or so fucking angry.

We hit traffic and it's tested every ounce of my patience to get to my townhouse, but finally we're here.

My heart aches for Ivy. She's curled up in the passenger seat shaking like a leaf. Her eyes are vacant and unfocused.

Seeing her like this, shattered by her father's cruelty, makes me realize how horrific things must have been growing up. She's never shared much about this part of her home life, other than what happened to her brother and how traumatic it was for her parents. Jesus Christ, with all their wealth and status, they've done Ivy such a great disservice.

How am I going to help her through this?

My own mind is reeling from what happened. The things her father said. The venom in his words...I've never seen this side of him before. For the past three years, he's been tough but also fair and kind. It's hard to reconcile the monster we encountered with the man who laughed and joked with me and my folks at Ivy's birthday party a couple of weeks ago.

Now's not the time to dissect it, though. I park the car and rush around to help her out. She attempts to stand, but her legs buckle immediately. Without another thought, I scoop her into my arms, cradle her quivering body against mine and carry her inside all the way up to my bedroom where I gently lay her down on the bed.

The townhouse is blessedly silent, a stark contrast to the chaos we experienced at Ivy's house. It's hard to believe she's never been here before—we couldn't make it happen after we got back together with her father's setback. As I tuck her into bed, I hope the unfamiliar surroundings won't scare her.

"I'm here for you, baby," I whisper as I unbutton her blouse. "Let me help you get comfortable."

Ivy's eyes are almost blank as I undress her and help her into one of my sweatshirts. My clothes are far too big, but at least she'll be warm. I pull back the duvet and gently slide her under the blankets. Then, I undress and slip in beside her, enveloping her in my arms. She's cold. Or in shock. I don't know, but her body shivers uncontrollably. I press my lips to her forehead, wishing I could take away what just happened.

Once I've gotten her tucked tightly in the crook of my arm, I search for information on my phone about how to help someone experiencing a traumatic shock. I read about the symptoms—chills, dizziness, shakiness, rapid heart-beat—check, check, check, and check. *Shit.* Apparently, her brain is trying to protect her from the emotional abuse she experienced. For now, all I can do is provide her with comfort and support.

I'm not a patient man, though. If she doesn't settle within the hour, I'm bringing her to the emergency room.

Thankfully, Ivy begins to relax a bit. I kiss her forehead and whisper soothing words. "I'm here, Ivy. I'm not going anywhere. I love you."

She turns and nestles against me, wrapping her arms around my waist. Almost like a reflex, her entire body stiffens and with one final full-body shudder, she finally let's go, collapsing against me. I hold her tighter, feeling a surge of protectiveness.

I'll do whatever it takes to help her heal. She deserves to be happy and loved without conditions or judgment.

Ivy's breathing steadies and she falls asleep. I wait until she's completely out and, careful not to wake her, gently slide out of bed.

My da answers on the second ring. "Cillian? What's going on?"

"Not good news. Stan caught us...uh, in the office in the most humiliating way. It was horrendous. He demanded Ivy come home immediately, so I went with her for support—to stand by her and face the consequences." I pace outside the bedroom door, phone pressed to my ear, quietly recounting the evening's events in a frenzy. "Fuck, Da. He accused me of being a predator, corrupting his daughter, and ruining her life. Even worse, he slut-shamed his own daughter in the most despicable way."

There's a pause on the other end before he responds, "Jaysus, Cillian. Are you okay?"

"No. He fired me on the spot. I'm supposed to get everything off the Bright jobsite immediately. Before morning." I wince saying it out loud. I've never been fired from anything in my life.

"Kill." My dad sighs loudly. "I don't give a feck about the job. Are you and Ivy okay?"

How can I answer? I can't even begin to process the horror we endured—it was the most gut-wrenching moment of my life. Stan's accusations about me sting, but it's the venom he spat at Ivy that truly tears at my soul. Hearing him degrade the woman I love has crystallized how far I'm willing to go to ensure her happiness.

"Ivy's not doing well." A sob escapes before I can choke it back. "He kicked her out. Her whole life has been shattered. I can't leave her alone."

Da doesn't hesitate. "Aye. Of course. I'll handle Bright. You focus on Ivy."

"He's in the hospital." I shake my head in disbelief. "Her mom texted Ivy a couple hours ago. It seems like he's stable but he'll be there a few days. My information is coming from a flash on a screen, though. I'll know more after Ivy wakes up."

"For fuck's sake. Take care of her, I've got your back, son." Da says goodbye and we hang up.

I return to Ivy's side to cuddle her while she sleeps. My mind races with thoughts of our future and how we'll navigate this mess. What will become of her family? Bright Shipping? McGloughlin Construction?

I have no answers.

The entire situation is a disaster.

Shit. I must have fallen asleep.

Ivy faces away from me. I'm spooning her tightly as she snores softly.

It's morning. The first light of dawn filters through the blinds and a heavy sense of dread settles over me.

The memory of her father's vicious tirade rushes back. His savage words echo like a relentless drumbeat. Ivy is strong, but I'm terrified. This isn't how I envisioned us starting our lives.

I have no idea what comes next.

Ivy stirs in my arms and rolls onto her back. A few minutes later, her eyes flutter open. For a moment, she looks disoriented, but then she sees me, and a small smile crosses her lips.

"Good morning." I comb my fingers through her hair.

"I don't remember coming up here," she murmurs. "Are we at your townhouse?"

"Yeah. How are you feeling?" I trace a finger along her shoulder.

"I think, better..." She scrunches up her nose. Her eyes still hold a shadow of the night before. "I'm sorry..."

"No, baby." I gather her to me. "You have nothing to apologize for. None of this is your fault. What your dad said was unhinged. I think he needs help. I've never experienced anything like it."

Tears pool in her eyes then spill down her cheeks. My heart breaks for her. "Last night was as bad as it's ever been."

"*Ivy*." I cannot believe anyone, let alone her father, would ever be nasty to such a sweet soul. "Has he really spoken to you like that before?"

She takes a shaky breath. "Well... after my brother died he was angry all the time. He'd lose his temper with me over stupid things. My grades. Doing the dishes. Cleaning my room. I generally tried hard not to do anything to set him off. He rarely loses control around other people."

"He yells at your mom the same way?" I cannot imagine, in my wildest dreams, speaking to my daughter cruelly, let alone my wife and family.

Then I remember how I spoke to Ivy once...

"Well..." Ivy pauses and her eyes grow distant. "I've never seen him do it. Look, I'm not trying to defend him, but losing a child is possibly the worst thing to happen to someone."

"Sure, and..." I hold my tongue, she's been through enough for now. I'm not going to rip her dad a new asshole...*yet*.

"He and my mom reacted differently in their grief. He lashed out. She clammed up." Ivy squints into the distance, as if trying to recall. "Honestly, I guess it's possible. He never spoke to me like that in front of her either, so maybe that's how he gets away with it. No witnesses."

I'm incensed but try to keep my shit together. "Still, she let him take it out on you."

"No, she truly wasn't around," Ivy says this matter-of-factly. "Before yesterday, the worst he'd been was three years ago, when he found out I hadn't been spending nights at home while I was with you. He screamed at me for days. Called me similar appalling names. It's why I left." Her voice breaks and tears well up in her eyes. "But last night... I thought we'd moved past it. To have it happen again was worse than anything I ever imagined. I think I blacked out."

"I feel sick about it," I admit. "I wish we'd have told him after your birthday. I can't unhear what he said to you."

"I thought he'd changed," Ivy murmurs. "We tried every-thing. Went to family counseling..."

Ivy doesn't say anything more but I know from the shud-dering of her body she's crying. We lie there for a while longer, holding each other. There really isn't much more to say. Now is my time to be there for my girl and, hopefully, make her feel safe.

At some point, my stomach roars. We didn't have dinner last night and I'm starving. "How about I make us some breakfast?"

"Sounds good. I don't think I can handle anything heavy, though." Her voice is weak, defeated.

I kiss her forehead. "How about some scrambled eggs and toast? Something light to start the day."

"Yeah." She looks up at me and I'm relieved to see bit of color returning to her cheeks. "Perfect."

I lead Ivy, who wears only my sweatshirt, through my townhouse. "It's hard to believe you've never seen this place." I open the door to the spacious living room. "To think we planned on you moving in after your birthday."

Ivy looks out the window into the backyard, not really paying attention. "I probably should talk to my mom. Despite everything, I can't stop worrying about my dad. I need to know he's okay."

"Here's your phone, it was on the charger." I move behind her and clasp my arms around her middle. "You can call her while I make the eggs."

"I'm scared." Ivy leans back against me. "I'm not sure what to say. Or, how I'm supposed to feel."

I kiss the back of her head several times. "Let's try to take it one step at a time. Food first. Decisions later."

Taking her hand, I lead Ivy to the kitchen and get her settled at the counter.

Ivy immediately scans her messages. Her eyes widen and she looks up at me and tells me what I already know. "Mom's been texting since last night. Dad's stable and resting. She wants to see us. To check on me and talk to you too. She wants to understand what went down."

"Do you want to talk to her?" I set her eggs on the counter.

Ivy hesitates. "Um...I don't know, I don't feel up to facing more anger or disappointment."

"Let's take the day for ourselves, then. Better yet, we'll make it a self-care day for you, baby." I gently rub her back.

Ivy spins around on her stool and hooks her heels around my knees. She takes my hand and brings it to her bare pussy and moves my fingers through her folds. My finger finds her clit.

"What do you need, baby?" I circle her nub. "Do you need to come? A little relief?"

Ivy nods furiously. "*Yeah*. Does that make me a slut?"

Anger burns deep in my soul.

"Of course not. If an orgasm will help release some tension, it's the ultimate self-care." I caress her face as I slide my fingers through her wetness. "Let me make it better."

Ivy nods but looks away, almost like she's ashamed of expressing her needs.

I slip my fingers inside her and rub. "Enjoying pleasure with the man you love is normal. Don't let your father's vile words make you feel less-than. When we have sex, it's sacred. Every time."

Ivy spreads her legs, allowing me better access. Soon she's writhing against my hand.

I pick up the pace. "Does that feel okay?"

"You fucking me will feel even better." Ivy tugs my sweatshirt off, leaving her naked, splayed on the stool, with my fingers plunging in and out of her.

My breath catches. "Are you sure…"

"Yes." She yanks my joggers down and my cock springs free, standing at full attention.

Okay, then. Everything else can wait.

My woman needs me.

Thirty-Seven

Later That Afternoon

I'M GROGGY AND DISORIENTED.

My body tingles.

I'm confused about where I am, then realize I'm alone, naked on the couch in Cillian's living room covered by a fluffy throw.

We've made love for hours today and I feel empty without him inside me.

I need him. *Now.* There's probably some sort of psychological explanation why I'm insatiable, but I don't care to dissect. I want what I want.

Cillian.

I wrap the blanket around me and get up to find him. I hear the faint sound of running water, which seems to be coming from upstairs so I move in that direction. Aha! He's in the shower.

Perfect.

At the same moment I walk through the door, Cillian emerges from the bathroom, a towel slung low around his waist. His hair is wet and tousled, droplets of water cling to his chiseled, bare chest. He's magnificent. I can't believe this man is finally mine.

All mine.

Heat swirls through me like a torrential storm, whooshing its way through my core, up my chest, and down my limbs. My pussy clenches. My nipples pucker.

A devilish grin spreads across Cillian's face. He steps toward me. "Did you miss me?"

"A lot." I drop my blanket and look into his eyes. I'm completely bare and vulnerable. Three years ago, I stood before him exactly like this and he rejected me. Today, his eyes sweep over me with such deep regard, it feels like he can see into my very soul.

This time his reverential gaze is filled with complete acceptance.

Love.

Cillian lunges toward me and his mouth claims mine. Hard. Insistent. His towel falls to the ground and I jack his cock as our kisses grow deeper. His rough hands roam all over my body, cupping my ass, palming my tits, pushing into my hair, where he fists it tight against the base of my neck.

His thumb finds my clit, circling it as I caress and fondle his balls. Cillian lowers his mouth to my breast, sucking my nipple in between his teeth, triggering slithers of pleasure through my body.

"Tell me if you want to stop. If you're sore," Cillian rasps. "Otherwise, you're at my mercy. I'm gonna make you forget everything."

"I never want to stop." I pump his cock faster and his mouth finds mine again.

We devour each other roughly until I sag and nearly fall over, but Cillian is ready. He lifts me and carries me to his bed, laying me down gently. I reach for him and he moves over me, kissing me deeply as he aligns his body with mine. His cock glides through my wetness and finds its way home.

We stare into each other's eyes, the intensity of our con-nection makes me feel floaty. He's buried to the hilt. I wrap my legs around his hips and angle up until he's so deep there's no difference between Cillian's body and mine. A surge of emotions consume me then every stress falls away and I'm laser focused on what's happening between us in this moment.

The warmth of his body against mine. The stretch of my pussy around his throbbing cock. The taste of his mouth as he kisses me long and slow. Every roll of his hips.

Raw passion takes over and we move to a rhythm all our own. Rolling and thrashing on the bed with abandon as our bodies and needs take over. We're wild. Groping and moaning. Demanding and pleading. Loving and tender. Awestruck and ecstatic.

Before I know it, I'm riding him. Swiveling and rolling my hips. My tits bounce and jiggle and he squeezes them and pinches my nipples.

"*Ohhhhhhhh*" His crown hits my spot perfectly. He releases my breasts and grabs my ass with both hands, enabling him to drive up into me hard. Fast. Punishing. *Incredible*. It's too much. Too good. My entire body tenses as the most intense sensation of my life courses through me. It's a euphoric wave beginning deep in my core and radiating outward, leaving me utterly consumed by the sensation.

"*Ohhhhhhhmmmmyyyyyyyygoooooodddddddd*. Come with me. Cillian..." I beg, rubbing my clit furiously in time to his fucking.

With a long, tortured groan, Cillian flips me onto the bed. He pistons his hips like he's burrowing himself into my body permanently. Every nerve ending is electrified, each pulse of ecstasy builds upon the last until I'm suspended in a moment of pure, unadulterated bliss.

Suddenly, my pussy gushes like a geyser, drenching us. Cillian's entire body shudders and he growls out my name, emptying everything he has until I'm overflowing with our combined release.

I'm a moaning, writhing mess, unable to comprehend how my body is capable of such pleasure, but he's not done. Cillian pulls out and kneels between my legs, placing my thighs over his shoulders. I'm unable to move, but he lifts my hips up to his face, buries into my pussy, and laps us up with a feral abandon.

His tongue is everywhere, in every crevice, through every fold, settling on my clit. His entire mouth engulfs me. I shudder through yet another mammoth orgasm.

This the single most intimate moment of my life.

We're finally free.

Unbothered by our mess, Cillian eases me down and gathers me in his arms. "You squirted, I've never seen anything like it. I had to know what we tasted like."

"Let me sample." I can barely move but I manage to tilt my face up to him. We kiss, swirling our tongues together. "I love it. I *loved* it."

Completely satiated, I rest my head against his chest. My leg is flung over his thigh and my arm is draped over his stomach. He kisses my temple and holds me tighter. "I'll do whatever it takes to make you happy, Ivy. I've never loved someone like I love you. I never will again."

"I've always known you were meant for me. My soul connected with yours the second we saw each other." I snuggle closer and peer up at him. "When you're inside me, I feel free and alive. *Complete*. I'll love you forever."

Cillian looks at me with such intensity, it makes my heart skip a beat. "You're my everything, baby. I have something to say, though."

"*Mmmmmkay*." I kiss his chest.

"After hearing your dad berate you viciously...I'm still so fucking ashamed for saying things you'll never unhear. I will never, ever, *ever* speak to you out of anger or fear again. No matter what I'm going through." He kisses me softly. "I *want* you. I've *always* wanted you. I'll want you *forever*. *Mo shíorghrá.*"

"The way you say 'muh-heer-grah' is so beautiful. You've never told me what it means." I trace his eyebrow with my finger.

He cradles my face in his hand. "It means 'my eternal love' in Gaelic."

"*Ohhhh*." I take a deep breath and let his words sink in. "It's the first thing you ever said to me when I saw you at Kells."

Cillian nods. "*Yeah*."

Tears well up, but this time they're because I'm grateful. "You're nothing like my father. I know you were hurt and said things you didn't mean, but you weren't being vindictive or ruthless. It was a painful blow to learn I'd lied to you about things that were so important. You still took accountability, apologized and meant it. We've both made mistakes and now we're past it. Let's put it behind us."

"And, in that vein, I think we should pack up your stuff so you can move in while your dad's in the hospital." Cillian squeezes me tightly. "That way, you won't have to face him until you're ready."

The reality of what happened settles in. The thing is, I'm not the only one who endured my father's wrath. Cillian took a lashing too. "What about you? You've been focused on me all day, what's going on at the jobsite?"

"I have no idea. My dad is handling it. My only focus today is making sure you're okay." Cillian gazes into my eyes.

"Well, if fucking me senseless is making sure I'm okay, I'm lucky to have you." I comb my fingers through his hair.

He chuckles, but looks thoughtful. "Ahh, well, I'm lucky you enjoy being fucked senseless." He cups my breast and runs his hand down my side. "Promise me, if it gets to be too much, let me know. I don't want you to feel overwhelmed. You're dealing with a lot."

"I'm good." My heart swells at his care for me.

He feathers kisses on my jaw. "We'll pick up the pieces, baby. We're going to be happy."

"I'm *already* happy," I assure him. "It may seem strange, but I feel relieved. I keep thinking—if my dad reacted badly about our current relationship, thank God we didn't tell him you're the guy from my past."

"Yeah..." Cillian doesn't finish.

"To be clear, I don't feel the need to hide anything. But I also don't owe him an explanation or require his permission. It's none of his fucking business. He tore me apart yesterday and I'm not sure how we come back from it." I trail my hand across Cillian's arm.

"Yeah...I have to say, I feel the same way." His eyes blink closed. I realize he must be exhausted.

I rest my head against his chest, feeling the steady rise and fall of his breath. "It's our time now."

We lie in silence, savoring the moment of calm. I can't help but believe in fate.

Meeting Cillian changed the trajectory of my life. He showed me how to love. Taught me to believe in myself. No matter how we got to where we are today, I think he and I would have always found our way to each other.

Mo shíorghrá.

It was always meant to be.

I'm where I belong and I'm never leaving again.

Thirty-Eight

CILLIAN

The Next Morning

HOLY SHIT.

What the actual fuck has happened over the past couple days?

Yawning, I roll over toward the window. I slept hard. Ivy's warm body is pressed against mine, which means she's where she belongs.

I'm glad we both got some rest. It was probably inevitable. I fucked her so many times yesterday, we eventually collapsed with exhaustion.

Christ.

Until the day I die, I'll never forget the look on Stan's face when he spotted Ivy's panties under the couch in my office. His reaction was exactly what I'd feared. I wish to God he hadn't found out about us the way he did—but there's no turning back time. At least there's no more sneaking around.

We're free to be together.

Finally.

I gently kiss Ivy's forehead before slipping out of bed to let her sleep a bit longer.

Stepping into the hallway, I check my phone. I've missed quite a few texts from my da and I really need to speak with him—I can't abdicate my responsibilities forever. I briefly glance back at Ivy—who stirs slightly but doesn't wake—then quietly slip downstairs to make the call.

"Morning, Da." I sink into my recliner to prepare for the worst. Considering all the logistics, pulling off this particular jobsite won't be easy, there are too many components to the whole operation.

Except, he seems almost cheery. "Morning, son. How's Ivy holding up?"

"She's sleeping. Yesterday things seemed to stabilize. At least as far as she and I are concerned." I realize my anger has dissipated slightly, if not completely. "We're heading to her house so she can pack. She's moving in with me."

"Good man yerself," Da encourages. "Now, then. It might be a bit premature, but tomorrow is family dinner. Everyone's in town and I think you should bring Ivy. Might as well jump into the deep end."

"I'll ask her." Ivy's been through a lot, adding a dinner with my entire family may not be something she's up for yet. "Anyway, I'm calling for a reason. Tell me how things went down yesterday."

My dad takes a deep breath. "Business as usual."

"Da! Stan fired me." I clench my teeth. "I don't want to rub salt..."

"Cillian, listen. Let cooler heads prevail. I met with our lawyer, Joe Finney, who walked me through the contract." Da describes the analysis. "Bright Shipping can't fire McGloughlin Construction without us breaching our agreement. Dating his daughter is not a breach, so he has no legal authority to fire us. Technically, the contract doesn't allow us to walk off the job either. For now, I'll take over and try to talk to Stan once he's released from the hospital."

It feels like I've shed a heavy coat on a hot day. "What a relief. I'm still worried. How are you holding up with all this?"

"I'm alright. I don't mind hard work." I can feel him smile through the phone.

"Thanks, Da." I feel grateful to have his help and support. "I'll check on the other projects Monday. Ivy's putting on a brave face, but she's shaken. What happened is a lot to process. I'm putting her first." I lightly pound the railing with my fist for emphasis.

My father's voice softens. "You're doing the right thing, son."

"Well, we're heading back to the scene of the crime to get her things soon, so I'd better go. I'll let you know if we'll be there for dinner on Sunday." I hang up and head back upstairs, finding Ivy awake and sitting on the edge of the bed, staring at her phone.

"Everything okay?" I sit beside her.

"Yeah, my mom's been texting me." She turns her phone to show me. "She's home and wants to talk. I think we have to face her before I pack. I plan on coming clean. About everything. I really don't care what my parents know at this point, I need to move on from these secrets."

I stand, hold out my hand and waggle my eyebrows. "It's your choice, baby. First, let's shower. I'll make sure you 'come clean.'"

"Oh, I'm counting on it." Ivy actually giggles, which sounds like music considering the heaviness of the past two days.

One long, sexy shower later, I load a couple of empty suitcases into my truck and we depart. On the way, Ivy's fingers drum nervously on her thigh as she stares out the window. I reach over and squeeze her hand, offering silent reassurance. None of this is easy for her, but she's resilient.

Ivy's mom, Allison, is waiting for us outside.

"Hi, Mom." Ivy's voice is wary when she gets out of the truck.

Allison embraces her but doesn't look at me. "Ivy, are you okay? I'm confused about what's happening. Let's go inside and talk."

I follow her into the house and notice the tension is palpable, which is to be expected, I guess. It's funny, I've always liked Allison when we've interacted but she's giving me the cold shoulder. It makes me nervous.

Ivy sits down on the couch opposite her mother. For a second, I contemplate sitting in the chair next to her out of respect. On second thought, if we're going to present a united front, I'm staying by Ivy's side. I sit next to her on the couch.

The three of us stare across the coffee table for a few long moments.

Finally, Allison breaks the silence. "Ivy. Please tell me what happened last night. Your father is furious."

"Mom, Dad walked in on Cillian and I yesterday. We've been seeing each other and it's serious, but I need to tell you the entire story." Ivy takes a deep breath and looks at me. I nod my encouragement. "We don't want any more secrets."

Allison's eyes widen. "Secrets? What do you mean?"

Ivy's voice is steady as she explains our history from the day of her birthday to us meeting at Kells, the development of our relationship to the demise. "The thing is, Cillian is the guy I never identified to you. He and I have never gotten over our breakup. When I got back into town, we realized our feelings hadn't diminished. We're still deeply in love and were planning to tell you and Dad after my birthday weekend, except Dad had the setback and we decided to wait until he felt better. The other day, he showed up to the job site unexpectedly and found us in Cillian's office after we'd..."

"Oh." Allison's expression softens, but there's a hint of worry. "How embarrassing."

"Embarrassing doesn't even begin to cover it," I admit, looking at Ivy's mom directly. "If it's any comfort, I've loved your daughter from the moment I met her and I've never stopped. I broke it off back then because I thought our age difference was too great..."

"...because I lied and told you I was twenty-four," Ivy interjects, then looks at her mom. "I've told you most of the story over the years and now you know the whole truth. I don't want you or Dad to be angry at Cillian. I'm the one who deceived him."

Ivy's mom looks between us, crestfallen. "All these years you've kept this a secret?"

"I was scared of what Dad would say. How he'd react." Ivy leans forward. "We're done hiding, now. Cillian and I are in this for the long haul. I'd love your support, but even if I don't have it, I choose him."

Ivy reaches over and takes my hand and threads her fingers with mine. Our eyes lock and, in this moment, the invisible weight we've been carrying seems to dissolve, leaving only clarity and strength between us.

Allison takes a deep breath to compose herself. "Your father is a stubborn man, but he loves you. He'll come around eventually."

"Can we address an elephant in the room?" I try to keep my voice steady. "Mrs. Bright, I know this is a lot to take in, and you don't know me well—what shocked me to my core was the way Stan spoke to Ivy the other day. It was unbelievably cruel and demeaning. I won't stand by and let it happen again. Ivy deserves much better from her father."

Ivy squeezes my hand and looks at her mom. "Ever since Forrest died, I've endured Dad's outbursts. I've lived in fear of setting him off. Of disappointing him." She stops for a moment and looks up at the ceiling. "I came back this year thinking things had changed. I was ready to step in and take my place at Bright Shipping, but now I can't bear to be around him. He can be the most generous, loving person in the world, but the flip side is scary."

"Don't be so judgmental, darling. He's never going to stop grieving. Losing Forrest shattered us—he got angry. He takes it out sometimes..." Allison trails off.

"*Judgmental*?" Ivy raises her voice. "I'm the one who was being judged. *Everything* I did."

"Until you have children of your own, you can't understand what it's like to learn your eighteen-year-old daughter—your only living child—put herself in a potentially dangerous situation. We didn't know the circumstances or who the guy was. He *could* have been a predator. How could we have protected you? You broke our trust." She shakes her finger at Ivy, then her demeanor changes. "I knew he was angry with you—it didn't warrant how he handled it, though. When I came home, you couldn't even get out of bed, a shell of my beautiful, vibrant girl. I thought sending you to Italy would give you and your father a fresh start, but I see now it wasn't enough."

Shocked, I glance at Ivy. She never told me about the aftermath and what she endured. It makes sense given how she reacted to his vitriol the other day.

"I was crushed." Ivy's voice breaks. "And it sucks to learn nothing's changed. At this point, I'm not interested in revisiting the past. We're here to talk about the future."

"I can't lose you." Her mom buries her head in her hands.

Ivy gets up and sits on the other side of her mom and hugs her tightly. "You and I will be fine, but unless things change with Dad, I can't risk allowing him in my life. I don't want to live in fear. If he gets help, I'm willing to try and rebuild our relationship. If not, then I need to cut him out of my life."

Observing Ivy and her mom gives me some perspective. All families all go through their ups and downs. How you navigate the obstacles is what's most important.

"Until yesterday, I respected Stan immensely. If he's willing to put in the effort and make some serious changes, this can turn itself around." I stand up and move toward the door. "Ivy, I'll grab the suitcases."

When I return, Ivy and her mom are talking softly. She's smiling, at least. I move closer and relief washes over me. Her mom extends her hand.

"Cillian, I look forward to getting to know you," she says warmly. "I'm sorry this isn't the best of circumstances. I always thought meeting Ivy's first serious boyfriend would be different."

Ivy and I glance at each other and she looks back at her mother. "Mom, to be clear, Cillian is my first and last boyfriend. There won't be anyone else."

"*Oh*. I see." Her eyes widen.

Ivy joins me and takes my hand, giving me a small, hopeful smile. "Let's pack my things."

I can't help but admire how strong she is.

Ivy's room is elegantly furnished with antique white furniture, a plush canopy bed, and walls adorned with classic artwork. In other words, sterile. There's nothing to indicate anyone under forty had anything to do with the decor. We work quickly, filling suitcases with her clothes and personal items.

I know we're both relieved the sneaking around, stolen moments, and fear of getting caught is behind us now. Ivy and I are finally free to be a couple. Openly. Honestly.

On our way out, as I load the suitcases into the trunk, Allison stops Ivy. "I want you to know I'll support you and Cillian. I want you to be happy."

"Thanks, Mom. It means everything to me." Ivy hugs her and the embrace lasts a long time.

Eventually, Ivy gets in the passenger seat and we drive off.

Whether we're ready or not, we've chosen each other.

I can't wait to begin our new chapter.

Thirty-Nine

4 Months Later

Families are weird.

Weird and wonderful.

As usual, the drive to Rory and Maureen's house is filled with excited anticipation. Sunday dinners are part of our regular weekend routine these days. Sometimes it's the four of us and other days, like tonight, the whole gang is here. Every now and then my mom joins us if my dad's out of town.

Considering my own family is still broken, I look forward to connecting with Cillian's family each week. All of them have welcomed me with open arms and the warmth filling this home reminds me of my family before Forrest died.

Cillian and I always seem to be the last to arrive and today is no exception. There's no parking on the street and Cillian is forced to block Connor's SUV in the driveway. I'm happy they're in town, it's always fun to hang out with Ronni, she's become like a big sister to me even though she always jokes I could be her daughter.

I guess, technically, it's true—the ribs about my age are lighthearted now. Everyone can see how much Cillian and I love each other, and his brothers tease us more to get under his skin than mine. Anyways, these evenings are chaotic, loud, and filled with laughter—I look forward to them every week.

We walk up to the door and before Cillian can knock, it swings open. Connor stands there with a wide grin, holding sleeping Teagan in his arms. "Look who finally decided to show up!" Connor teases as he pulls Cillian into a one-armed hug. "We were starting to think you got lost."

"Ha ha, very funny." Cillian rolls his eyes but smiles as he kisses Teagan on the head. She peers up sleepily. "How's wee Teagan?"

"Perfect," Connor says proudly, handing her to my man. "Yer niece is a handful but I like being a girl dad."

Watching Cillian cradle his niece with such tenderness sends a pang of longing through me. I can't wait for us to have a child. The way he gently rocks her, his eyes full of love, makes my heart ache in the best way possible.

Ronni appears behind him, looking a bit frazzled and tired but glowing with happiness. "You're just in time for the third season premiere."

"Congratulations, Ronni! How amazing." I'm genuinely thrilled for her. "We missed you while you were filming."

"Well, one more season to go." She shakes her head, smiling. "We're going out with a bang. Next summer we're all spending the summer with the band in Europe. All the wives. All the kids. It'll be mayhem. I can't wait."

As we move farther into the house, Rory, Brennan, Seamus, Liam, and Padraig are gathered around the television. The Seahawks are having yet another fourth-quarter comeback. Cillian joins them and I move along to the kitchen.

I find Maureen bustling around, checking on various dishes and making sure everything is perfect. The aroma of roasted chicken and fresh herbs fills the air, making my mouth water. I'm absolutely starving.

"Need any help, Maureen?" I step up beside her, glancing around to see if there's anything to graze on.

"Oh, Ivy, dear, how wonderful, I can always use a spare set of hands, so I can." She hands me a bowl of boiled potatoes and a masher. "Smash those up, the milk is heating on the stove. "Now tell me, because I've been wondering, how are things with your dad?"

I never get sick of her Irish lilt. "It's a work in progress. He hasn't accepted my relationship with Cillian yet, which breaks my heart."

"Aye. My dad was a stubborn sod too." She hands me a couple of sticks of butter for the potatoes.

"At least he's still in remission. We may not be speaking, but I want him to be healthy again." I put a bit of elbow grease into the mashed potatoes until they're smooth, buttery, and creamy. Maureen has been teaching me how to cook, and if I could eat these mashed potatoes every day and not be three hundred pounds, I would.

Maureen gives me a sympathetic smile. "Family can be complicated, but it's worth the effort. Rory and I have been through sheer madness and we've managed to make it through. Jay-sus, with the accident, his drinking, and then health scares, we got through it all. Don't get me started on our boys. They've all had their own trials and tribulations."

"Oh, Cillian has told me stories." I laugh.

She takes the potatoes from me and hands me a block of cheese and a grater. "Next task."

"Put me to work. It makes me happy." I begin shredding the cheddar.

We continue preparing dinner and as usual, our conversation flows easily. Maureen's unconditional acceptance of me as part of the McGloughlin family has meant the world to me. Especially considering she wasn't a fan of me lying to Cillian and didn't hesitate to scold me about doing it again. I love this big, loud family and I want Cillian and I to have the same thing.

Sooner rather than later.

"Can you go let the folks know dinner is ready?" Maureen takes the chickens out of the oven. "It's gone quiet in there, the game must be over."

I make the rounds but can't find Cillian or Rory. While the rest of the family gets seated, I hunt for them in all the usual places. Finally, I locate them out back. They're deep in conversation, leaning against the railing of the deck overlooking the sprawling garden.

"We finished the Bright construction job this week. Two months ahead of schedule, which means a significant bonus." Rory has his arms crossed. "Stan let me know they're going with someone else for the Tacoma project. He wasn't open to meet with you, Kill. I'm sorry, I tried."

I don't mean to eavesdrop but I can't help it. It makes me sad my dad is still being petty.

Cillian nods, not surprised. "I figured as much. It's unfortunate, but we've got a ton of work lined up so we won't miss it. Ivy's gotten us organized, we're going to scale on similar projects up and down the coast."

"Excellent." Rory claps a hand on his son's shoulder. "I'm proud of you both for getting through a tough time."

"Thanks, Da." Cillian turns and I step out from the doorway. "Hey, babe." A smile spreads across his face.

I give Rory a hug. "Dinner's ready."

"Aye, well, let's get inside." Rory leaves us in the dust.

We gather around the table and the usual buzz of chatter fills the air. Maureen always prepares more than enough for the entire family. As we dig into the food spread out on the table, the lively banter I look forward to each week begins.

"Cillian, Ivy." Brennan smirks. "When are we going to hear wedding bells?"

He asks the same question every week. This time, though, I feel my cheeks heat up and I can't help but smile. Cillian and I exchange a secret look, knowing we're going to shock the life out of him.

"Yeah, Cillian," Connor chimes in. "What's the holdup?"

"We're taking things one step at a time." Cillian takes a sip of iced tea, smoothly deflecting the question. He squeezes my hand under the table. "But who knows what the future holds?"

I nearly laugh out loud, he says the same thing every week. We smile at each other and share a moment of silent understanding. A few days ago, we found out I'm pregnant. Cillian put an offer on a lot in Madison Valley, where he's going to build our forever home. Our future is shaping up, even if our families don't know the details yet.

Our plan is to tell everyone at Christmas. We're hoping my dad will come around by then, but we're not holding our breath. He hasn't been receptive to any outreach since I moved out.

The attention shifts to Brennan, who fills us in on a financing round he closed. His AI company is poised to take off in a big way. Seamus details how stressful taking his medical boards was. Padraig and Liam seem a bit subdued. They're back from recording in LA, but something's clearly off. Cillian swears they have their own language, but I've never seen evidence of it in the time I've known them.

After dinner, we play Rory's favorite game, Pictionary. It cracks me up every time because the family gets so competitive they make me draw with my left hand. Cillian and I usually win anyway.

On the drive back home, I rest my hand on Cillian's thigh, feeling content despite the challenges we're facing with my dad. Our relationship feels effortless, like it was always meant to be this way.

"Tonight was nice." I gaze at Cillian's profile. The passing streetlights cast fleeting shadows across his handsome face. Every highlight and shadow enhances his strong jawline.

God, I love him.

"Yeah, it was." He glances at me with a smile. "Were you spying on me a bit earlier? Tell the truth."

I suppress a giggle and shake my head. "No, of course not. Just, you know, paying attention to your every move. It's hard not to when you're so...captivating." I slide my hand up to the bulge in his pants.

"Captivating, huh?" Cillian raises an eyebrow. "You have a way of making me feel like the luckiest guy in the world." He shifts slightly, trying to focus on the road. "For transparency, I asked Da to see if your dad would speak with me one-on-one. I don't want to go too much longer without fixing things. I know you want his blessing before we get married."

A flutter of hope and anxiety stirs in my chest. "Yeah, I'm glad you're making the effort because I won't feel comfortable being in his presence until he gets help for his anger. Mom can't get through to him, either. It's upsetting to think he still feels justified in his reaction to our relationship."

"Yeah, it's hard." He pulls into the driveway of the townhouse. "I keep thinking if he knows how much I love you and how serious we are, he'll come around. I'd like it to happen before you start showing."

God, I love everything about my life with Cillian. It's everything I thought it would be and more. Even the quiet of the townhouse as we walk through the front door wraps around us like a comforting blanket.

Cillian locks the door and without a word, takes my hand and leads me upstairs. As usual, the anticipation in the air is palpable. Tonight—and every night—is more for us than a physical connection. Every time we make love it reaffirms our commitment to each other and the life we're building.

"Ivy." Cillian turns to me, his eyes dark with passion. "No matter what happens with your dad, I'd like for us to get married before the baby comes. But, if you want to wait we can wait."

"I want the same thing," I reassure him. "Let's focus on us and on our family, and everything else will fall into place."

He bends down and captures my lips in a slow, deep kiss, which sends shivers down my spine. We waste no time, shedding our clothes and slipping under the covers, where we lose ourselves in each other.

As we lie entwined afterward, I feel a profound sense of peace.

Our path hasn't been easy.

Soon, we'll be focusing on our own family and it fills me with a happiness I can't quite describe.

I drift off to sleep with Cillian's arms around me.

Knowing whatever comes our way, we'll be able to face it.

Forty

CILLIAN

Three Months Later

I HAVEN'T BEEN THIS nervous in years.

I'm waiting at a small, cozy café near Madison Park. The aroma of freshly brewed coffee fills the air. The soft murmur of conversations and the occasional clink of cups is comforting, but my heart races as I wait for him to arrive. This meeting has been a long time coming and weighs heavily on my mind.

I know it's my last chance to make things right for Ivy and her family before our son is born.

The bell above the door chimes, and I look up to see Stan walk in. He looks a million times better than the last time I saw him. He scans the room until he spots me then strides over, his presence commanding as ever. I stand to greet him, extending my hand.

"Stan, thank you for meeting me." I try to keep my voice steady.

He ignores my hand. "Cillian," he replies curtly, sitting down across from me.

Well, then.

We order our coffees and there's a heavy silence between us as we wait. Finally, the server sets our cups on the table. Stan takes a sip before looking at me with a mixture of curiosity and suspicion.

He cuts straight to the point. "What is it you want to talk about? I'm pretty sure I've said all I want to say."

"You must know Ivy's pregnant." I take a deep breath, organizing my thoughts. "You've made it clear you don't approve of our relationship, but I thought we could talk man to man because we had a great relationship for years. I love your daughter and I'm going to always take care of her and our child, which means I don't want her to be sad. She misses you."

Stan's eyes narrow slightly, but he doesn't interrupt, so I continue. "I know you're angry about how things happened.

I also know I've made mistakes. I'm not sure how much Ivy's mother has told you about Ivy's and my relationship, but it's the real deal. She's it for me and I'd like to ask for your blessing to marry her before the baby is born."

"You think you can ask for my blessing, and everything will be fine? Do you have any idea what you've put my family through?" he scoffs, shaking his head.

I meet his gaze and don't take the bait. "I'm not here to make excuses. I'm here to make amends."

Stan leans back in his chair, his expression hard as nails. "Oh, really? And how exactly do you plan to unwind the clock? Seems like you can't undo what's been done. My daughter isn't even twenty-two and she's already knocked up by a man pushing forty. Her brilliant mind—wasted."

"I understand why you're furious, Stan." I take a deep breath and try to keep my composure. "I know you had different dreams for your daughter, but I think if you'd stop being angry, you'd realize she's living her own life now. There's nothing I won't do to support her. You and I are alike in this way."

Stan's eyes narrow. "How do you expect me to trust you?"

"I earned your trust in business. I'd like the chance to earn it in my personal life. I love her." I lean back and open my arms up. "I love her more than anything in this world."

Stan scoffs, shaking his head. "You've got a lot of nerve. You love her? No, you snuck around with her. Put her in a compromising position in your office. You got her pregnant. Why should I believe anything you say?"

"Because I'm devoted to her and she's happy. Happier than she's ever been." I shrug. "I feel the same. I'm building our new home. We're planning our future. I'll be by Ivy's side for the rest of our lives. It's why I'm here now. Ivy needs her family and you need Ivy. We want you to be part of your grandson's life."

"Grandson?" Stan looks at me for a long moment. The anger in his eyes dims.

"Yes," I confirm, feeling a surge of hope. "We're naming him Forrest. We want our son to know his entire family loves him."

Stan's shoulders slump slightly. "A grandson," he murmurs, almost to himself. "I never thought..."

"Ivy loves you," I say gently. "We truly didn't want you to find out about us the way you did. I'm trying to make things better."

Stan's hands clamp into fists. "You have no idea what it's like to see your daughter..."

He shuts his eyes and shakes his head vigorously.

"She's not a little girl anymore." I reach across the table and touch his arm. "You, of all people, know how special she is.

Get to know her for who she is, not for who you want her to be."

He opens his eyes. Nods slowly. Every ounce of fight seeps out before my eyes. "Maybe it's time I faced some of my own demons."

"Thank you, Stan. You have no idea how much it means to me." Relief whooshes through my body.

Stan stands up and finally offers his hand. "I'm not doing this for you, Cillian. I'm doing it for my daughter. Maybe, in time, we can find a way to move forward."

"I can't ask any more of you. Thank you." I take his hand and shake it firmly.

On my way home, a sense of cautious optimism settles over me. If Stan is willing to work on himself, maybe Ivy can have the loving father she remembers from her childhood back instead of the acerbic-tongued asshole who tried to control her. I'll do everything I can to help them find their way back to each other.

I walk into the house and the scent of fresh paint hits me. Taking two steps at a time, I bound up to the nursery, eager to see what Ivy's working on. I'm blown away. I knew she planned on painting a full-wall jungle mural, but this is something else.

She's sketched it out in pencil—a majestic lion lounging under a tree, a family of elephants near a sparkling river, playful monkeys swinging from vine to vine, and vibrant parrots perched amidst lush foliage. She's filling in some of the details with color, bringing the scene to life with each brushstroke.

Ivy wears a snug white tank top and loose pajama shorts that cling to her curves, belly prominently straining against the fabric. To say I'm fascinated with her growing bump is an understatement. I can't believe we created a wee little being whom we already love so much.

"Hey, baby." I step into the room and gesture to the wall. "This is incredible."

She glances over her shoulder and smiles. "Thanks, babe. How was your meeting?"

"He was defensive, then he seemed to listen to reason.." I step toward her and notice I can see her nipples, which have enlarged and darkened, through the thin fabric.

My dick twitches. Ivy's pregnancy hasn't diminished our sex drive. If anything, it's increased.

Ivy's hand pauses mid-brushstroke. "Really? Forgive me for being skeptical, but self-reflection doesn't sound like him."

"I think he knows he needs to change for the sake of Forrest." She looks skeptical, hurt still lingers from his harsh words. "I didn't press him, but I told him he was having a grandson."

She presses her lips into a thin line. "Well, I'll believe it when I see it." As if on cue, our baby kicks, causing her to gasp slightly. "Did you see him move?" Her eyes light up.

I move behind her, wrapping my arms gently around her belly, feeling our child move beneath my hands. "Hey there, little one." My hands slide up and down her bump.

"He always gets excited at the sound of your voice." Ivy leans back into me and closes her eyes.

"I can't wait to meet him." I lower my head and kiss the top of her shoulder.

Ivy turns in my arms and our lips meet in a tender kiss. I feel love radiating from her, enveloping us both. Our kiss deepens, becoming more urgent, and my hands roam over her body, feeling every curve, every inch.

Carefully, I lift Ivy's tank top, revealing the smooth, rounded expanse of her belly. I lean down and press soft kisses to her skin, feeling the baby move beneath my lips. "Forrest," I whisper between kisses, "I love you."

"I think he already knows you're his hero. You two are going to have such a special bond." Ivy smiles down at me, her fingers threading through my hair as I continue to shower her belly with affection.

It's hard to explain how I feel—all I know is there's a deep, sweet connection to both Ivy and our child, which will never be broken.

"I need you, baby." I push Ivy's tank top above the swell of her breasts and cup one in each hand, pinching her nipples.

Ivy pushes down her pajama bottoms and steps out of them. "Let me ride you."

"Yeah." I make short work of my own clothes, sit on the rocker, which she's dragged to the middle of the room, and guide her to straddle my lap. "Climb on."

Ivy giggles and sinks down on top of me. She takes my hands and places them on her belly, guiding them over the firm, round curve. I can feel the baby's gentle movements under my palms as we make love. I trace the beautiful stretch marks that have started to form.

"You're incredible." My eyes never leave hers. "I love you."

"I love you too." Ivy smiles then closes her eyes and sighs with pleasure when I slide my fingers down to her clit. "And, oh how I love your magic fingers."

My God, she's beautiful. Funny. Smart. I'm the luckiest man in the world.

It's hard to believe Ivy was once my tender temptation. Against all odds, our relationship has grown into something solid and true.

Despite the obstacles we faced, we're living life on our own terms now.

I wouldn't change a thing.

IVY

Epilogue - Eight Months Later

GOD, HOW I LOVE these nights.

I never get tired of the three of us being surrounded by family.

Cillian pulls up to his parents' house. The familiar sight of the gorgeous four-story craftsman fills me with warm fuzzies. The two of us gather Forrest's diaper bag and essentials, Cillian hauls everything up the stairs as I follow with our son cradled in my arms. We're late, as usual, but we have good reason.

A quick wink and a kiss later, Cillian opens the front door.

"Welcome, lovebirds!" Rory's booming voice greets us the second we step inside. He takes one look at Forrest and his face lights up. He wiggles his finger on my baby's nose. "Jaysus, there's my wee man!"

"Hi, Mom. Hi, Dad." I give my mom a warm hug and then stiffly hug my dad.

It's been a healing journey with me and my father, but the fact my parents regularly join us at the McGloughlin family dinners is definitely progress. Of course, spending time with his grandson helps too.

Dad's gruff demeanor melts a bit whenever he sees Forrest. He gently pushes his finger into Forrest's tiny hand and watches in awe as my son clings to it. Dad smiles up at me. The moment is brief but significant. A silent acknowledgment of our efforts to mend our relationship.

My mom peers over my shoulder and kisses my cheek. "It's good to see you, baby boy," she coos as she reaches for Forrest. "Aren't you my beautiful grandson. Aren't you the sweetest boy." She looks at me "Can I take him?"

"Of course, Mom." I hand him to her. My heart swells with pure joy. Watching my son cradled in her arms, surrounded by love, fills me with a happiness I've longed for ever since my brother died.

This is the family I remember fondly. One I wanted for myself, and now I have it—and so does my son.

Cillian wraps his arms around me and kisses my head then lowers his lips to my ear. "I love seeing you happy, baby."

"You've given me everything I've ever wanted." I fold my hands over his and lean back into his embrace.

Maureen bustles over, her apron still on from preparing dinner, which is set out on the dining room table. "Let me take him, Allison. You need a break, so you do."

My mom reluctantly hands Forrest to her and Maureen snuggles him tightly against her chest. It's funny how everyone competes for my newborn's attention. I'm here for it. The more love the better.

As usual, the dining table is laden with a feast that could rival any holiday spread. Tonight it's roast beef, mashed potatoes, green beans, and a dozen other dishes. As we sit down, the banter begins. Dinner is lively, as always. Everyone's in high spirits, and the room buzzes with laughter and conversation.

Maureen is the most doting grandmother, she's reluctant to hand Forrest over to anyone else.

Rory teases her gently, "Now, Maureen, don't be greedy with the wee lad."

"Grandparents' privilege, Rory." She grins down at Forrest, whom she rocks gently.

Brennan, Cillian's only other brother here tonight, bounds down the stairs and joins us in the dining room, which is already filled with laughter and chatter.

"Sorry, folks, this financing is killing me." His smile is strained.

Cillian's been worried about him. Ordinarily, they hang out all the time but for the past year, Brennan is in Silicon Valley more than he's in Seattle. This financing round never seems to end.

"Ivy has a great mind for numbers," my dad says before he devours a fork full of roast beef.

"Aye." Rory nods. "She's brilliant. I can't get over how much she's done for McGloughlin Construction."

As I listen to Cillian and my father discuss my so-called attributes, I can't ignore the slight underlying tension lingering between our families.

The fallout from Dad discovering our relationship over a year ago still lingers. Rory stepped in and finished the Seattle headquarters in record time, but my dad hired a rival construction company for the Tacoma expansion.

I guess, despite the progress we've made, my dad's vindictiveness casts lingering shadows. Not that it's affected McGloughlin Construction in the slightest. My work with Cillian's company has helped streamline operations. He's made some key hires who have helped propel the company forward and it's doing better than ever.

Meanwhile, I've heard through the grapevine, my father's Tacoma project still is months behind schedule.

"You know." Rory nudges my dad. "Connor and Ronni have invited us to Ireland for Christmas. Why don't you two come too?"

"We should, Stan." My mom claps her hands.

"If Cillian would ever make an honest woman out of my little girl, I might consider it." Dad stabs his roast beef, but his lips curl up in a smirk.

Cillian leans back in his chair and puts his hand on my thigh. "Oh, we enjoy keeping you all in suspense. Besides, we've got our hands full with our wee man."

Maureen chimes in, "Blah. Blah. Blah. Seriously, son, when's the big day?"

I laugh, enjoying the lighthearted teasing. "We're working on it. We promise you'll all be the first to know."

My mom and Maureen exchange glances. "We'll believe it as soon as there's a date." Maureen winks at Mom. "Meanwhile, we're fighting over who gets to babysit next, so we are."

Mom's eyes twinkle. "I think we need a schedule. Every other day, perhaps?"

"Alright, alright." I shake my head, unable to suppress my grin. "You'd think the two of you had never seen a baby before. What if I told you in six months, we'll have another one to pass around?"

There's a moment of stunned silence before the room erupts into cheers and congratulations.

"You're joking!" Maureen exclaims, her eyes wide with excitement. "Irish twins?"

"Cillian! Ivy!" Mom claps her hands. "What wonderful news! The two of you didn't waste any time, my goodness!"

I never imagined I would get pregnant so quickly after Forrest, but we're overjoyed. The love Cillian and I share is beyond anything I ever dreamed was possible. He treats me with such tenderness and respect. Each day is better than the last.

Now, our family is growing, as is the love between us. I have no idea what the future holds, other than Cillian and I plan to have a lot more kiddos. As he puts it, his "swimmers" always find the target.

Rory leans forward and takes my hand. "Another wee grandchild on the way! How about that?"

My dad looks momentarily shocked, then breaks into a rare, genuine smile. "Well, I'll be damned. I don't hate the idea."

"Well, we don't hate the idea either." Cillian squeezes my hand under the table. "We're really fucking happy."

After dinner, we move to the living room. I sit on the couch, breastfeeding Forrest, who I keep under a blanket in order to appease the grandfathers. The room is cozy, with a fire crackling in the fireplace and our parents chatter away with mugs of hot chocolate. Once Forrest is fed and burped, he falls asleep in my arms.

Across the room, I notice Cillian and Brennan standing in the foyer, they're deep into what looks like an intense conversation. I can't hear what they're saying, but it's clear there's some tension between them. Cillian's brows are furrowed, and Brennan's hands are gesturing animatedly.

"What's going on with those two?" I ask Maureen, who's sitting next to me.

She glances over and sighs. "Ach, you know how brothers are. Probably some stupid miscommunication. I've learned to stay out of it. They'll work it out, my boys always do."

The evening winds down and we say our goodbyes. After we load up the car, the drive home is quiet. Forrest is asleep in his car seat and I'm exhausted. My pregnancy hormones are insane this time, probably because I never had a break between giving birth and getting knocked up again.

We get home and settle Forrest into his bassinet next to our bed, and I turn to Cillian. "What were you and Brennan talking about?"

He turns to face me. "He seems to be under too much pressure—but he's making some strange decisions. Apparently he's taking on a huge investment for his company, which could change everything, but not necessarily for the better. I actually think there's something else going on, but he's being tightlipped. It's frustrating. I want to help him."

"You're a good brother." I comb my fingers through his hair. "Your mom told me you'll work it out."

Cillian pulls me into his arms. "We will. Whatever happens, I'll be there for him."

"Families are messy and imperfect, but I'm learning messiness is our greatest strength." I rest my head against his chest. "Being each other's support system is what life's all about."

"Well said, *Mo shíorghrá*." Cillian kisses my temple.

As I drift off to sleep in Cillian's arms, with our precious Forrest beside us and another on the way, I can't help but feel grateful for our beautiful life.

We've faced many challenges, some self-imposed, but our love has only deepened over the years.

Reconnecting, healing family rifts, and building our future has taught me love isn't just about two people—it's about the bonds we create with those around us.

We're an unbreakable foundation.

Want more Cillian & Ivy? Scan the QR Code below for a Bonus Scene.

He had everything planned, until an unexpected reunion changed his future forever. Brennan & Astrid's story is next in Daring Destiny. Preorder now scan the QR code.

Connor's story launched the McGloughlin brothers' tale in Fearless.

'I've never met anyone like you, Connor McGloughlin. I'm in way over my head.' Discover more read it here.

Behind the Scenes

Hey Amazing Readers,

Grab a cup of coffee (or hey, maybe an Irish coffee!), and let's chat about something super close to my heart—the Charming Irish series. This journey has been a whirlwind of emotions and inspirations, drawn from a very personal place.

You might remember we kicked things off with Connor in the Less Than Zero series. He's the big brother who had to grow up fast, taking over the family after their dad's accident. That story opened up a whole world for me—and for you, too, from what you've told me! Now, I'm thrilled to dive deeper into the lives of Connor's brothers in the Charming Irish series, where each book peels back more layers of their turbulent yet heartwarming family dynamics.

You've just finished Tender Temptation.

Oh, Cillian! He was always the McGloughlin brother who lingered in the back of my mind, a bit elusive, a little undefined—until now. Like his dad, he faces his own battles with alcohol. But Cillian's story twists these challenges into a modern tale of resilience and redemption that I couldn't wait to get onto the page.

And let's talk about the romance—holy crap! Cillian and Ivy's connection puts a whole new spin on 'forbidden love' with their sizzling passion and significant age gap. Today's world throws a lot of shade at relationships like theirs, and I wanted to explore all that tension and passion. How does a couple navigate love when society keeps throwing barriers in their way? How do they hold onto their spark amidst all the noise? How do they navigate a little white lie that threatens to destroy both families?

This series, especially Tender Temptation, is so dear to me. Not just because it's fun to write about all that Irish feistiness (though, trust me, it is!), but because it digs into real issues—like dealing with past trauma, breaking down societal taboos, and, of course, the messy, beautiful fight for love.

I can't thank you enough for coming along on this journey with me. Your messages, your reviews, and your enthusiasm keep me motivated to keep digging deeper and pushing the boundaries with each story.

Thanks for sticking with me, for reading, and for being the best readers an author could ask for. Here's to more adventures with the McLoughlin's!

Love Tender Temptation? Don't forget to leave a review where the book is sold.

Big hugs and lots of love,

Kaylene

Maureen McGloughlin's
Buttery Colcannon Mashers

INGREDIENTS

- 2 1/2 - 3 lbs similar sized potatoes (Russets or Yukon Golds are lovely)
- 7 oz kale, stripped from stems & torn into pieces
- 1 cup whole milk
- 2 tsp sea salt (or to taste)
- 4 green onions, sliced finely
- 1 block KerryGold Irish butter

Serves 5-6

2x or 3x the recipe depending on who's coming to dinner.

DIRECTIONS

<u>Boil the Potatoes</u>: First off, give those potatoes a good scrub and pop them, skins and all, into a large pot of cold salted water. Cover the pot partially with a lid and bring it to a boil. Now, depending on the size of your spuds, you'll be cooking them anywhere from 40 minutes to an hour. You want them tender enough to pierce easily with a fork but be careful they don't boil to bits.

<u>Prepare the Kale</u>: While the potatoes are bubbling away, take your kale, strip it from those tough stems, and tear it into small pieces. Even if you've bought pre-chopped kale, it's worth a quick check for any stubborn stems. Cook the kale in a small pot of salted boiling water until soft, about 5 minutes. Drain well, squeeze out the excess water, and put it back into the warm pot, keeping it covered and set aside.

<u>Potatoes Ready</u>: Once your potatoes are tender, gently lift them out of the pot (you don't want them breaking up and getting soggy) and place them on a large board. Empty the pot of water, give it a quick wipe with some kitchen paper, and then return the potatoes to the dry pot to steam off for a minute or two.

<u>Mash Away</u>: Mash the potatoes right there in the pot. I love the texture the skins give, so I don't bother with a ricer. Warm the milk slightly, pour it into the potatoes, add the salt, and mash until smooth but not gluey (and don't you dare use a stick blender, or you'll regret it). Once mashed, fold in the cooked kale and check the seasoning and adjust as needed. Cover the pot to keep it warm while you move on to the brown butter.

<u>Make the Brown Butter</u>: Cut your butter into pieces and melt it in a heavy saucepan over gentle heat. Once melted, turn the heat up to medium and swirl the pan regularly. You're looking for the butter to turn a deep golden brown with dark specks at the bottom—this should take about 7 minutes. As soon as it smells nutty and delicious, take the pan off the heat and add the sliced green onions. They'll sizzle something fierce, but that's exactly what you want.

<u>Finish the Colcannon</u>: Pour about two-thirds of the brown butter into your mashed potatoes and beat it in well. Scoop your colcannon into a warm serving dish, making some lovely swirls on top with your spoon. Drizzle the remaining brown butter and green onions over the top.

Take it to the table with a smile, and enjoy every buttery, comforting bite of this Irish classic. Bliss on a plate!

Acknowledgements

Cover/Graphic Designer/Finder of HOTTIES: Regina Wamba

Editor: Grace Bradley Editing, LLC

Proofreading: Letitia Delan

Formatting: Willow Yanarella

PR: Wildfire Marketing

Literary Agent: Stephanie Phillips, SBR Media

Website Maven: Sherri Kiarsis, Ruby Moon Designs

My Right Hand: Willow Yanarella

YAY to KAYLENE'S KREW!!!

Dedication

To my husband Gareth. There's nothing like being part of a big, feisty, passionate, hardworking Irish clan, I hope the McGloughlin's capture the love and loyalty I've experienced in my found family.

About the Author

Kaylene Winter is an Amazon best-selling author of steamy, contemporary romance.

Each character-driven novel is filled with snappy dialogue, pop-culture references and enough steam to make you fan yourself. Kaylene weaves authenticity, emotion and angst into a turbulent rollercoaster ride of love, passion and soul-searing romance always ending with a delicious HEA.

Kaylene lives in Seattle with her amazing Irish husband and gorgeous Siberian Husky. She loves creating art of all kinds.

Other Titles

Scan the QR Code Below or follow this link.